HOUSE OF GLASS

DELIRIUM NOCTURNUM 1-4

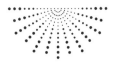

ROJANA KRAIT

HOUSE OF GLASS: CHIPPED

PROLOGUE

ELODIE GLASS

Maybe it's futile. Maybe it's far too late, and then again, maybe the world in my dreams never existed in the first place. Maybe we were all born to suffer. Maybe we're already in hell. Maybe there is no 'we' and maybe I'm a fool.

I don't belong to the light any longer, but that doesn't mean that I won't be drawn toward it like a moth toward a flame until the end of time. I slay the beasts that stalk this Earth in order to clear a path for the innocent. I free slaves and I destroy monsters, but if you think that I'm a heroine, you've got the wrong story.

I know the darkness that dwells in the hearts of mankind because I share it. It simmers under the cold, white surface of my skin, pulsing through my veins, waiting to boil over into the world. I unleash it on those who evade punishment for their atrocities and on those whose power and privilege exclude them from the laws of man and immortal alike.

This is my way to atone for the blood that never washes off my hands. I took a vow to myself and my sisters that I'd only ever harm the evil ones. The ones who would drag the entire world down with them into chaos and torment.

And I've kept that vow. I'm a hunter, and the predators of the world are my prey. I hunt them, I stalk them, and I end them. Depending on their nature I might even devour them. And my secret?

I love it.

I live to kill and I'm afraid that I was born this way, not just made this way like my sisters.

But I've got just enough humanity left in me to realize what a wretch I am, what a ghoul. If I wasn't hunting these creatures, I'd probably be one of them.

I know that there's always been something wrong with me, but I stay in the dark where I belong with the other demons.

Or at least I did.

Until her.

My Aya.

The only light in my life, though she's barely aware of my existence. I might not have a sun any longer but the sun I remember from my past life never burned with her luminosity. She never has much to say, but the way her eyes flicker and burn under her lashes testifies to her depths. Her skin smells like salt water and cinnamon and somehow reminds me of the ocean that I was never able to visit while I was still alive. I might be immortal, but she's otherworldly.

She's everything I'm not, and I'll do whatever it takes to keep her that way.

I watch her and wait for the right moment, a moment that I know will never come because she's too pure to ever be mine. I'm not a creature worthy of anyone's love, and especially not hers. I know this all too well as I watch her sleep or follow her on the rare occasions that she leaves her home. She's far too good for this world and she's still innocent despite the horrors of her past. I'm going to be the one to make sure that she stays that way.

That's what I tell myself anyway, as I follow her. That I'm protecting her. Making sure that she never again falls into the hands of someone who would hurt her. Truth be told, though, I'm doing it as much for me as for her. Just being near my Aya soothes me and give me a peace that I haven't known in... well, a peace that I've never known.

I made a promise to myself that I'd only watch her from a distance and that I'd never interfere with her life. All that changes when circumstances force my hand and she sees what I do. What I am. After that, she has to come with me, so I can keep her quiet.

And safe.

From everyone except me.

This is our story.

CHAPTER ONE

ELODIE GLASS

Every single week I wonder to myself why the humans can't find a nicer location for these meetings.

Don't get me wrong; there's nothing really terrible about the community center. It's spacious and, while I wouldn't describe it as clean, it's not too run-down either. There is plenty of seating and the parking lot has a full time security guard, which is a luxury downtown, especially for the attendees of this particular group.

Someone has even made a few little efforts here and there to make the place more inviting and homey. I can see a series of watercolors on the wall this week. They're new and they seem to be some kind of exhibit on local efforts to preserve our environment, which is rich in this town considering the damage that has already been done by a century of unregulated manufacturing followed by decades of political corruption and widespread deterioration due to the poverty that set in after the factories shut down.

I sometimes wonder if I'll be walking a literal hellscape in five hundred years thanks to the damage that's been done to the Earth. I already live in a state of what the humans would consider general decay; our house, which must have been majestic at one time, long before I was born even, had been abandoned for at least fifty years before we moved in. It's still standing and not in imminent risk of collapse, unlike the newer abandoned buildings, it will probably still be standing in a hundred years bar unforeseen disaster, but the wallpaper discolored and peeled from the walls long ago and a variety of creatures from rats to ravens have taken up residence with us in the attic and the basement. They can't smell us so they're regularly surprised by our presence, though we've been there longer than they've been alive. My youngest sister has made something of a game to try to befriend the ravens in the attic but so far they seem to naturally distrust her even more than they distrust humans.

I would have absolutely died of horror and shame if human me could have seen how immortal me lived. It's not that I prefer the decay now; far from it, I've always been a fastidious woman. But time passes so quickly when you live forever and housekeeping just tends to get away from you.

Still, the prospect of continuing to exist for eternity long after the Earth becomes uninhabitable for any lifeform is unappealing. I don't want to live on forever in a two hundred degree cave with nothing to look at except rocks and dust.

Thus I can appreciate the community center's efforts at increasing environmental awareness without missing the fact that the community center is just kind of a sad place to be. There's something institutional about it, with its yellowing linoleum floors, fluorescent lights, and rickety aluminum chairs. The walls are concrete block painted with a high-gloss mint colored paint that was probably meant to be easy to clean but really just looks antiseptic enough to constantly remind one of the need for disinfectant in such a public place.

I feel bad for the humans, having to come into this hospital-like environment to share their deepest troubles. I imagine that it would do them good to hold these meetings somewhere beautiful, like a garden. That had always made me feel grounded when I was living, returning to a place of natural beauty. I want that for them, a place full of sunlight and flowers where they could feel safe while they tried to heal. But then, of course, I would't be able to attend.

I've arrived early this Thursday evening — I always do — just in case *she* shows up early too. She never has, of course, but that doesn't stop me. Maybe one evening she'll get here at 7:45 and then I'll get the chance to…

What?

Talk to her?

She's never given me any indication that she wants to talk to me, or to anyone at all for that matter.

Every week after the meetings she flies off like a bat into the night, never hanging around for pastries and coffee like some of the other group members. I fly out right after her, literally, and follow her home. I make sure that she arrives safe and sound, keeping my distance, both for her sake and my own.

But it would be nice to be able to talk to her for once instead of just watching her. I have so many questions that I'd like to ask her.

So here I am, helping the other early birds to arrange our metal chairs in a giant circle. Our group leader Felicia, a big strong woman in her sixties with an extensive collection of larger-than-life natural stone jewelry and hip-length dreadlocks, prefers that we all face one another when we speak. She doesn't like the idea of people having to share the most intimate details of their lives with the back of other people's heads and I agree with her.

I knew better than to expect her to show up early but when the group starts to take their seats and she still isn't there I panic a bit. I glance at the door and briefly consider leaving, going out to look for her, having convinced myself that she might be in some kind of trouble and need me, but then she rushes in late at the last second.

My eyes scan the room and I hurry to a seat amidst several empty chairs, not because I'm trying to avoid the other group members but instead because I've strategized. I know that she likes to sit alone and so I've sat myself in the most sparsely-populated arch of the circle in the hopes that she'll choose a seat near me.

My plan works. She takes a seat only two chairs away from me.

I breathe in deeply to inhale her scent. It's the closest I can come to tasting her and I'm very practiced at doing this discretely. It's the same scent I know, salt water and warm spice, and I can also smell the pumpkin soup she's had for supper and the Meyer lemon soap that she uses to wash her hands.

"Can everyone please take a seat?" Felicia waves at the group members lingering at the coffee machine, chatting quietly. "I'd like to get started."

We wait as the stragglers seat themselves, and I wince as one of them takes a chair in between Aya and me. Now this stranger's cologne is poisoning the air, but at least I can take glances at Aya without her noticing.

"Good evening, everyone," Felicia begins as we all quiet down. "I see a lot of familiar faces tonight and a few new ones. Welcome to the PTSD Survivor's Support Group. We're here to grow and heal together in a safe, supportive environment. I'm Dr. Felicia Bosal and I'd like to lay out a few ground rules and expectations here for our new members."

Felicia continues with a rundown of the basics that we hear every week. Names are optional. Judgement is forbidden. No interrupting. Crying is okay, and so on.

Felicia opens the floor and a few of the new attendees introduce themselves. Some want to explain why they are there and some prefer to wait until they feel more comfortable. Next some of the regular members share updates, progress they had made in their therapy or setbacks they had encountered over the past week.

I wait quietly, hoping that she will share tonight. She rarely does and I'm not surprised when she remains silent, with her hands folded in her lap. I know it's hard for her and I know that she's trying to heal but it's not going very well. The very few times she has spoken about what's brought her to these meetings, she's revealed a world of pain and suffering.

I want to be the woman to relieve that suffering.

The meeting is about to draw to a close when one of the new attendees asks if she can say a few words.

"I'm sorry," the woman apologizes, already starting to tear up. "I'm sorry to hold everyone up but I just don't know what to do."

"You're not holding anyone up," Felicia assures her, my Platonic ideal of motherly nurturer.

"It's my babies," the woman cries. "I'm living at a woman's shelter with them and a judge has just granted my husband — sorry, my ex-husband — unsupervised visitation with them. He attended a one-hour anger management class and some kind of therapy session about inappropriate behavior with children and now he gets to take them out alone."

"Are you afraid that your ex-husband is going to hurt your children?" Felicia asks quietly.

"He's already hurt them," the woman cries. "I'm afraid that he's going to kill them."

My ears prick. This is the official reason I'm at this meeting. Several other members offer their sympathies and when the meeting is adjourned I can't slip out right after Aya. I have work to do.

"My sister is a lawyer," I approach the grieving mother as she's grabbing a bottle of water after the meeting. "I think she can help you."

"I have a lawyer from the women's shelter," the woman takes a sip without glancing my way. "But thank you for the offer. My lawyer says that there's nothing we can do to prevent the visit."

"My sister," I lean in close and make eye contact, "is very well-connected. I feel confident that she can help you to keep your children safe."

I can be very persuasive when I want to be.

"But Caleb," the woman says softly, not able to break the eye contact, "he's got so much money. He has an entire team, and his father belongs to the same country club as the judge and—"

"His money won't protect him if he's truly a bad man," I interrupt quietly.

"His money won't protect him…" the woman repeats, now lost in a fog. I know that I can only hold her attention for another moment before she gets so disoriented that she'll need help getting home.

"His name is Caleb?" I ask.

"Caleb MacLean," the woman nods.

"And what's your name?"

"Melissa. Melissa MacLean."

"Would it be alright with you, Melissa, if I referred your special case to my sister?"

"Yes," Melissa nods, already looking like she's been drugged.

"Then I'll do that. And she'll help you and your babies. So be brave, just for another day. Can you do that for me, Melissa?"

"I'll be brave," she agrees as I break the enchantment I have over her and slip out into the night.

Aya is long gone but I have a feeling I know where she'll be. I slip through the city streets to the bodega around the corner from her apartment. She likes to get herself a pint of brownie ice cream after our meetings. It's one of the few treats she indulges in and I can spot her examining her options in front of the freezer, though she makes the same choice every time.

While I wait for her to pay and exit I text my sister Jayden and ask them to look into this Caleb MacLean.

I know in my unbeating heart that Melissa was telling the truth but we always confirm before we act.

Jayden texts back in agreement just as Aya steps out of the bodega with her brownie ice cream and I slip back into the shadows so that I can follow her home.

CHAPTER TWO

AYA LACHAT

How can it be that the more empty the streets are, the less alone I feel?

I fight the urge to stop walking and turn around yet again, to scan the sidewalks trying to find the eyes that I can feel on the back of my neck. Instead, I pull my hoodie tighter around me and pick up my pace, eyes locked on the lamppost glowing on the corner just ahead of me. Just another hundred yards or so and I'll be home, locked safe in my apartment.

Not that I ever actually feel safe there.

I was at home when I lost everything and I *had* felt safe in that home, with my parents and my sister and my two brothers. And that house was definitely more secure than my shitty apartment. I don't even have any kind of home security system, though I desperately want one. They're just way out of my price range while I'm living on disability and can't work.

All the more reason to get better, I try to give myself another pathetic pep talk. I can't help it though. I feel like I'm barely treading water with my recovery, but I still want all of the shiny new opportunities that are supposed to come with getting better. All of the experiences that normal, healthy people my age take for granted.

Once I get over my PTSD I can go to school and make friends and get a job and do all those things that I had assumed I would do until everything including my own future got ripped right out of my hands by Olsen Leonard. I'll stop panicking every time I go out in public and I'll make enough money to pay my own bills so that I don't have to prove to the social security office how fucked up I seriously am over and over and over so that they don't discontinue my benefits and make me homeless.

I'm not even to the lamppost yet before I'm stopped dead in my tracks, my train of thought derailed by pure instinct. The hair rises on the back of my neck and I can feel cold sweat prickle all over my skin. My breath turns shallow and my ears strain.

I heard something. I know I did.

I try to listen harder as my eyes dart around, looking for a safe place to run. This part of the city isn't even the 'bad' part but there are still several abandoned row homes I can spot on this block alone. I could try to hide in one of those, or I guess I could scream and hope that the person who hears me is less dangerous than the person who is following me.

I hear the noise again, but this time it's accompanied by a quick movement I catch in the corner of my eye. I glance over and feel like an idiot. It's a mangy-looking orange cat digging through a pile of trash on the street, probably trying to find a meal. He briefly glances over at me, confirms that I'm not a threat, then continues his seemingly futile raid.

Great.

Even this half-dead stray cat is less of a coward than I am.

Dr. Brothers says that it's just my lingering feelings of paranoia and it's nothing to be ashamed of. Anyone would be on high alert, she assures me, after something like what I've been through. I can tell by the way she says it, though, that I'm supposed to be doing something to get over these feelings. To recover from them. As though I can just bootstraps myself out of PTSD. Declare myself cured and move on being a productive citizen.

At least my meetings aren't too far from my place. I unlock my front door and the light in the apartment building's foyer automatically flicks on, illuminating the hallway with a flickering yellow glow. I grab my mail and bring it upstairs so I don't have to be out in a public space any longer than necessary.

"Honey, I'm home!" I call out to no one as soon as I've made my way inside, best joke ever. I lock the door behind me and kick off my sneakers.

All of my bowls are in the sink. I only own one big one and one small one, so this happens to me a lot. I grab a spoon instead and flick on the light in my living room.

After confirming that every object I own is exactly where I left it, I sink down into my old sofa and pry the top from my ice cream. I've been looking forward to it and sometimes I tell myself that my ice cream reward is the only thing that keeps me going to these meetings. God knows it isn't for any kind of healing. Every week is the same, these poor people who already suffered unspeakable things just get more and more beaten down by life, including me. Often it seems like we're not there to support each other as much as we are to marvel together at life's cruelties.

This one at least wasn't particularly bad. That poor woman shared her fears about her ex and her children and that was hard to hear. I hate feeling helpless, and I can't imagine what would make one feel more helpless than being ordered by the state to hand your children over to your torturer. I wish that there was something that I could do to help her and her kids but I can't even take care of myself.

Every week some new fresh hell is shared with the group, every week it's a fresh dose of pain and suffering. There are always new people, and old people disappear, as far as I can tell no better off than when they first started attending. It's a revolving door of victims, most of whom are victimized once by their attackers or abusers and then repeatedly by the legal system or the healthcare system or just plain bad luck.

I don't even really know why I go. Attending these meetings used to be a requirement that my therapist placed me under in order to continue receiving benefits, but now even Dr. Brothers doesn't really think that the meetings are doing me any good. I rarely ever share with the group and I certainly don't have any wisdom to offer any of the other attendees.

Actually, there is one thing drawing me back week after week.

Well, not one thing. More like one person.

It's her.

I call her Angel.

That's not entirely true; I've never called her anything at all out loud. I just named her Angel in my imagination, which is where the vast majority of our interactions have taken place. I made that up because she did introduce herself to me once but I got so nervous speaking to her that I blanked and missed her name, then I was too embarrassed to ask her to repeat it. I've been trying to catch her name ever since because I want to see if I can find her on the internet, even if it's just to gawk at pictures of her and daydream.

She's been coming to the meetings even longer than I have and she shares even less with the group than I do. I know that she attends because her mother was an alcoholic and addict who sold her to strangers as a child but other than that I don't really know anything about her other than what I've observed. She rarely ever speaks about herself, though I've seen her approach other members of our group occasionally to offer her help. Her sister is some kind of lawyer or something.

That's part of the reason I call her Angel, but the real reason is that she's so beautiful that she looks like she's not human. I absentmindedly mine my ice cream for brownie chunks while thinking about her white-blond curls and her glassy blue eyes. Her skin is so pale that she looks like her slight frame is crafted from marble, but that's not entirely unusual in such a rainy part of the world. I'm very pale myself. It just somehow looks strong on her but sickly on me.

I wonder what she looks like naked. I've only ever actually seen one other adult naked in person and it's not something I like to recall.

I'd like to see my Angel though. I bet she lives in a fancy apartment. I can tell that she's got money. Her manners are so elegant and I don't think I've ever seen her wear the same outfit twice, and believe me, I'd notice.

What if I had some reason that I had to go to her apartment?

Like, what if she was missing from our group meeting one week and everyone was super worried about her so that Felicia sent me to her apartment to check to see if she was okay?

I set my ice cream down on my end table.

So I'd go over to her place and I'm not wearing my standard black leggings and hoodie. Instead I'm wearing a pink floral sundress that's so lightweight that it's almost transparent, because of course it's summer and the weather is perfect when this scenario occurs. I show up at her place in my sundress with my hair washed and curled and she answers the door in her underwear. She looks me up and down and licks her lips. It's a good thing that I'm at her doorstep because she really needs to talk to me...

CHAPTER THREE

ELODIE GLASS

I f the police catch me like this, I'm definitely going on some kind of a list.

Hell, who am I kidding. I belong on a list for this.

I lean my back against the rear wall of Aya's apartment building and work my right hand into the waistband of my pants while the other hand steadies my phone and tries not to touch the screen. If I touch the screen, the video feed will cycle through the other cameras that I installed in Aya's apartment, and I definitely don't want to lose this particular feed. I very rarely get to see her... relax like this.

I know that I'm taking a risk, out here in public with my fingers on my launch button, even if I am concealed amongst the shadows in an alley that is used primarily to store the dumpsters that belong to the buildings that line this street. It doesn't matter to me, not a bit. Not at the moment, though I'm sure I'd be filled with regrets if I had to kill anyone who saw me like this. I need to relieve the urgency coursing through my body. I can't see Aya like this and walk away.

I realize how this situation makes me look, but I'm not a total dirtbag. I initially installed the surveillance system because Aya looks up home security systems online all the time. She likes to read reviews and testimonials, but then when she gets to the pricing information she always closes the tab on her computer.

I know that she's dead broke and I feel terrible about it. I've spent hours trying to think up ways that I could help her without her knowing it. I've thought about just leaving her bags of cash, but I'm afraid that she'd get frightened or turn them in as lost property to the police who would undoubtedly then just help themselves. I've also considered trying to fake some kind of sweepstakes that she 'wins' so that I can just write her a check but I couldn't figure out a way to do that without her finding out where the money came from. It's actually one of the most difficult things about living inconspicuously as an immortal, dealing with bureaucracy. Obviously our finances don't make sense to banks or governments, and the more regulated financial systems get, the more difficult it is to seem like an ordinary woman on paper.

So for the time being, I sometimes just buy her things without her knowing. Like this state of the art security system, for example. She doesn't know it, but her entire apartment building is under 24 hour surveillance. Her apartment has a lightweight yet heavily reinforced titanium door with a locking system that is powerful enough to keep out a small invading army, let alone a home intruder. She's also got infrared thermal sensors that send an alert directly to my phone whenever anyone enters her place and the pantry in her kitchen can even be used as a panic room if she enters and hits a button I installed behind the baseboard near the door.

It was easy for me to install all of this stuff after I bought her building. I just had to put her (and the rest of the residents, all of whom were hand-picked by me to make her feel as safe and comfortable as possible) up in a hotel for a week under the guise of tenting for termites.

I like to tell myself that I installed that security system for Aya's safety and comfort, but in reality that's not how I'm using it. At least not at the moment.

Sweet little Aya has peeled off her leggings and, as usual, she isn't wearing any panties underneath. She's cast her ice cream aside and her head is tossed back into the cushions of her sofa. She wets one of her slender fingers in her mouth and then slides it down her body, into her auburn curls and slowly up her mound until her soft flesh gives way and her finger disappears.

I'm so glad that I went for color video instead of black and white because, my God, it's worth it. The creamy skin of her thighs flushes with excitement and I'd love to bury my face in between her legs. She's on the second floor above me but she's got a window open and I can smell her pussy, ever so slightly, like a shark can smell a drop of blood in the ocean. She's peaches and iron and a little something spicy and I'd do anything to taste her right now.

My canines are already extended and I run my tongue over them, tasting my own blood and pretending that it's hers. The images that flash through my mind make it abundantly clear to me that I can never, ever touch her in real life. I wouldn't be able to restrain myself and she'd end up dead. It's like I'm starving and she's the only thing that can save me, I can't stop myself and I need every drop of her.

I don't just want to drink her, I want to drain her, and I want to possess her in every way possible. I've got the overwhelming urge to get inside her, to feel her tight body contracting around me, even though I haven't been with a woman that way in decades.

She's so lively tonight and I wish that I could read her mind. What's she thinking about that's got her so hot and bothered? She's really going at it on her sofa; she's got her head thrown back and her back arched. One hand is working her clit and the other is in her mouth. I want to turn on the volume to my feed but I don't need to attract any unwanted attention to myself in this state.

I've never wanted a woman like this. I've certainly never had such a desire to feed one. I know what my blood can do to a girl but I also know what kind of responsibilities come with sharing it and I've never had that particular craving before meeting Aya.

I don't have to think for a moment whether I'd want to keep her forever. I'd do anything to have her and only my vows to myself and my sisters are protecting her from me right now.

I don't want to be a beast but it's my nature.

I'm about to cum when my precious feed is interrupted by an incoming call.

Fuck.

It's Jayden so I have to answer.

I pull my hand back out of my pants, fingers still slick from the folds of my lips so I have to wipe my hand off on my trousers.

"Hey," I answer, still adjusting myself.

"Everything okay?" Jayden asks, their boyish voice suspicious.

"Yeah, why?" Suddenly I don't want to be standing in an alley behind a dumpster coated in my own lifeless, sticky fluids, but I'm not feeling particularly terrible either. I'm not sure what Jayden is hearing in my voice.

"You sound like you're out of breath."

Ah-ha.

"I was out jogging."

I wait for Jayden to laugh, but it doesn't happen.

"Dude, I was just kidding. So what did you find."

"Your man is a real piece of shit."

"How bad?"

"I think he's actually possibly quite worse than the mother knows. He must be worse; otherwise she'd do anything to keep the kids from him. He's perfect for us; irredeemable and it looks like his family's money has been allowing him to skate through the legal systems without consequence for years. He's even been traveling overseas to pursue his... interests... in person."

"Fuck. Okay I'll pay him a visit."

"I recommend that you go before this scheduled time with his two little girls."

"It's that bad?"

"It is."

"I'll go now then."

"Be careful. He's heavily armed, I see here in his internet history that he's made a great deal of purchases recently, all top of the line weaponry. Nothing that can permanently injure you, but a lot of stuff here that could hurt bystanders and attract a lot of attention. He might be planning something big, actually."

"Got it. I'll scope the scene out and slip in quietly."

"Perfect. I'll text you this guy's info right now."

"Thanks, babe."

"Hey, that's what I'm here for. Good thing you caught this lead tonight. Good luck, dude."

Jayden disconnects the call and I wait for Caleb MacLean's address to pop up in my text messages. It appears and I roll my eyes. Of course this guy lives all the way across town in one of those shitty gentrification-gone-wild million dollar high rise apartments.

Oh well. I was a mess anyway. It's not like I could walk across the city looking like this.

I relinquish my materiality and shift into my non-corporeal form, a small wisp of smoke, and dissolve into the night air on my way to work.

CHAPTER FOUR

ELODIE GLASS

According to folklore, a creature like me can't enter your home without an invitation. Depending upon the tradition you follow, I might be able to enchant you or maybe I have to rely only on my natural charm. Maybe I just get lucky and meet a lot of people who have no sense of self-preservation or maybe I have to be clever and trick people into offering up that necessary invite before I can feed.

The truth is that I can go wherever the hell I want.

There's no magic spell protecting you from me or my kind while you lie in your bed at night. As a matter of fact, I'm very, *very* good at getting into all sorts of buildings where I'm not welcome. I can pick locks and scale walls and, if I really want to, I can usually just knock down doors with brute strength if I'm in a hurry and I'm not concerned about whether or not anyone can hear me.

But there's no need to panic. I generally don't enter people's homes unless it's absolutely necessary. People's houses and apartments are full of their personal belongings, which tend to fill me with a visceral sense of disgust. All of the physical manifestations of the memories of a lifetime line the floors and walls and fill the closets. The smell can be overwhelming, especially if the home has been lived in for a very long time, and it's usually not very appetizing.

These days in particular, I only feed on the most vile of men (and the occasional woman) and I have absolutely no interest in getting to know these people intimately. I don't want to see their family photos or smell their dirty laundry. These beasts stink, and their blood is oily and sour. Feeding on them is joyless; it's something I do to quench my thirst and to protect people like my Aya, or, in this case, Melissa and her children.

It's part of my penance.

I'll never taste the sweet blood an innocent again.

Even before my vows, though, I preferred not to enter human homes. I don't like to play with my food. I never really enjoyed getting to know my victims, though I'm not really capable of empathizing with them deeply. I feel primarily desire and rage. Grief and regret are for the daylight hours, when I'll be tucked back in safely under-ground, deep in my dreamless sleep.

I much prefer to catch my prey outdoors, where the cool night breezes can carry away the scents and screams that are inevitable when I inflict my horrors.

But that's not always possible.

Tonight, for example, I'm sitting on a fire escape, watching an overweight, balding man in his mid thirties snore away on his sofa. He's illuminated by the glow of a laptop that's still playing a video and I can tell by the half-empty bottle of Japanese scotch that he's probably out cold.

I pop the screen from his window and climb in, not even really bothering to keep quiet, and I'm surprised when a fluffy white cat immediately approaches me and butts his head against my leg.

I lean down to give him a scratch behind the ears. Usually animals are wary of me. They can't smell me and that unsettles them. This little guy seems to be desperate for a friend, though. He's got bright blue eyes and long, snowy hair and such a precious animal strikes me as incongruous with the rest of Caleb MacLean's aesthetics.

I glance around the nondescript apartment and guess that MacLean probably rented the place already furnished. All of the tables and sofas and chairs are in forgettable neutral shades, and, most telling of all, the apartment smells like a public place rather than a private home. I can tell that many, many people have occupied this space, none for a very long time.

I can hear a small child crying.

The sound is coming from the laptop. I glance over and my eyes flash with rage. Buried memories over a hundred years old threaten to bubble to the surface of my consciousness and I have to cover my mouth with my palm to keep from roaring in anger.

It's a video of a small child, a toddler even, suffering unspeakable abuse at the hands of a faceless man. Only the man's revolting gut is visible in the video, well at least that's the only part of him that might be recognizable, and I slam the laptop shut before I have to see any more.

Was that MacLean himself in the video? It might have been him. Same skin tone, same physique.

I'm certainly not going to take another look at the video to try to figure that out, though. Plus, it doesn't matter. Just watching something like that is a death sentence in my book, and my book's the only one that matters right now.

I had initially planned to slip in, drain MacLean, and then leave within minutes. Now I've decided that a quick death is too good for filth like him. Suddenly, I've got all the time in the world.

My first order of business is to keep him quiet. He's still sleeping, but I choke him out to make sure that he won't wake up until I'm ready for him. His own pet cat watches me as I strip him completely naked and tie him to a chair in his kitchen, which turns out to be more difficult than I expected because of his size. Even with my inhuman strength. He really does look like a little pink pig with a goatee, and I end up having to tie the chair to a table so that it doesn't topple over under his heft.

It takes several slaps and a glass of ice water to wake him up, then once he's conscious I'm glad that I had the foresight to tie the chair to a table because he's struggling and throwing his weight around. I stand still with my arms across my chest, watching him grunt, waiting for him to settle down.

"Comfortable?" I finally ask him when he stops fighting his binds.

He grunts back, his eyes wild, darting around the room. He's probably trying to figure out if I'm working alone.

"Good," I grin, allowing him to see my canines. This sends him into a tailspin and I wait patiently while he struggles again.

"Are you surprised to see me, Caleb?"

MacLean frantically looks me over and I can tell that he's trying to figure out if he knows me from somewhere.

"It's me," I offer him a hint. "The girl from your video."

It may as well have been me, though when it actually was me home videos hadn't been invented yet.

Now MacLean is in a moaning, sobbing panic. Good.

"I bet you didn't think that we'd meet like this. I'm so much bigger now. And stronger."

I flash my canines again and now MacLean is so hysterical that he's choking on the rag I stuffed in his mouth.

"You have a debt to pay. Do you want to die right now, Caleb?"

He shakes his head 'no' so vigorously that I have to laugh. I'm going to make him wish that he said yes.

"Okay," I pretend to agree. "I'll cut you a deal since I'm in a good mood. You seem to be struggling with your manhood. So I'm going to give you the opportunity to remove it."

Now MacLean is staring at me in a way that makes it clear that he has no idea what the fuck I'm talking about.

"Let's see," I glance around the kitchen, then open some drawers. "I've got a pairing knife here or a pair of kitchen scissors. What do you think?"

Now we're back to the hysterics.

"Oh, come on. Don't be such a baby. What do you think, I'm going to feel sorry for you if you cry? Did you feel bad when I did? And I don't know what you're so wrought up over, you barely have anything to remove anyway."

It's true, I can't even see his little worm-dick under the overhang of his belly. He seems to think that he has *a lot* to remove though, because he's thrashing about so much now that he's almost pulled the table *and* the chair over.

"Okay, if you don't want to choose, I will. Here, let's try these kitchen scissors. They'll probably be faster. I'm going to untie you, and I'll give you one chance to cut before the deal is off."

I kind of want to see if he'll really do it, but I'm already growing tired of this game. The moment I untie his hands, he puts me in a bear hug and tries to go for the scissors.

"I had a feeling that you'd change your mind," I say quietly in his ear before I pierce him, draining him as he sobs and moans.

It doesn't take more than a few minutes and then I'm left with nothing but a sack of fat tied to an ugly chair. I wipe my mouth on my sleeve and toss the scissors to the tile floor.

CHAPTER FIVE

ELODIE GLASS

I should clean this up.

I don't want to, but I don't want Melissa MacLean to be somehow implicated in this mess. And she's the first person that the police would investigate, being the ex-wife embroiled in the middle of a nasty custody battle. It's ludicrous, really, to imagine that a woman like that could cause this amount of destruction, she's literally not physically capable.

But that doesn't mean anything to the cops.

I untie the late Mr. MacLean from the chair and let him drop to the kitchen floor, which was stupid because the little bit of blood he has left splashes on the cabinets and now I'll have to clean those too.

This always happens to me.

It's a kind of post-orgasm clarity, but instead of post-orgasm it's post-kill.

This man, who looked so demonic and evil to me a mere ten minutes ago, now just looks pathetic and weak. He's been reduced to a sack of gelatinous fat and bone and now it's hard to believe how much pain and terror he was able to cause when he lived.

Oh, don't get me wrong. I don't have any regrets. If I do regret anything, it's the fact that I got impatient and didn't torture MacLean all night. He certainly deserved it; I believed that when I killed him and I believe it now.

It just always puts me in a melancholy mood, the banality of evil.

I strip down naked so that I don't get my clothes any more dirty and drag whatever is left of MacLean into the bathtub to take him apart with his own high-end chef's knives. It would be easier with a bone cutter or hacksaw, but I don't want to waste time running home to get my supplies, so I just have to put in a little elbow grease.

By the time I've got him stuffed into several heavy duty garbage bags and I'm sure all the blood is bleached clean, I'm feeling filthy. I pull on my pants, grab his keys, and run the bags down to the incinerator in the basement, tossing him in without a second thought like the spoiled meat he is.

I ought to just leave but I don't want to go home, so I let myself back into MacLean's apartment and take a shower in the tub where I just dismembered the former resident. It doesn't improve my mood, but at least now I can't smell that fat sack of shit on my skin any longer.

My sister will probably want to take a look at MacLean's computer. I understand modern technology, but Jayden's a genius and they can often dig up all kinds of dirt that these monsters think they have buried so deep that it will never see the light of day, or the light of the moon in our case. I pack it in a messenger bag leaned up against the sofa and I'm about to let myself back out onto the fire escape when I hear a plaintive meow.

It's the white cat, sitting at my feet and looking up at me expectantly.

"You hungry? Okay." I put down the messenger bag and return to the kitchen to find the cat food. God only knows how long it will be until someone misses MacLean and the cops come to look for him. I don't want the cat to suffer or starve.

"There you go," I fill a small bowl with dry cat food.

The cat looks up at me and meows again.

"Go ahead."

The cat just continues to stare, ignoring the food.

Against my better judgment, I pick up the cat and carry him out the window with me into the night. That seems to make him happy; he snuggles against me and doesn't try to run off.

I have an idea and I know it's a bad one but that doesn't stop me.

Back across town we drift, back to my Aya. I check the video feed in her bedroom. She's deep asleep in her bed now, tossing and turning so that her thin sheet has become wrapped around her pale legs. I let myself in the front door with my key and lock it behind me. She's forgotten her ice cream in the living room and it's almost entirely melted but I put it in her freezer so she can still have it later if she wants.

"You be quiet, okay?" I try to negotiate with the cat, who just stares back as I set him on the floor in her kitchen.

He follows at my heel when I crack the window in the bathroom. I know that Aya would never leave it open but I want her to think that's how the cat got in so she doesn't panic. I'm not sure that she'll even like the cat, but she seems so lonely.

Next I slip into her bedroom, and I half hope that the cat will just jump right onto her bed and wake her up. Then she'd see me and I'd have to act. I'd be forced to…

I don't know what.

Introduce myself?

Try to explain in a non-threatening manner what I was doing in her bedroom?

I'm lying to myself. I know exactly what I'd do. I've been envisioning a scenario like that for months and I'm ready for it. I've prepared a special home for her just in case she needs to be kept safe, for her own good.

At any rate, the cat's not cooperating. He's just sitting at my feet, watching Aya with me like we're now partners in crime. She's snoring softly like a little bear cub and clutching her pillow as though it was a life raft. I get up and quietly move the hair from her face and she doesn't stir so I indulge myself and stroke it gently, rubbing it between my thumb and forefinger. It's so soft and thick, I just want to tangle my fingers in it and pull her toward me, then pull her head back and expose the length of her throat. My thumb runs down the side of her alabaster neck and she shivers so I carefully untangle her legs from her sheet and cover her.

I'm glad that she's able to sleep so soundly and I hope that her dreams are sweet, though I've got my doubts. I know that she's tortured by her own memories, though she rarely ever speaks about them to anyone. I lay down beside her and breathe in deeply, inhaling her scent like I'm devouring her, which is what I actually want to be doing. She's so tender and precious and delicate. She's everything I'm not and I'll do whatever is necessary to keep her this way. She's already been through so much, way more that her share of pain and suffering. It's remarkable that she's able to face the day each morning, let alone try to go out and better herself.

I almost don't notice that her old manual alarm clock is set for 6AM.

That's wrong. She never leaves the house the day after our group meeting. She needs at least an entire day to recover and she doesn't set her alarm unless she has some kind of appointment.

I briefly consider just turning the alarm off so it doesn't disturb her in the morning, but instead I decide to get up and check her computer just in case. I slip out of her bed and into her living room, where it's still sitting open on the coffee table. I tap it to wake it up and enter in her password, Rose-Gold313.

She's got her emails open and I congratulate myself on resisting the temptation to read them all, which is a bit absurd since they're almost entirely spam save for a few messages from her therapist. Instead I open her calendar, where I see it: she's moved her therapy appointment ahead two days. It must be because her therapist is going on holiday or something because the rest of her calendar is almost entirely empty and her therapy session is back at its regular scheduled time next week.

It'll be morning soon and I'm tired. I check Aya's fridge and pantry and make note of some things that I ought to top up the next time I stop by, then give in to my urge to crawl back into bed with her for just one more moment before I head out.

She's tangled up in her sheet again, silly girl. The darkest hour is just before dawn so I gently untangle her once more to cover her, though I know she'll probably be wound up again before the sun rises. I wish that I could warm her up, though I know it's impossible because of who and what I am.

"If only we could have met in another life…" I stroke her cheek and then lift her fingers to my lips to kiss them gently.

This sets the cat to meowing and I shift back into my non-corporeal form so that I can drift off into the night before he really does wake her and all hell breaks loose.

I don't want to leave but it's okay. I know I'll be back soon.

CHAPTER SIX

AYA LACHAT

I'm woken again with the sense that someone is watching me, but this time it's different. I open my eyes and I swear to God something moves in the corner of my field of vision. It's been a long, long time since I've been this terrified and I lay still as a cold sweat beads all over my skin. I'm expecting to be attacked at any moment.

Then I see it again, a flick of white. It's too small to be a person.

"Holy shit," I cry, pulling the sheet up to cover my body.

It's got to be a rat. My apartment is in a really nice albeit old building and I keep it clean, but maybe these things are inevitable in this city. I've seen them digging around the dumpster in the back alley and I don't know for sure but I think they can climb pretty well. Well enough to scale the side of my building?

Quickly my mind races through my possible next moves. I could try to trap the rat with my laundry hamper and throw it back outside? Or I could shoo it out the front door with my broom. Obviously the most sane course of action would be to call my landlord and ask for help, but that would probably mean letting strangers into my place, which obviously is a no-go.

Then my eyes focus and I'm even more confused.

It's not a rat, it's a cat. A fluffy white one with blue eyes.

"Um... cat?" I say in way of introduction, not sure what I'm supposed to do in this situation.

The cat meows back at me.

"Are you lost?" I ask, as though the cat can answer me.

To the surprise of absolutely no one, he stays mum on the subject.

"How did you get in here?"

Still no response.

Now I have to get up and check the front door. Even I know that bad guys don't break into people's homes to drop off fancy cats, so I've got to assume that I left something open. It doesn't really make sense to me since I'm obsessed with confirming that everything is locked up tight, but that explanation makes more sense than the alternative.

To my great relief, the front door is locked. All five locks are fast and tight. Then I do my rounds checking the windows, starting with the fire escape, and I find the point of entry. It's my bathroom, which has no screen and is just barely open. I'm shocked that the cat was able to squeeze into such a tight space, but I've heard about cats getting themselves stuck in all kinds of places so I guess it's possible. I'm going to have to be more careful in the future; I must be getting careless.

"Where did you come from, kitty?" I ask him, bending down to scratch his ears. "You're a fancy boy. I don't believe that you're an alley cat. Did you get lost?"

The cat seems happy and healthy. I've never really considered getting a pet, but I'm embarrassed to admit to myself that I've already started thinking of ways to hide the kitty so I can keep him and his real owners don't claim him back.

"What's your name?"

I decide that I'm going to have to make some posters just in case a family is looking for this guy. Then if I don't find them in a month, I can keep him.

"How about Yeti? Because you look like a snowman?"

The cat doesn't object, so Yeti it is. I pop open a can of tuna for him and dump it into a bowl, since I don't have anything else to offer him yet. Fortunately he seems to be a big fan.

I've got plenty of time this morning before I have to leave for my therapy appointment, so after I shower and dress I pop open my laptop to make a grocery delivery order for the afternoon. I browse through the pet section and order cat food and a litter box. I want to order a bunch of cute toys too, but I'm on a budget so I settle on a single mouse on a little fishing pole that has a ton of good reviews.

Yeti has finished his tuna and jumps onto my lap as I browse the news. My therapist has warned me that the news tends to be triggering for me, so I'm supposed to avoid it, but I'm not exactly the world's best patient.

Unfortunately I find exactly what I'm looking for. Last night a man was dismembered and thrown into his luxury high rise's incinerator just across town. The police found him this morning when the building's superintendent smelled something weird and immediately phoned 911. The man's body was so badly damaged that they can't figure out his exact cause of death, but that doesn't stop me from copy and pasting his name into my browser so that I can read every single news article about the murder.

I hold Yeti tight and put on my amateur detective hat, searching the scant news articles for any indication that this was the work of Olsen Leonard.

I can't tell my therapist this, but I'm sure he's still out there and I'm also fairly sure that he's 'working' this city. The proof I have is just overwhelming, at least to me. I don't know much about O but I do know that he drains all the blood from his victims, sometimes slowly as he tortures them. I will never, ever be able to scrub the memory of him lapping up my parents' blood like some kind of sick, rabid dog from my brain.

But for such an animal, he's also very clever. He never leaves any evidence like fingerprints or his own DNA, and he seems to be an expert at breaking and entering. There are never any witnesses to his crimes and I know that he must be someone important because the house where he kept me captive was palatial. Sometimes I'd hear other girls screaming and I could tell that they were also inside but it sounded like they were several hundred meters away.

I know it's him whenever the police find another body drained of blood. How many serial killers could there possibly be who even have the know-how or the resources to do that? It must be him, and I've spent the past several months assuming that, any moment now, he'll be back to finish the job he started with me.

My therapist thinks that obsessing over Olsen Leonard after so long is not doing my recovery any good, but I don't know what else I'm supposed to do. She tells me to let the police do their job, but the police don't even seem to want to consider that all of these murders are actually him. They certainly don't have any leads. If I wait for the police to capture Olsen Leonard, I'm going to be waiting until the day I die, which probably won't be long from now if O has his way.

I can't say for sure whether this latest murder is O's work. There isn't enough evidence for me to feel confident, but it's possible. I slam my laptop shut and carry Yeti back into my room. I've got to clear my head before my therapy session or else my therapist is going to pick up on something wrong and I just don't want to deal with telling her that I've been looking for O in the news again.

I set Yeti down on my chair and set to work making my bed. Keeping my things tidy makes me feel more in control over my life. Then I see it: there's a hair on my pillow, and it's definitely not one of my long, auburn ones. I pick it up to study it.

"Is this yours, Yeti?" I wonder aloud. I know that cats shed a lot and I'll probably have to get used to more vacuuming.

Yeti meows back.

"Yeah I didn't think so. This one is wavy."

It's true; there's a wavy, white hair on my pillow. That's weird because I've never had anyone over to this apartment. I pick it up and study it, trying to put my finger on why it looks so familiar to me.

I can't let my imagination get away with me. My therapist has already warned me that if things get worse, I might have to go back to the hospital.

This hair probably belongs to one of my neighbors, and that's why it looks familiar. We have a single shared laundry room in this building and those machines are used by everyone because they're free.

I strip the bed and pile the sheets and pillow cases into my hamper. I need to keep moving, to distract myself before I spiral into a panic.

I feel like I'm in a riptide, being pulled under, like I never really escaped. O may not have killed me (yet), but he has stolen my life. I don't want to spend the rest of my days looking over my shoulder, but I can't help it.

I'm sure that someone is watching me.

HOUSE OF GLASS: CRACKED

CHAPTER ONE

AYA LACHAT

I'm going to end up back in the hospital; I know it.

I hated it there and I'd do anything to avoid it, but at this point even I am beginning to wonder if that isn't the best place for me. I can't even function at a basic level anymore. I constantly have the feeling that I'm being watched. Followed. Stalked.

But I never see anyone.

In fact, I seldom encounter any other people. I never leave my apartment anymore except to attend my group meetings and my therapy sessions. I have trouble falling asleep at night, and when I do drift off my sleep is fitful and restless. I'm plagued by nightmares. My memories are the kindling and my imagination the fuel for the fires that burn through my soul every night, and I wake up more tired than I was when I went to bed.

I'm so isolated but I never feel truly alone. It's like there are invisible eyes on me at all times, though I never do anything very interesting these days. At least if I was back at the hospital, I'd be able to rest assured knowing that I actually *am* under surveillance at all times, by someone who is watching me because it's her job.

But then who would take care of Yeti?

Sometimes I feel like this cat is the only reason I have to go on living. He's my only joy and a true friend, sleeping in my bed at night and never leaving my side during the day. He trusts me, which is something that I've never experienced before, and taking care of him is the only thing that makes me feel not entirely useless.

Things aren't going well, but I'm still trying. I haven't yet reached the point where I stop taking care of myself or my home entirely, though my lack of appetite and physical activity has made me weak.

Today is laundry day, which has become a big event for me. I collect my pile of faded black rags and prepare to leave my apartment for the first time in 72 hours.

"Do you have any clothes you want me to wash?" I joke with Yeti. He doesn't. He doesn't even wear a collar, that libertine. He meows back though, acknowledging that I'm stepping out for a bit. I think he understands that I'll only be gone a minute when I'm carrying the hamper.

Going down to the laundry room used to be a high-stress situation for me but now I've got a strategy. I wash all my clothes and linens at 2AM in the middle of the week. That way I know that I'll have the laundry room to myself.

It's not that I don't feel safe around my neighbors in particular. Quite the contrary, this building seems to be full of exclusively very sweet women. Very sweet, very friendly women who love to chat and get to know one another. They're definitely the kind of girls who I could imagine myself being besties with, if I wasn't a complete loser.

At it stands, though, I'm deeply, deeply ashamed of my failure to thrive. There's nothing I hate more than meeting someone new and then quickly having to explain that no, I don't have a job. No, I don't study anything. No, I didn't finish school. No, I don't have any hobbies. No, I don't have friends. No, I don't have a family.

What *do* I do? Mostly look over my shoulder and imagine implausible scenarios in which I am again the victim and this time I don't escape.

Who would want to be friends with someone like me?

Every single time I read about some other girl who survived something, I'm reading about how that girl overcame every setback and became an astronaut or a doctor or something else really impressive that the world needs.

I never read stories about girls who survive and then become recluses who scrape by for the remaining years they have left on Earth on public benefits.

So down I head, into the laundry room in the basement, at the witching hour on a Tuesday. Carrying my pile of black tunics and leggings so that I can at least wear clean clothes when I spend another week sitting alone on my sofa, reading about local crimes on the internet.

My therapist thinks that I need to stop triggering myself and she's probably right. But how can I stop? When O is still out there and this city is practically under siege? Just this past week two women were attacked within four blocks of my building.

The motion detector in the basement activates the lights as soon as I open the door. It's one of the many things I like about this building even though the fluorescents give me a bit of a headache. The hallway is bright and clean and there are no places for someone to hide, so I'm feeling pretty confident when I approach an empty washing machine.

My clothes don't even fill the machine halfway. I'm adding detergent when I hear it. There is some clanging metal sound behind me. I spin around to look at the empty hallway and freeze. There's nothing there. I know that it's my imagination playing tricks on me because it happens constantly. Best case scenario is that some pipes were making noise, someone started a shower or flushed a toilet or something. The worst case is something that I've been fearing for a while now... what if I'm actually starting to hallucinate?

I resume loading my wash and the machine rumbles to life. Sometimes I just hang around and wait for the wash cycle to end so I can move my clothes into the dryer, but now I've given myself the heebie jeebies so I head back to the stairs.

As soon as I open the door there are arms around me. I scream and some kind of sour tasting, rough textile is shoved into my mouth. My legs kick out but the person holding me is much stronger than I am and seemingly twice the size. I can't see who has me but I can feel a big belly behind my back and I can smell stale menthol cigarettes.

This is it. The moment I've been waiting for. The Olsen I remember was slender and smelled like decaying roses, but I guess we've both changed a lot over the past years.

Instead of leaving the building like I expect, I get dragged to the door of a maintenance room that is always locked. Now it's open, though, and I'm being shoved inside. I land on the ground with a thud and hit the side of my head.

I'm scrambling around, trying to gain my footing when I look up and see that it's not Olsen who has me, it's Lou, the building's new-ish handyman. The same one who greets me every time I go out or come in. The same one who probably has a key to my place.

Still, I'm not sure. It's technically possible that Olsen has aged a lot over the past months. I was just so sure that it would be him that ended me. My brain doesn't want to accept that it's another man entirely.

Just when Lou lunges for me, someone grabs him from behind. I can't see exactly what's going on now because the maintenance room is dark and the figures are backlit by the hallway. I can only see the shadows struggling.

The new figure is tall but far more slender and is administering a savage beating. I can hear the thump of fists hitting soft flesh over and over and I feel a spray of liquid on my face that I'm afraid is blood.

I scamper back into a corner in a crab walk and wrap my arms around my knees. There's no way that I could make it past these two and out the door. My eyes dart around, looking for a better hiding spot, but this maintenance room isn't that big.

Lou is clearly losing this fight. His body is slumping and now the other man is kicking him in the side. I'm still trying to make out what is going on and the only detail I can see at first is light shining through pale blond curls. And then I see, it's not a man at all.

"Angel?" I say quietly out loud, mostly to myself. Now I'm almost sure that I'm hallucinating.

She doesn't answer. Instead she opens her mouth wider than seems humanly possible and rips out Lou's throat with her bare teeth. She doesn't just bite, though, she's tearing out strips of flesh and she seems to be eating them.

I know that I'm screaming but I can't hear my own voice. The only thing I can hear is the sound of my own blood pounding in my ears.

It's the same all over again, Olsen tearing at my parents, but this time it isn't Olsen.

And this time I'm surely not going to escape.

CHAPTER TWO

ELODIE GLASS

I never wanted Aya to see me like this.

I can't help what I am, but that doesn't mean that there aren't more elegant ways to feed. I know that what I just did was beastly and I know how I must look right now. I can feel the blood on my face and I can feel bits of flesh stuck between my teeth.

I know that I've horrified my Aya because she's unconscious. Her little body is lying in a slump on this dirty basement floor and my top priority is getting her somewhere safe and comfortable where she can recover.

I've got just the place in mind.

At least I don't have to deal with the body of this cockroach immediately. I drag the handyman into a corner of the maintenance room and leave him there for now, trying to see the bright side of this situation. I can come back later to dispose of him because the only people who have a key to this maintenance room are me and him and he's not going anywhere anytime soon.

I can't believe I was such an idiot, risking Aya's life like that. I'm the fool who hired this animal. I did a thorough background check on him and nothing in his past indicated that he'd try to pull something like this, but here we are. I guess you just can't trust anyone these days.

I give his lifeless body another kick just for good measure, taking out my anger at myself on him.

For now I've got to get Aya out of here. I pick her up like a rag doll. She weighs almost nothing and her head rolls back as I hold her in my arms, exposing the slender length of her neck. This is the closest I've ever been to her and I don't know if I can control myself.

I lift her up closer to me and I can feel my own body shaking with need and hunger. I'm slick with desire and ravenous, though I just fed. I want to fuck her and drink every last drop of her at the same time. I'm too old to be this lacking in self control and I'm glad that my sisters can't see me now. I know that they'd be worried about me. I haven't felt hunger like this since I was freshly turned.

I know that I shouldn't, but I nestle my face down into the soft skin where her neck curves into her shoulder. She feels feverish and I can smell the fear in her, the sweat and tears. I can also smell the rich, metallic edge of her blood and the tang of her cunt. She's so alive and so deep; the closer I get to her, the more there is to discover. I know that it would take lifetimes to know her, and luckily lifetimes is what I've got.

My lips part and my tongue darts out instinctively. My breath catches in my throat as I draw it into the dip in her Plender gap, up her neck, and behind the tender flesh of her unpierced ear. I feel her shake in my arms and I'm afraid I'll wake her. I pull myself away from her and wince when I see what I've done; there's a streak of blood running up her body like a stain where I kissed her. It's not hers, though, thank God. It smells sour like the handyman. It must have rubbed off my face and I'm glad that she can't see the mess I've made.

We need to leave.

I carry Aya out to the street and I'm grateful for two things. First, that she does her laundry in the middle of the night. No one is awake to see me carry her out, and I hate to imagine what might have happened to her if this attack happened during the day. Second, I'm glad that I drove. I bring Aya out to the Mercedes that I've been driving since I bought it new back in the 1960s and I hesitate.

I'm loathe to do this, but I cringe and pop the trunk. If she wakes up while I'm driving I'm afraid she'll hurt herself trying to escape and we don't need any unwanted attention. I don't want her to think that I mean her harm but I have to confine her for her own good. I'm used to throwing bodies in my trunk but I lay Aya down gently and hope that she doesn't wake up before I get her home.

"Sorry," I say mostly to myself as I quietly shut the lid.

I slide into the driver's seat and I have to take a moment to myself. I take a few deep breaths and rest my forehead against the steering wheel, trying to calm my mind, which is spinning out of control.

I've pictured it so many times, the moment when I have to act and claim Aya for myself. In my dreams she's rushed into my arms and begged me to protect her. Now I have her locked in the trunk of my car.

Adrenaline is the only thing propelling me forward. It's certainly not a plan or anything resembling good decision making. I drive Aya out of the city and toward the outskirts of town, out of the revitalized part of the city into the still-decaying part, then far enough that we're back in another nice part, then farther still toward the abandoned mansions where I live with my sisters.

Our place is an hour out of town, but that's not where I'm taking Aya.

My sisters don't know anything about her. If they did, she wouldn't be in my trunk right now.

I keep driving to the antique stone farmhouse that I've prepared for her. It's been my secret project and my passion for the past several months and I hope for her sake that she likes it.

From the outside, it looks like any other abandoned stone farmhouse. It lays on five hundred acres surrounded by a tall stone wall with a rusted iron gate and the house itself and surrounding structures are covered with ivy.

The inside is a different story.

Like Aya's apartment, this farmhouse is actually a highly secured fortress with all of the most modern, state-of-the-art security features including iron doors, bulletproof windows, a video surveillance system that covers every square inch of the property, infrared heat detectors, and soundproof walls.

Unlike Aya's apartment, though, this fortress locks from the outside.

Every single feature is controlled via my phone. I'll be able to see and hear what Aya is doing at all times. She'll be safer than the crown jewels.

But I haven't committed all of my efforts to security.

I've also gone to extreme lengths to make the home comfortable for Aya.

I've been watching her for so long and I've made an identical copy of her bedroom, but with top of the line furnishings. Her cheap pink sheets are now 400-thread count Egyptian cotton. Her pressed wood furniture is now imported teak. The posters she had hanging on her wall have all been replaced by original artworks.

I've even replaced her stuffed animal collection, arranging her little menagerie exactly like she had it on her own dresser at home.

I want her to feel at ease and I've decorated the entire house in a manner that I believe will appeal to her, but for the time being I've decided to lock her in her bedroom. I want to give her the opportunity to settle in before giving her run of the house. I don't want her to get frightened and wander off somewhere so I have to hunt her down and catch her.

When I pop the lid to the trunk I'm happy to see that Aya is still sound asleep. Her breathing has slowed and her temperature is lower. I carefully pick her up and carry her into her new accommodations, setting her gently on her bed.

She immediately stretches out and grabs the pillow tighter, hugging it to her body. I can still smell the sweat on her clothes and I get a pair of clean pajamas from her dresser, a set of floral shorts and matching camisole. At first I mean to change her clothes myself, but then I think better of it.

She might not feel comfortable being undressed by a stranger and I can no longer pretend that stripping her naked is absolutely necessary for her own good, though I want to desperately. I set the pajamas on the bed next to her so she can change herself if she wants to when she wakes up.

I brush my thumb across her cheek and I can feel the crust of her dried tears. I want to carry her to the bath and wash away all her troubles, assure her that her life is in safe hands now and she never has to be afraid or lonely again.

I want to comfort her and show her with my body how much I love her.

For the time being, though, I let her sleep. I leave her room and lock it behind me. The dawn is approaching and I've got to go to ground.

CHAPTER THREE

AYA LACHAT

" ... **Y**eti?"

I'm in my bed.. but it's more comfortable. I've never been this comfortable in my entire life. I pull my sheet up to my chin and it's softer than it was before, I'm sure of it.

I'm in my room, but it's different. It's my room, but my furniture looks heavier. I don't know how to explain it. The colors look richer too. It's like I was previously viewing my room through the lens of a disposable camera and now I was viewing it through a top-of-the-line digital camera.

I sit up in my bed and call my cat again. He's not here and he doesn't answer, which is out of character for him.

I'm safe in my bed but I don't think that I've ever been so afraid in my entire life.

I just woke up from the worst dream. I was doing my laundry and I got assaulted by my building's superintendent, a man who had never been anything but polite and friendly. Then my crush from my group meeting showed up and beat him to death before turning into the monster who murdered my family and abducted me.

And now my perception of the world is different. I've lost my mind; I'm absolutely sure of it. I've graduated from feeling like I'm always being watched to feeling like my room is not my room.

I definitely need to call my therapist. I can no longer keep up this facade of semi-normalcy. I'm pretty sure that I'm having some kind of psychotic break and I need help before things get worse.

I'm about to get up when I notice something on my bed. It's a set of pajamas that doesn't belong to me. They're folded up neatly on the corner and I suddenly realize that my clothes are the only things that don't seem weird. I'm wearing my same old ratty black leggings and tunic. I don't even think they're clean because I can smell the faint odor of my BO.

My heart is racing and I sit for a moment and stare at the pajamas. They're very pretty, a pair of cotton shorts with tiny rose buds and lace trim and then a matching camisole. But they're not mine and I have no idea where they could have come from.

"Yeti?" I call again, as though the cat might appear and explain what's happened.

No such luck.

I get up and glance at the window and it's then that I know for sure that either A. I've gone completely insane, or B. I'm actually not in my room.

My apartment is nice and I'm happy with it but views are not one of the things that it has to offer. My bedroom window looks out directly at a brick wall four feet away. I kind of like it because at least no one has a view inside, but it's not exactly idyllic.

This window is in the same location in my room, but instead of a brick wall I'm looking at an oak tree. I glance around the room to confirm that nothing else looks amiss and I get up to look outside.

I'm no longer in a city.

Somehow my room has evolved. My belongings are nicer and now I'm in the middle of a lush forest. I can see trees and what looks to be what was once a lawn but has now gone to meadow. I'm only on the second floor and I can see little wildflowers bending in the breeze. I'd like to open the window to get some fresh air, but that's apparently the one thing that hasn't been upgraded from the original. It's still stuck shut.

I still can't tell if I'm physically in a different space or I'm mentally in a different space.

I can tell that I need to speak to my therapist though. I'm going to call her and make an emergency appointment.

I try my bedroom door and it's stuck. It's never been stuck before. I rattle the handle and push my weight up against it and then I realize: it's not stuck, it's locked.

"Hey!" I scream, now quite sure that I'm not imagining things. I slam my shoulder into the door and I'm immediately met with searing pain. My door in my apartment is thin wood but this one is obviously some kind of metal. "Hey!" I cry again, trying not to panic. "Hello?"

There's no answer.

Now that I'm up I take the time to look around the room more carefully and I feel dumb. This is obviously not my real room. All of the stuff in this room looks like my stuff, but it's really, really, really nice. Like stuff that I could never afford, not in a million years.

I'm fighting back tears and struggling with a flashback.

It's that same claustrophobic feeling that I got when I was locked in the small, dark room where O kept me prisoner. This room is bright and luxurious but it's still a prison.

I'm back at O's and he's toying with me. He must somehow know that I never recovered mentally from what he did and now he's purposefully trying to make me think that I've lost my mind.

This sends me into a flying rage and I slam my body into the door over and over, not caring if all I'm doing is wrecking my own shoulder. I shriek until my voice is gone and my body is too bruised to continue. Then I sink to the floor in a crying heap.

Is there anything in this room that I could use to break the window?

I look around and don't see anything useful. Just furniture and my stuffed animal collection, the only things I have left from my childhood. Did Olsen go into my room and pick up my stuff when he kidnapped me? I pick up my old Pound Puppy and confirm that no, it's not mine. I put mine on a hot stove when I was a little girl and burned it so that my mother had to patch it. This one isn't patched. It's the same model but not the same toy.

This sicko. What kind of man would do something like this?

I knew exactly what kind of man. The same kind who would cannibalize a child's parents in front of her.

There's another door in my bedroom. In my real bedroom, it leads to my bathroom. Maybe this one leads somewhere else.

I try it and it's not locked.

I enter and this door leads to a bathroom too, but O hasn't created an exact copy of my real bathroom. I guess that he felt that the bedroom copy was sufficient to make me think I'd lost my mind.

This bathroom is far more luxurious than the one in my apartment. It has a huge corner tub with jacuzzi jets and a separate shower with multiple shower heads. Fluffy white bath sheets are stacked high and I can see an assortment of luxury bath products in scents that would have made me drool if I wasn't very aware that they were provided by the man who was going to kill me, probably slowly and painfully.

The window here is stuck too, and upon closer inspection I discover that it's not just stuck, it's sealed shut. And the glass is some kind of special glass, super thick.

I'm not going to be able to break out of this room, that much is immediately clear.

My only chance will be to make a run for it when O opens the door. I'll have to be ready to charge him and hopefully catch him by surprise and knock him over so I can try to escape that way. It's not ideal but it's all I've got.

I sit on the edge of the bed and keep my eyes trained on the door for so long that I begin to fear that O's plan is just to lock me in this room alone permanently like a tomb.

After about an hour, a small slot at the bottom of the door that I hadn't previously even seen slides open and a tray appears. I make a leap from the bed to try to catch the hands that slide it though but of course I'm too slow, I'm not a cat and I don't have the reflexes of one.

They're a woman's hands, I think, beautifully manicured. I also notice a heavy gold wristwatch and I might be imagining things but I'm pretty sure it's not O. I would have remembered him having such long, feminine fingers. Maybe he has someone working for him, or maybe this is another woman he's captured and forced into servitude.

The tray is laden with food and it smells incredible. There's an entire half of a roast chicken and a mix of spring vegetables but I won't touch any of it.

I notice that there are also two vials and I leave my perch on the bed to go take a closer look, the curiosity is killing me.

They're labeled Tylenol with Codeine and Valium.

He must be watching me. I glance up from the floor and my eyes search the room for cameras, but I can't see anything.

I leave the food and the 'gift' of medicine untouched on the floor and take a seat on the chair next to the bed, waiting for something to happen.

❧

CHAPTER FOUR

ELODIE GLASS

T his isn't going the way I always imagined it would.

It's funny how that happens no matter how long you've been walking this Earth... you start to daydream about a particular fantasy for long enough and then your fantasies begin to seem more like memories. Memories that just haven't happened yet. Then when reality doesn't match those future-memories...

Let's just say that reality can sometimes come as quite a shock to your psyche. A real kick in the gut, if you will.

I should have known better. Hell, I did know better. I always knew in my head that Aya might have some trouble... adjusting... to her new life. It was a long time ago for me, but I can still remember how I struggled when my life changed. Or ended, rather.

It's just that In my dreams Aya was always so grateful. Grateful that I saved her life, grateful that I rescued her from her terror and drudgery. Grateful that I provided her with the luxury, security, and comfort that she deserves. Grateful that I loved her so, so much. More than life itself.

When I pictured our future together, things were different. I'd swoop in whenever was necessary and carry her away in my arms into the night, off to the home that I'd already made perfect for her. She'd somehow already know what I am and that she'd be safe with me. She'd accept me and grow to love me.

I already know that she wants me, or at least wanted me. I know that at least that's not just a fantasy of mine because I can smell the slight changes in her body chemistry whenever I greet her at the group meeting. I can smell her sweat a little bit and I can smell the wetness of her sex.

There's nothing I'd love more than to give her exactly what her body begs for.

It's just that her mind is playing tricks on her. Instead of taking what she needs, she's denying herself.

I've been sitting on this sofa, watching her on my phone for over two hours. I'm going to be honest here: her stubbornness is infuriating. She's been sitting on her little pink chair, not moving since I dropped off her meal.

I'm especially annoyed because I went to the trouble of learning how to cook so that I could prepare that meal myself. I don't normally eat, at least not chicken, and I haven't had any reason to prepare food... ever. Even when I actually was alive I never cooked.

"Eat the God damned chicken, Aya," I say quietly to myself. I know that the problem is not the food because I chose this recipe because she herself had bookmarked it on her laptop.

I'm sure it's cold by now and I'm beginning to worry that if she does decide to eat it now she'll get food poisoning. I don't need her getting sick. She'd probably just assume that I poisoned her.

I head back upstairs and slide the panel in the door open quickly so that I can pull the tray back out.

"Hey!" Aya yells, and then I can hear her little feet pounding as she traverses her room. "Hey open the door, asshole!"

I immediately decide to just take the food and push the tray back in with her medicine. I hope that she just comes to her senses and at least takes the damn Valium so she can calm down but I'm not getting the impression from her current behavior that my hopes are going to be fulfilled.

She tries to grab for me again, but she's not as quick as I am and she's certainly not as strong. I push her meds back inside and slam the panel shut.

Fortunately for me the room is soundproof so I'm spared her tirade of insults.

I head back downstairs to the sofa, check out her video feed, and immediately turn off the sound feed. I can see that she's throwing herself at the door again and screaming and I really don't feel like listening to her opinions about my behavior right now.

I can't soothe her anyway.

Well, I think I can, but at the moment it doesn't look like she would welcome me entering her room and offering her the kind of comfort that my body craves.

I watch her throw herself around the room in a fit for a while and I feel sorry for her. I don't feel responsible, of course, because I only did what needed to be done for her own good. But I do feel sympathy. She's obviously so distraught, and it's so unnecessary.

I wish that there was some way that I could make her understand that there is no reason for her to work herself up like that. She's afraid, clearly, and she's angry too.

I can't blame her, really. Aya doesn't have a very good track record with my kind, between what happened to her family and what happened just now with that piece of shit handyman. I can tell that she's afraid that I want to hurt her. I'm going to have to make her understand that I would never do that. Not on purpose.

My video feed is interrupted with a call.

It's my older sister Adrienne.

"Yo."

"Where are you?"

"I'm out."

"Out where?"

Shit. Adrienne is in one of her moods. It's the time she spent working as a mercenary; she thinks that we all need to know each other's business at all times. You know, synchronize watches and all that.

"I'm fixing up an old farmhouse I found."

"You're what?"

"Fixing up a farmhouse."

"Why are you doing that?"

"Because I want to?"

"So what, you're getting into house flipping now or what?"

"No, I just saw it and liked the way it looked. Sometimes I like working with my hands."

"Then why don't you fix up our place?"

"Is there something you wanted, Adrienne? Or you just missed me?"

It's not that weird for me to be gone for a while. We all do it occasionally. I'm not sure why Adri has a bee in her bonnet.

"Yeah," Adrienne seems willing to let the subject of my farm drop. "What's the deal with this MacLean? Jayden told me that was you."

"Yeah, it was."

"What happened? This guy wasn't on the list."

"I got a tip off and it was a time-sensitive situation. Woman in the PTSD Victim's Group was beside herself over a court order that allowed her ex unsupervised visitation with her little girls. Guy had already been done once for child exploitation and Jayden checked it out. I didn't have time to go through the whole process."

"You know that there's a reason that we have a 'whole process,' right Glass?"

"Yeah, I know. You're right, I'm sorry. I should have at least called you. I was too fired up about it. You know how I get when it's kids, A. And I caught him red-handed."

"Yeah, Ma, I know. We just have to be careful. It's the security risks. Get impulsive like that and you'll get sloppy. We don't need any attention from the feds and we definitely don't need to draw any attention from other vamps. I don't know about you but I like it here. I don't want to have to start over somewhere else."

"I know Adri, and I'm sorry. I burned him. No way for anyone man or beast to know that it was us."

I'm going to need God to save me if Adrienne finds out about the 'security risk' that I'm keeping at my farmhouse, which would mean I'm in deep trouble because God turned his back on me over a hundred years ago. I can't even imagine what my eldest sister Aravella's reaction might be. She'd be in a white, frothing rage, for sure. Angry enough to kick me out of our coven? Maybe. Angry enough to end me?

I don't know.

Best case scenario, she'd tell me that I have to get rid of Aya. I made a vow to my sisters to protect the innocent, and I don't think that Aravella — or any of my sisters for that matter — would appreciate my new, creative interpretation of what that 'protection' entailed.

They'd think that I'd lost my mind, and maybe they'd be right.

But now that I have her I can't let her go. It's just not possible. I've waited my entire life for Aya and I won't give her up now that she's finally mine, even if she doesn't quite understand that yet.

I don't want to be forced to choose between Aya and my sisters.

But if I am forced to choose, I already know where my still heart lies.

CHAPTER FIVE

AYA LACHAT

My stomach growls and my vision is blurry. Something fuzzy is coating my teeth and I've got a sickly sweet taste in my mouth.

I don't know how long I've been in this room.

I'm starving.

The trays of food arrive at regular intervals, a new meal each time, every one smelling delicious. I haven't touched a single one. Every one sits for an hour before it's removed. Then later another fresh plate takes its place.

At first I was afraid of being drugged. I wouldn't eat because I was afraid that if I did eat, I'd lose consciousness and not be able to protect myself. I'd get raped, or worse.

Now that fear no longer makes sense because I've been losing consciousness anyway, only from exhaustion and hunger instead of from some drug. I sit for long, boring hours on this stupid chair and then suddenly I'm startled awake and I discover that some amount of time has passed and I'm still in the damn chair. Nothing has changed and the only way to mark time is by the movements of the sun out of my window and the meals coming through the doors.

It's been at least a week, but I'm struggling to measure time because I'm no longer on any kind of sleep schedule. The meals appear only during the night, and instead of sleeping at regular intervals I just fight to stay awake until my body gives out.

Then there's no telling how long I've been asleep.

At this point I'm refusing the food out of pure stubbornness. I'm sure that I'm being watched, though I haven't been able to find the cameras, and I don't know if my captor intends to let me starve or at some point he'll come in and force feed me.

Both options terrify me.

I've read before that it's horrible, starving to death. It could take three months or more and along the way my hair and teeth will fall out. Has O figured out a way to make me torture myself to death?

I remember the way he toyed with my brothers, Hugh and Gabe. He tore my mother and father apart like animals, but he took his time with my brothers. He taunted them and let them beg for their lives. Then he offered to let them live if they decided who should die first — myself or my older sister Nala. They refused to choose and then he let them think that they had a chance at escaping before catching them again. He cut the tendons in their ankles and allowed them to try to drag themselves away before pulling them back over and over.

It went on and on and on.

Of course O can never torture me quite like that again.

It would be impossible now, because there's no one left alive who I love.

No one alive who loves me.

I'm still not exactly eager to suffer alone, especially not for his sick entertainment.

I'm already in pain from trying to break out of this room. I know now that it's futile, but I still throw myself against the door. It feels better than sitting and waiting for my own death, though I think I may have damaged my shoulder.

I want to take a bath in the big tub to soak it, but I don't want to give O the pleasure. I'm sure he's got cameras in both rooms and I have no illusions about him respecting my privacy in the bathroom.

So I'm still wearing the same clothes that I was wearing when I arrived and I haven't washed myself. I stink and my hair is stringy and greasy. I've discovered a closet full of pretty dresses but I haven't touched them.

My plan was to wait until O opened the door, and then charge him. That plan is fading further and further into the distance now though. I no longer can fool myself into believing that I have the strength for something like that.

So now I just curl up on my chair and wait for something to happen. I've been avoiding the bed entirely, first because I feel gross being this dirty and getting into bed, and second because I'm afraid if I get back in that comfortable bed then I'll fall so deeply asleep that I won't be able to wake up if there's a sound.

Time stands still and I resign myself to existing in pain. It's daylight out and there's no food, just the tray of medicine which I also haven't tried. It's tempting now that I'm so weak anyway but I'm afraid that my cognitive function has declined to the point of no longer functioning to reason.

Then it happens.

The sun sets and the door opens. In enters...

Angel?

I lift my tired body from the chair, barely, and try to figure out if I'm hallucinating.

Angel locks the door behind her and she seems very real. I don't know what to make of this situation and I blew my chance at running anyway so I sit silently in my chair and watch her.

"I brought you something," she says quietly and offers me what she's holding in her hands.

It's a pint of chocolate brownie ice cream and a spoon.

I continue staring silently and don't accept her offering.

"Still not hungry?" she smiles slightly.

"I want to go home," I whimper.

"Why would you want to go home? Your home is just as much a prison to you as this place and it's not as nice. Plus it's worse because it's a prison you made yourself."

"A prison I made myself is not worse than a prison that O made."

Angel is confused. I can tell by the look on her face.

"Is he paying you? Do you work for him?"

"What? Is who paying me?"

She genuinely seems to have no idea what I'm talking about.

"Olsen Leonard. Is he paying you to keep me here and take care of me until... until he does whatever it is that he's planning to do with me?"

"Nobody is paying me, Aya." Angel shakes her head.

"Then why are you doing this? Who are you?"

"My name is Elodie."

That's right. I knew her name was something weird.

"Elodie, I want to go home."

"I'm sorry, Aya, that's impossible."

"Please," I cry.

I had spent the last several days planning to be a complete badass and break out when I got the chance, but instead here I am, crying and begging like a little dog.

"Please don't do this to me. I've never done anything to you. I don't want to stay here. I want to go home."

Elodie looks sad and I think that I might be getting through to her. I continue trying to appeal to her humanity.

"Aya, sweetheart, I'm truly sorry but you have to stay here. It's for your own safety."

"My own safety from what?" panic flashes in my eyes.

"Do you want me to explain everything?" Elodie offers, leaning against the dresser full of sleepwear and lingerie.

"Yes," I practically beg. "Why am I here? I didn't do anything."

"It's not something you did," Elodie approaches me and I flinch as she reaches out to touch me. She withdraws her hand. "It's what you are."

"I don't understand."

"Okay, I'll explain. Everything. But I'm going to make a deal with you."

"What kind of deal?" I'm skeptical. If she tries to coerce me into submitting to some kind of situation like I was in with Olsen, I'm just going to tear her eyes out. She'll probably kill me, but then at least I'll go down fighting.

"This hunger strike is over. You join me for dinner and I'll talk. You have to eat, Aya, you're weak and your health is failing. You're going to make yourself seriously ill if you keep starving yourself."

"That's it? I just have to have dinner with you and you'll tell me what's going on?" I'm still very suspicious.

"That's not it."

A-ha. There it is. I wait for the other shoe to drop.

"You also have to take a shower," Elodie continues. "And change your clothes."

"Do you think I'm stupid?" I snarl.

"What?" Elodie seems shocked again. "Absolutely not! Why would you say that?"

"I know that you're watching me. I know that there are cameras in the bathroom. I'm not going to do a little strip show for you. Are you streaming this on the internet or something?"

Elodie cringes slightly.

"I'll turn them off."

"How will I know that you turned them off?"

She considers the question for a moment.

"I guess you'll just have to trust me," she shrugs.

I consider my options for a moment. I don't trust her, not at all, but I also don't really have a choice. Plus, I reason, if she wanted to assault me she could just attack me and do it right now. It's not like I have the strength left to defend myself.

"Fine," I agree. "I'll take a shower and have dinner with you. But you have to explain everything."

"Everything," she promises.

CHAPTER SIX

ELODIE GLASS

"She's going to be happy to see you," I reach down and scratch behind the cat's ears. "She was asking for you, you know."

I can't believe that I forgot the cat. I had to go back to Aya's apartment to get him when I saw her on my video feed wake up and ask for him. He was pretty angry at first, he didn't like being left alone and he seemed to know that I was responsible. I was able to get back into his good graces with a bowl full of fresh sardines and he's been living the good life ever since he arrived.

At first I considered just putting him in Aya's room so that she'd feel more comfortable, but since she wasn't eating or showering I was afraid that adding an animal to the mix would be a bad idea. So I've been taking care of him in the main house for the past week, waiting for the perfect opportunity to reunite the two. We've become quite the pair, the two of us.

Though I freely admit that I was planning to use the cat as a bribe if needed.

"You think she'll like the steak?" I ask the cat.

He meows back. Clearly he'd like to try the steak. I toss him a bit of fat that I trimmed off and he grabs it and makes a run for under the sofa.

I hope that Aya likes what I've prepared. I suspect that she will because I've used all recipes that she herself has looked up previously. I've got a reverse-seared ribeye, Hasselback potatoes, and sautéed mushrooms. I've also prepared a fruit tart and stocked a full bar.

I want this dinner to impress her. It's our first date, if you think about it, and I want everything to be perfect. I cut some wildflowers from the growth outside and I've placed them in several vases on the table and around the room so that the air is sweet and fragrant. I've also set the table with a cloth, fine china, silver, and candles. It might be a bit over the top, but I've been waiting all my life and all my afterlife for this night.

My phone is lighting up in the corner of my eye and I struggle to ignore it. I'm receiving notifications from the security system: the cameras in the bathroom are disabled.

I know, phone. I desperately want to turn them back on. Believe me, no one wants to activate the cameras more than me at this point.

But I made a promise and I intend to keep it.

The phone dings me again; Aya is back in her bedroom. I pick it up and I can see her on my little screen. She's wearing one of the dresses that I bought her, though I can't tell which one in the small image, and toweling off her hair.

I watch as she gazes at herself in the mirror in her room. I promised not to spy on her in the bathroom but no agreements were reached over her bedroom. She fixes her hair and leans in closer to the mirror. I think she's checking out the circles that have formed under her eyes.

"Don't worry, Aya." I've taken to talking to her image on my phone. "You'll feel better once you eat something and get some good rest."

I wait patiently while Aya finishes running her fingers through her hair and rubbing in some of the face cream I left her. I also provided her with makeup, which she sometimes liked to play with at home, but she leaves it alone aside from a bit of tinted lip gloss.

When she sits herself back down in her chair I plate up dinner and go upstairs to get her. I've got the same shot of adrenaline rushing through me as when I have a hunt, but this time it's complicated by feelings of lust and hope.

I knock on her door before opening it, a new courtesy I've just thought to extend.

"Aya," I greet her. "You must be starving."

I know that she is, literally. I can smell that her stomach has been eating itself and I feel a twinge of sorrow for her, poor thing.

I offer her my elbow and I can't explain how delighted I am when she takes it. I lead her down into the dining room and we almost trip on the cat.

"Yeti!" she exclaims, the first time I've seen her smile since she arrived. I wait as she reaches down to pick him up and give the two a moment to get reacquainted.

"I picked him up for you," I try to score some brownie points. "I thought that you'd like to have him."

"I was so worried," she says, more to the cat than me. "But you look like you're fine!"

It's then that she notices my efforts in the dining room. She looks bemused for the briefest of moments, then her brows furrow.

"You look stunning," I compliment her. It's true. She's wearing a white cotton sundress with little eyelets all over. She looks so fresh and pure, like a package waiting to be opened.

"Elodie," she starts, her voice suddenly hard, "this looks like you think you've set up some kind of a date. A forced seduction is still rape."

"No one is forcing anything!" I put my hand up to show her that I'm not going to touch her without her invitation. Then I turn her to face me. "Aya," I begin, "I didn't bring you here to hurt you. Listen to me. I'm not going to rape you. I'm not going to torture you. I'm not going to let anyone else hurt you either."

"Then why did you bring me here?"

"Please. Sit down and have some dinner. I'll tell you."

I manage to finally get Aya to the table in front of a plate of food. She thanks me graciously and, to my relief, begins eating.

"Aya," I start, "I have a lot to tell you. I had to bring you here after what you saw me do to that man who attacked you. I couldn't risk you running to the police."

"What were you even doing in the basement of my building?"

For a moment I'm going to confess it all. I'm going to tell Aya that I'm desperately in love with her and I've been watching her for a long time. That she's the other half of my soul.

But no. I break my promise to her. I don't tell her everything. I can't. Not yet.

"I own that building. But also: that's what I do. I stop bad men from doing bad things. I've made a vow with my three sisters to destroy monsters like that."

"By destroy you mean kill?"

She looks horrified and I'm disappointed and slightly ashamed but not surprised. Normal people don't consider murder a possible solution to their problems.

"Yes."

She considers what I've told her for a moment. "I think there are some people who can't be saved or rehabilitated. Some that need to die. Is that why you come to the meetings?"

"Mostly."

"So everything you said about yourself was made up? That stuff about your childhood? Your alcoholic mother selling you?"

"No, that was all true. It all happened. A very long time ago."

"Is that why you're like this?"

I consider the question but I don't want to explore it. "Maybe," I answer, wanting to change the course of this conversation. My life should remain buried. No good will come from digging it up.

"But you're a good person? You consider yourself a good person?"

I have to laugh at this question. "No," I finally reply with a tight smile.

"You're not? Are you an evil person?"

"Aya," I look her in the eye, "I'm not a person. Not anymore."

"What is that supposed to mean?" Aya looks annoyed.

I take a deep breath before continuing. "I was a woman, a long, long time ago. Now I'm a beast."

"Because you hurt a lot of people?"

"Well, yes, but I mean it. I'm a monster. I'm not speaking in metaphor."

Aya looks at me like I'm crazy and I can't blame her.

"Look," I hold up my left hand and make a long cut across my palm with my steak knife. Aya gasps and covers her mouth. I put the knife down and hold up my palm so that she can see the cut. It's deep and now my blood is dripping down my wrist into my coat. I wonder already if she can see that my blood is much darker than hers, but to make sure she understands me I spit in my palm and then clean it off with a napkin.

The cut is gone.

This is apparently a little bit too much explanation for Aya because she gets up from the table and makes a run for it.

God damn it.

This is not how this dinner was supposed to go.

CHAPTER SEVEN

AYA LACHAT

This can't be real. My heart is racing from the adrenaline and from the food I just ate. I feel light-headed and my stomach is roiling but I have to keep moving. I have to find a way out of this nightmare.

It's so dark in this house. I rush to the windows but I'm not surprised to find that they're the same thick material as the ones in my room. There's no way I'll be able to break them and they're tightly sealed.

What the hell is this place? It looks like a regular home inside, with furniture and pictures on the walls, but it's locked down like a fortress and under surveillance like a maximum security prisoner. This can't all be for me, can it?

My only hope is that I can get out the door before Elodie catches me. I've already noticed that she isn't chasing me, and I know in my heart that's because she doesn't think I'll be able to escape. I'll be damned if I don't even try though.

This old farmhouse is pretty big inside and I run from the dining room into a living room that looks eerily like I decorated it. My eyes adjust to the light and I can make out a poster that's just like the one I have at home, a print of a Rodin painting of a couple in a boat. Wait. No. That's not a poster. That's an actual painting.

I can also see a bookshelf with a bunch of books I own and a couple candles in scents I have at home too.

I can't deal with this. It's too weird. Recognizing all of my personal belongings has momentarily distracted me and before I know it I feel a pair of arms slip around my waist. I know who it is, of course, and if I didn't I'd be able to figure it out by the blood-stained cuffs my captor wears.

"Aya," I can feel her cool breath on my ear, "calm down. You're okay."

"I'm pretty fucking far from okay!" I shriek, feeling a panic attack coming on. "Why are you doing this? What do you want from me? I swear to God, I won't tell anyone what happened. Just let me go!"

"I already told you, Aya, I can't."

Elodie's grip tightens around me.

"What do you want? I'll do whatever you want!"

I won't and I know it. There are some things that I've done in the name of self-preservation that I don't think that I can ever do again. But that doesn't stop me from making promises that I can't keep. At the moment I'd say anything for my freedom.

"Aya please. I can take care of you. I can make you happy, I know I can. You just have to stay here. I can provide you with anything, absolutely anything on Earth that you want. You'll be living in unfathomable luxury if that's what you want. You can have all the jewels or pretty dresses or books or anything that you desire. Anything."

"I want my freedom!" I argue.

Elodie sighs and I can feel her nestle her face in the back of my hair.

"That's the only thing you have to give up. You can have anything but that."

"My freedom is the only thing I have," I cry.

"Your freedom is what you had. And I'd argue that you were never free. You were a prisoner of your own fear. Now I'm what you have."

Elodie is holding me tightly from behind even though I'm no longer struggling to escape from her. I think she's trying to comfort me now, or who knows, maybe she's trying to comfort herself. She's strong, so strong, her arms are like iron bars around me. She's not crushing me, but there's no way I can escape her grasp either.

Can I convince her that she's wrong? On the one hand she's a big enough psycho to think that I'd agree to this arrangement, being her caged bird. On the other hand, she seems to be genuinely forlorn about my despair. I don't get the feeling at all that she takes pleasure in torturing me. Not like O.

O.

Just thinking of him steels my resolve.

"I don't accept. I'll never, ever accept this arrangement," I suddenly locate my spine. "I don't care about all the stuff you can buy me. I don't want it. The only thing I care about is my freedom. I've already escaped one psycho, and I'll escape you too eventually. I'll never stop trying, so you can forget it."

I can feel Elodie's body stiffen behind mine and she sucks in her breath. I know that I've made her angry.

"Fine," Elodie's voice is short.

She grabs me by my upper arm and drags me through the room. I'm stumbling after her and I'm beginning to worry that I was wrong about her not wanting to hurt me.

I'm surprised when we reach a door that seems to lead outside. Maybe my speech worked and she is just going to set me free? At this point, anything seems possible.

Elodie uses her fingerprint to open the door and I'm met with a face full of sweet, fresh air. I suck in deeply, not realizing how much I had missed the breeze. Before I can take a good look around, she's pulling me outside.

The grass is wet on my feet and little stones and rocks are sending shooting pains up my legs. The closet in my room was full of dresses but there wasn't a single pair of shoes so I'm still barefoot.

Elodie is pulling me around outside and I think she means to show me something. I'm stumbling along after her as best as I can.

"Can you at least slow down please?" I don't want to tell her that she's hurting me but my feet are getting torn up. "I'm not wearing shoes."

Elodie looks down at my feet like I've just reminded her of something. Instead of slowing down, though, she picks me up in her arms.

Now she's carrying me through the yard like I'm a small child. It's surreal but my feet hurt and I don't know what kind of stuff is living in this tall grass.

She's got one arm under my knees and the other under my shoulders so I wrap my arms around her for support. Now it's my face that's so close to her neck. I can feel her skin, which is just a little bit too cool to be natural. I've also noticed that she's got no scent at all.

It's strange, really, how you don't notice the way every person has her own scent until you meet someone who doesn't have one. Despite this uncanniness I feel myself drawn to her. I've got an overwhelming urge to touch my lips to her neck but my pride won't allow it. I wonder if she was able to cast some kind of magic spell on me to make me want her.

There's no telling what she's capable of.

"Look," Elodie finally gestures with her chin, still not putting me down.

We've walked pretty far around the perimeter of the house and I've seen a few outbuildings but nothing else but empty fields that have gone to meadow and a forest.

"There's nothing out there," Elodie continues. "You could walk for days before you reached anything, and there's no telling what you'd reach out in a place like this. There's nowhere for you to run. You're not going anywhere. Accept it and you'll be a lot more comfortable."

I struggle against her chest. I don't want to be held anymore.

She must think that she's made a very convincing argument because she puts me down. I immediately make a run for it, leaping over a wooden horse fence and taking off into a forest.

This time she does chase me. I run for all I'm worth, like a deer being pursued through the woods.

That's exactly what I feel like — her prey — and it thrills me. I'm darting around trees and over boulders and she lets me go for a while before she makes a leap at me and knocks me to the ground.

Elodie rolls me onto my back and I squirm under her, trying to get away, which only results in her being able to force her hips between my legs. I keep thrashing and bucking as she pins my wrists over my head.

I'm not even trying to escape her anymore. I can briefly feel the jut of her hip grind up against my sex and I thank God that there's no way for her to tell that I'm just as turned on as she seems to be.

Elodie's lips press against mine and her tongue forces my lips to part, to open up and let her in. She tastes like iron and wine and her kiss is hungry and urgent, searching my mouth and teasing my tongue until it somehow finds its way past her own lips into her mouth.

I've forgotten what I was upset about until her fingers slide under my dress and push my panties to the side. I don't want her to feel how wet I am and so I manage to wriggle away.

I'm about to try to leap up and make a second run when she jumps on me again, this time pinning me on my stomach. I can still feel her hand, this time pushed between the cheeks of my ass because my dress has been pushed up over my waist.

"Do I need to put you in chains, love?" her gravelly voice sounds in my ear. "Don't think I won't do it. It's for your own good."

I want to keep fighting her but I'm also very aware that this situation could go in a very different direction and I no longer trust my own body not to betray me. I'm not even sure if I want to keep fighting so that I can escape or I want to keep fighting to provoke her to take things further.

"Fine," I finally decide to quit and let my body go limp. "You win. I'm not going anywhere."

Elodie is visibly disappointed. I'm disappointed too, but I'm not going to let her see that.

"Come on," she makes a move to pick me up to carry me back to the house.

"No thank you," I stand up on my own and brush off my dress. "I prefer to walk."

CHAPTER EIGHT

ELODIE GLASS

Instead of taking Aya back to her own room, I take her to mine. It's actually a mirror image of her's layout-wise, but without all the girly furniture. I don't mind having flowers on everything and in fact I find it charming that she's drawn to such femme aesthetics but it's nice to have my own space that's a little more minimalist to retreat to if I'd like to be alone.

I use the room primarily as an office and space to relax, of course I feel most comfortable sleeping in the basement when I stay here. I'm pretty sure Aya's not ready to see that room, if she ever is, and I have no intention of showing it to her.

I carry her into the bathroom where I have a first aid kit, which I acquired specifically for her, just in case. Now I'm very glad that I was prepared because her feet are totally fucked.

"Aya," I scold her, "you really need to take better care of yourself. Or let me take care of you. Look at this, you're a mess."

I begin by picking all of the stones and sticks out of her feet. They're both bleeding and I'm struggling to ignore the scent. It takes all of my willpower to resist the urge to lick her blood from my fingers, or, better yet, directly from her feet.

I know that I can use my own blood to heal her immediately, but I don't. First, because I don't want to upset her further. I can tell that she's still disturbed by the information that I shared with her earlier and I'd like to give her some time to mentally and emotionally process it. Second, I know what will happen if I allow my blood to mix with hers. She'll be bound to me, even if it's just a slight amount, and I don't think that would be fair.

I want Aya to love me. To choose me. I don't want to force her.

"Just so you know," Aya addresses me while I'm washing her feet with a warm, wet washcloth, "I'm never going to give you what you want."

I stare down at her feet and fight to suppress my smile. It's a real struggle and my lips are pinched in a tight line.

"What is it that you think that I want, Aya?" I finally manage to ask without laughing.

Silly girl. I have to remind myself that she doesn't know what I'm capable of, that I can smell her wet little pussy and I know that she wanted it just as badly as I did. She must have not been aware of how her back was arching up to meet me, or how tightly she had her legs wrapped around me. I'm getting wet again just thinking of it.

"I think," Aya starts in an accusatory fashion, "that you want some kind of sicko, sociopathic version of domestic bliss. I think that you think that you can keep me locked up here like Homemaker Barbie and you can come play with me whenever you want. You can dress me up and have fun with me when you feel like it, then leave me here when you have something else to do. And I'll just be waiting for you to return, not having a life of my own."

I feel like I've been punched in the gut.

"Go ahead," Aya taunts, "tell me I'm wrong. Tell me you aren't imagining that I'll be your little wifey."

I need a moment to collect myself. I have to admit, she's right. That's exactly what I was imagining, but it didn't sound so dehumanizing from my point of view.

"You're right," I finally reply. "I'd love to make you my wife. I'd love to come home to you waiting for me with your legs spread wide open and no panties on, wet with anticipation."

I pause and we both turn our heads to look silently at the bed visible through the bathroom doorway. I can tell that the scenario I've described interests her. She wiggles a little bit in her seat on the edge of the bathtub and I know I'm going to have to snap out of it before I lose control of myself.

I force myself to finish cleaning up her feet and I rub them down with antiseptic cream. She's all patched up. I stand up and lean down to lift her when she pushes me away and stands up on her own. She tries to stumble out of the bathroom but she's slipping on the tile.

"You're smearing antiseptic cream everywhere," I curse and lift her struggling form. She tries to wiggle away the entire walk from my room to hers and it's driving me mad.

When we get to her room I have to practically throw her onto her bed. It's the only thing I can do to keep myself from ripping her panties off and licking her pussy to its limits until she screams with pleasure.

I can't even look at her like that so I immediately turn on my heel and slam the door behind me. I only need to make sure it's locked tight before I lean my head against my forearm, braced on the door, and reach into my pants to release the tension from my own clit, which has been aching with desire.

It's in for a thrashing, but it doesn't take long. I imagine what she's doing there, just a few meters away on the other side of the door. Pouting. I'd love to get my pussy onto those pursed lips and drip my juices into her throat, forcing her to swallow my cum as I ride her face.

For now I'm going to have to be satisfied with wiping it on the outside of her door like I'm marking my territory. I pull my handkerchief from my pocket and clean the mess I've made from my fingers, tossing it down the laundry chute on my way back downstairs.

I have the need to create some physical space between Aya and I, but I can't get her out of my mind.

So I do something that I've never allowed myself to do before:

I internet stalk her.

Usually that's Jayden's job, anything to do with the internet. It's not because I don't know how to use it, I do, but they're an expert. And we generally don't have any reason to research anyone but our targets.

I certainly couldn't ask them to dig up the dirt on Aya. I'd have no explanation for why I needed this info and they'd probably tell Aravella. Plus, in my own twisted way, I've been trying to respect Aya's privacy. I haven't dug up any information that she hasn't shared with me about her personal life.

Thus far.

Now I've completely abandoned any pretenses of being decent and I'm indulging my curiosity. I have so much I want to know about her and I have a feeling at least some of it will be searchable online.

For example: who the fuck is Olsen? Why did she think that I was working for him?

I know from our group meeting that she witnessed the murder of her family and was held hostage for several months so I'm pretty sure that I'll be able to find news stories about her past.

I do a search on her name and I'm a bit surprised when it pops right up. There are dozens of articles about her and I'm surprised that she hasn't changed her name. Maybe she wants to change it now. Maybe to something like... Aya Glass?

The news articles are harrowing and I feel guilty for reading them. According to every source, Aya witnessed the violent murder of her parents and her two younger brothers in her family home. Then she and her older sister Nala were abducted and held hostage by this sicko for months. Aya was able to escape while her captor was occupied with murdering her sister.

I'm torn. On the one hand I'm overcome with sympathy for Aya. I knew that she'd been through a lot, but I don't know. Not something this bad. Seeing the specifics of her case has filled me with a sense of horror. On the other hand, I'm so proud of her. She's overcome so much, it must have taken so much bravery for her to save her own life like that. It must have taken so much for her to continue living completely alone in the world.

So Aya is a survivor. That's what all the reputable news outlets have to say. To get the sordid details, I have to click over to the tabloid rags.

From these I learn that Aya named her captor Olsen Leonard, but there are no official records of such a person existing. Some of the articles imply that the police are questioning Aya's testimony. Some outright accuse her of being so mentally ill that she can't be trusted. But this Leonard was a real sick fuck. Aya told the police that he seemed to be eating her parents and brother, and he used to force her sister to play the piano while he cut her. Then he would drink up her blood.

I read these details and I immediately know what Olsen is. My heart drops.

Aya will never be able to love me.

Olsen Leonard is a creature just like me.

CHAPTER NINE

AYA LACHAT

I wake up blushing from my dreams.

I haven't got any real-life experience with sex but that apparently isn't stopping my brain from having a lot of very specific ideas about what I want to do with a certain woman. Or a certain not-woman, I guess.

How long have I been asleep?

Long enough to soak my sheets through with sweat, though the temperature in my room is pleasantly cool. I take a deep breath and untangle the Egyptian cotton linens from my legs. Just five minutes ago, in my dreams, that sheet was Elodie. I was tangled up under her, struggling. She threw my legs over her shoulders and dragged her tongue down my body until she had her face buried in my sex.

I sit up in my bed just in time to see a metal tray slide through the open panel in my door. Then the panel snaps shut and I'm alone again.

Crap.

It looks like I've lost my run-of-the-house privileges.

I'm not surprised after last night. I wish that I had planned my escape better, been sneakier. I should have pretended that I was going to cooperate so that I could gather intel. Maybe I could have seen how Elodie controlled the door or maybe I could have even convinced her that I had no intention of leaving so she didn't need to lock it.

Oh well. Too late now.

At least my hunger strike is over. There's no point in denying myself now, all I succeeded in doing was making myself weak. I would have been better off if I had just eaten. Then I could have fought Elodie off when she attacked me.

I'm nearly rolling my eyes at myself now. *Ha*. When she 'attacked' me. Like I wasn't kissing her right back.

I don't know what got into me.

I've already decided that I'm not going to be too hard on myself. I've channeled my therapist (is she wondering where I am?) and accepted the fact that I've been under an intense amount of physical, mental, and emotional stress. I might react in weird ways.

Breakfast smells good. I'm about to carry my tray over to my little desk when I get an impulse. I try the door.

To my surprise, it's unlocked.

For a moment I'm so confused that I just stand there. I gather my nerves about me, slide the tray aside, and open the door.

She's right there, sitting on the bannister at the top of the stairs. I wasn't expecting to run directly into her.

"Um, it was unlocked."

I'm not up for another run. I wait for her to respond but she doesn't say anything. Is she giving me the silent treatment?

"Am I free to go?" I ask, not sure how else to approach this conversation, especially since Elodie doesn't seem to be participating at all.

"You're welcome to use the entire house, but you can't leave. The doors to the outside won't open without my biodata. It's a complicated, military-grade security system and there's no use trying to disable it. But you don't have to stay in your room any longer if you don't want."

So I'm still a prisoner. Now it's Elodie's turn to stand there and wait for me to reply, but I give her some of her own treatment. I'm not going to thank her for giving me a bigger prison.

I grab my breakfast tray and carry it past her without another word.

When I get downstairs, the dining table where we ate supper last night feels too formal. I'm uncomfortable sitting at a chair at that big table all by myself, so instead I carry my breakfast into the living room and set it on the coffee table.

Sweet. There's a TV.

I haven't really realized how bored I've been locked alone in that room all that time. Maybe that's why Elodie seemed so interesting yesterday — maybe my brain was just melting from lack of use.

At any rate, I'm excited to have some entertainment.

I click on the TV and immediately do the one thing that my therapist has warned me time and again not to do. I click over to the 24-hour streaming news channel.

Talking heads blabber in the background as I lift the lid from my breakfast tray. I'm immediately impressed. The smell is heavenly and I've got French toast stuffed with something, bacon, sausages, scrambled eggs, and a bowl of fruit. I've also got coffee and orange juice.

I notice that there's no Valium on the tray anymore.

The bacon is crunchy and the eggs are creamy. The French toast is stuffed with orange cream cheese and it hits me — this is just like a recipe that I meant to try! I'm in the habit of looking up super complicated recipes that I never actually make and I'm impressed. Elodie must really like cooking.

I wonder if she eats.

Other than people, I mean.

Now that I'm feeling relatively safe and comfortable, my mind is racing. I have so many questions for her. Is she immortal? Does she go out and drink people's blood every night? Can she turn into a bat? Is garlic poison to her?

What a mind-fuck. Now I'm wondering what other kinds of things exist that are hidden in the shadows. I suddenly remember a story that one of the guys at our group meeting told. He was there because someone broke into his apartment and attacked him in his bed. He said that he *knew* that this person wasn't human and everyone thought that he was crazy. He'd been attending therapy to address the 'irrational beliefs' caused by his trauma.

Poor guy.

Now I wish that I could tell him that he *wasn't* crazy, that what he thought he saw was real.

The way things are looking right now, though, it doesn't look like I'll ever get the chance.

I turned on the news with the vague hope that I'd hear something about my own disappearance. I watch as I eat mindlessly and the anchors drift from one subject to the next, with no mention of me.

There is, however, a brief mention of an investigation into Lou's murder. I listen intently but the anchor only explains that it's unsolved and will remain under investigation as department resources allow. That last part makes me think that there are no leads and the police have done all they intend to do to solve this crime. He must have been alone, like me, with no family or friends pushing the police to try harder to solve his murder.

I wonder how long it will be until someone realizes that I'm gone?

It's normal for me to go days at a time without leaving my apartment, so none of my neighbors are going to think it's suspicious that they haven't seen me. I'm currently being held prisoner by my landlady, so I guess she's not going to care when I don't pay my rent. I go to my group meeting every week, but people disappear from our group every week and we've never conducted any kind of investigation into their whereabouts. My therapist mentioned that she gets ghosted by her clients all the time too. She brought it up once when she was trying to convince me that I was brave for trying to heal.

My only hope, as far as I can tell, is StarBurnz.

I know how stupid that sounds.

StarBurnz is my online friend from a gaming site. I've been chatting with her for a couple years but I've never met her in real life. I don't even know her real name or where she lives, and she doesn't have that info on me either. It used to make me feel comfortable, to have someone kind to talk to who doesn't know anything about me or what my real life is like or whatever happened to me.

Now I realize how vulnerable I've made myself.

How would StarBurnz even know that I needed help? She'll probably just assume that I drifted away, as online friends tend to do.

I'm suddenly faced with the reality of how very, very alone I've been in the world. Both by my own choice and by O's actions, when he stole everything that I loved and destroyed it all.

I hadn't meant to upset myself, but I can feel the tears welling in my eyes. I don't actually like being alone. I put my breakfast tray down and wipe my eyes, and I'm startled when Yeti jumps into my lap.

"Well hello," I smile through my tears.

He meows back and he's looking at something behind me. I turn my head and there's Elodie, leaning on the bannister of the stairs, watching us quietly. How long has she been there? Now that I catch her, she turns around and retreats in the direction of her room.

Is she serious about taking care of me? If I agreed to her terms, I wouldn't be alone in the world anymore.

But I also wouldn't be free.

Unacceptable.

CHAPTER TEN

AYA LACHAT

E very day is the same here, but I've started marking time. I'm not even sure why I do it. I'm no longer really holding out hope that someone will miss me and come looking for me. I guess I really was a nobody out there in the world. No one even notices that I'm gone.

I don't know why that comes as such a hard truth to me, since I know very well that I've spent my entire life avoiding people. I don't make friends, and whenever someone tries to get close to me I run.

Still.

It's not pleasant to be confronted with the truth that I don't mean anything to anyone.

I guess at least when I was free I had some minor interactions with other humans, in group meetings or at my therapy appointments. I also encountered other people when I was out on my rare trips into public, buying ice cream or running errands. I never expected to miss the guy who worked the register at the bodega, but here I am.

Now I'm really, truly alone.

But every day, as the sun rises, I scratch a little notch into the corner post on my bed. That's how I know that it's been fifteen days since what I have come to think of as The Big Night.

I can't really say that things have gotten either better or worse since then. I'm allowed to wander around the house but now Elodie is avoiding me.

I know that she still watches me. I know that every room has cameras and I still see her here and there sometimes at night. I don't know if she's angry or disappointed or what but she doesn't talk to me anymore. She goes out a lot at night and leaves me home alone, and I have no idea where she goes during the day. She doesn't sleep in her bed. I tried to find her a few times but I was unsuccessful.

I'm beginning to get a serious case of cabin fever.

I wander listlessly out of my room and into the living room. There I click on the TV. This is part of my routine every night now. I click through every channel and see the usual late-night suspects: reruns of The 700 Club, a pair of ladies selling jewelry on the home shopping network, talking heads arguing over politics, and an old episode of The Addams Family.

I crack a smile. I wish Elodie was more of a Morticia and less of a Nosferatu.

At least she's hot.

I shake those thoughts from my head and glance around the room. There are a few other entertainments available. I could read a book or do a puzzle. I saw a watercolor painting set and I guess I could try to teach myself to do that.

Nothing is really appealing to me. It all just looks so boring.

I flop over as dramatically as possible on the sofa, hoping that Elodie sees. Yeti jumps up on my stomach and meows.

"This sucks," I scratch behind his ears. I'm afraid that I'm going to lose my mind from the monotony and boredom.

That's it.

I'm going to find Elodie.

I get up from the sofa with a look of determination on my face. Why am I going to find Elodie? I don't know yet. What am I going to tell her when I find her? I also don't know. I just know that I suddenly feel like it's absolutely necessary to confront her.

I storm through the house, a woman on a mission.

She's not in the kitchen or the dining room. She's also not in my room or hers. There are several other bedrooms that are all empty and she's not in any of those.

I've got it: the reason I need to find her. I need to learn about my enemy. How does that old saying go? Keep your friends close and your enemies closer?

Maybe if I get to know her better, I can figure out what makes her tick and then persuade her to let me go. Or at least maybe I can see what she's capable of doing. So far I know that she can heal cuts fast and she's faster and stronger than a human. I have no idea what other tricks she has up her sleeve.

I finally find her in… a gym?

Vampires need to work out?

She's sitting on a mat in the middle of the room cross-legged with her eyes closed. I think she's meditating, that weirdo. I approach and stand directly before her with my hands on my hips.

She doesn't move.

Is she sleeping?

Maybe this is how she sleeps.

I wave my hands in front of her face to check if she's awake and she pulls me down into her lap.

"I was trying to concentrate," her eyes open and give me an admonishing look. I try to wiggle out of her lap but she holds on to me tightly.

"Concentrate on what?" I'm skeptical.

"Inner peace."

I guffaw. Then I look at her.

"Oh my God, you're serious," I honestly thought she was joking. Sometimes it's hard to tell with her.

"Yes, I'm serious," she seems slightly offended.

"How does your pursuit of inner peace jive with being a cold blooded killer?"

She considers my question. "It's a work in progress."

"But why do you do it?" I ask quietly. "Why do you have to kill those people?"

"I'm atoning," she answers, not explaining further.

I just realize that I'm still in her lap. My face is very close to hers and I'm made very aware of this because she's staring at my lips. I hop away before I can give in to the temptation — and I am tempted.

My God, I'm so lonely.

"Is this your meditation chamber?" I ask, gazing around.

The room is mostly empty in the middle but around the edges I can seem some stuff. My eyes focus and I can spot swords and axes and a selection of bows and arrows. All kinds of weapons.

"It's my training room," Elodie replies.

"Why do you have to train? Don't you just kill everyone like you did Lou?"

"Not everyone can be killed like Lou," Elodie informs me.

"What do you mean?"

"People like me, for example."

"How do you kill people like you?" I think I'm being pretty slick.

Elodie smiles. "You'd have to take off my head, Aya."

I look around the room. "Like with that ax?"

Elodie also glances around. "I'd go for the garrote if I was you. It's easier to use, if you're able to get the element of surprise. The ax takes some practice."

She doesn't seem very worried that I'm going to kill her, and honestly I can blame her. Now that I'm surrounded by all these weapons I don't really see myself doing that either.

"Are you going to train now?"

"Yes."

"Can I train?"

It's worth a shot.

"You want to learn how to throw the ax?"

"Can I?"

"I can show you."

I wasn't expecting her to say yes. I'm even more surprised when she gets up and pulls me by my hand over to her weapons. She selects three axes and takes me out to the yard.

"Let's try outside first," she says in a way that somehow lets me know that she's more afraid that I'm accidentally going to throw an ax into her wall than she is that I'm going to throw an ax into her.

"Look," she lines me up in front of an old oak tree. "You hold it like this, toward the bottom of the handle, then draw it back over your shoulder, throw, and flick your wrist at the release. It's that flick of the wrist that really makes your throw lethal."

She throws the ax and it lands, embedded directly in the center of the tree.

"Wow," I'm genuinely impressed. "You're really good at this."

"I've had a lot of time to practice. Now you want to try?"

Elodie hands me an ax and it's much heavier than I anticipated. I don't want her to see me as weak, though. I try to throw it just like she showed me and I miss the tree entirely but at least it was a pretty strong throw.

"Not bad!" she lies. "You want to try again?"

I do. I want to try over and over until I finally land one in the tree.

"Wow!" Elodie has been cheering me on like she's a mom at a Little League game. "Watch out! We've got an assassin on our hands!"

I'm shocked by how much fun I'm having. I haven't even thought once about running or trying to hit Elodie with the ax. I'm so caught up in the moment that the words are coming out of my mouth before I even have a chance to think about them:

"Elodie can we have dinner together tonight?"

She seems stunned.

Did I do something wrong?

"I'd love to, Aya," she replies without looking at me. "Do you have any preferences?"

"Maybe Italian?"

Elodie nods thoughtfully and slips back into the house, leaving me alone outside to practice some more.

CHAPTER ELEVEN

ELODIE GLASS

A second chance!

Who knew that the key to my Aya's heart would lie in my weapons cache?

I'm on cloud nine and I catch myself singing in the shower. It's "The Best Is Yet to Come," an old Sinatra tune that my dark father liked. I haven't thought of it in ages, but I also haven't thought of my dark father in ages, and now I'm feeling bouncy and optimistic.

Italian is the only cuisine I know from my own life.

When I was sold as a little girl for the final time, I began my life as a thrall to a vampire who had roots in Italy. Some of my best — actually my only — good childhood memories are of my dark father preparing me feasts before I was old enough to turn. I don't eat much anymore but I still have fond memories of those meatballs and that Sunday sauce.

I hope that Aya is going to be impressed.

I spent the earlier part of the night shopping for groceries at the 24-hour supermarket. I know that I went overboard but I don't care. I hope that Aya's hungry because I've made her a huge homemade lasagne from scratch, including homemade meatballs in the filling. I also made garlic bread, a salad, and cannolis.

I'm just putting the finishing touches on the table when she comes downstairs wearing a form-fitting short emerald green dress that I picked up for her on a lark. It's not her usual style at all, I've never seen her wear something like that, but I saw the color and I thought that she just had to have it.

"Aya," I can't tear my eyes away from the curves of her waist and her tender neck, "you look stunning. That color really suits you."

"Thanks," I see her blush. "Wow," she notices the table. "Is all that for us?"

Well, her actually. But I don't want to make her uncomfortable.

"I hope you like it."

"It smells delicious. I guess you can eat garlic after all," she comments to herself.

"Sorry?" I'm not quite following her.

"Garlic. I was wondering if it was poisonous to you."

"Aya," I smile softly. "Are you trying to kill me again? No, it's not poisonous. Some of us don't like it because we have a highly increased sense of smell and it's so pungent, but it's not poison."

"Is it bothering you?"

"I grew up with it. It's nostalgic."

I pull out a chair for Aya and she takes a seat. Then I pour her an absolutely enormous glass of red wine. I've got high hopes for this evening.

The food is a hit. Aya's so occupied with her lasagne; she doesn't seem to care that I don't eat much. I enjoy watching her and get a deep sense of satisfaction from feeding her. I also notice that she's enjoying the wine; I've already refilled her glass once.

"Where did you grow up?" she asks.

I'm reluctant to answer. I don't want to ruin the night talking about my life, but I also don't want her to think I'm hiding it from her.

"I was born in Chicago. I spent my childhood being dragged around by my mother though."

"The alcoholic?" Aya asks while chewing. "You mentioned her once at a meeting."

"Yes," I acknowledged. "My mother struggled with addiction her entire life."

"That must have been difficult."

Aya has no idea and I hope that she never has to suffer like that, feeling betrayed by the only person she loves. If I can make her love me, I can make sure that nothing like that ever happens to her.

"It was a long time ago," I answer instead.

"So how did it happen?" she asks, sipping her drink. I can tell by the way she's relaxed that she's slightly drunk.

"How did what happen?"

"How did you... you know. Become like you are?"

"Ah. It's kind of a long story. And not a very happy one, I'm afraid."

"Could still have a happy ending," Aya suggests.

I hold her in my gaze. What did she mean by that?

I know how I want to interpret it, but I'm afraid that my wishful thinking is leading me to conclusions that have no basis in reality.

"It could," I finally agree. That's not likely, not for me, but I'm not going to ruin our night.

"How's the food?" I try to change the subject. "That's one of my specialties."

"Oh, it's delicious," Aya nods enthusiastically. "Lasagne was my favorite when I was little too."

"And your room? Are you happy with it? Is there anything you need or want to change?"

"Well," Aya starts, "I don't have much to do when I'm alone all the time. Do you think that I could have my laptop back?"

I sit back in my seat and cringe.

"I was thinking of taking some online classes."

"Aya," I begin. I hate to deny her anything, but internet access is out of the question. "You know I can't."

"You can't," she repeats and puts her fork down.

"I can get you whatever books you need," I suggest, trying to diffuse the situation. "If you want to study..."

"I swear to God that I won't tell anyone," Aya takes a different tack and pleads. "You rescued me. I won't turn you into the police."

I glance at my hands.

"Please," Aya begs. "What if I promise not to tell anyone that you have me here? I'll just do my online classes and not say anything to anyone about my personal situation. I promise."

I want to believe her but I can't.

Actually, that's a lie.

I *do* believe her.

I'm just not willing to take any risk. Having Aya finally to myself is too good. I can't bring myself to do anything that could risk me losing her.

"You know what?" Aya continues, her eyes and voice sharp now. "I think you like this. I think making me beg is getting you off. I think you like watching me suffer. You're just like—"

"Aya! I'm nothing like him!"

"How can you say that?"

"I'm nothing at all like the man who kidnapped and held you?"

Her eyes get big and she looks like she's going to cry.

"Okay, maybe we do share some commonalities. But my intention isn't to hurt you! I don't enjoy watching you suffer! I want you to be happy here in your new life."

Now the tears are streaming down her cheeks. She's sitting back in her chair sobbing in front of her half-eaten lasagne.

"Aya, stop, please. I only want to protect you. I love you!"

"How can you love me?" Aya shrieks. "You don't know me! I'm a complete stranger to you! You saw me a handful of times from across the room and then you just decided to take me. You don't love me. You don't know what love is."

"You're so wrong, Aya," my voice gets dark. "I already knew that lasagne was your favorite food when you were a little girl. Don't you think it's funny the way I keep preparing recipes that you meant to try yourself? And don't you think it's funny that I was able to prepare a room for you that's identical to your bedroom in your apartment? Have you taken a look at the books on that shelf? They're all on your wishlist. And your deodorant in the bathroom? What a coincidence; it's the kind you buy yourself."

Aya's eyes widen and now I know I've really done it but I can't stop myself.

"Aya, I've been watching your every move for over two years. I know your schedule better than I know the back of my own hand. Your apartment, which I own by the way, is wired up just like this house. I have a direct feed from the cameras I installed to my phone. There's nothing I haven't seen. When you browse the news, I'm there, and when you touch yourself, I'm there. And now I'm really here! We can finally be together. I love you more than life itself and now you're mine."

"No," Aya sobs. "No, no no."

She's absolutely hysterical now. She pushes her chair away from the table and gets up, making a run for the stairs.

I'm afraid that she's going to hurt herself. I want to give chase, but after my idiotic confession she'll probably think that I'm doing it because I want to force myself on her, physically as well as emotionally.

I bring up the video feed on my phone and see that she's curled up in her bed, crying.

I want to go try to comfort her, but I need to give her some space. It's killing me to watch her like that, and the worst part of it is that I know that it's all my own fault.

I told her everything for two reasons.

One was blind hope that she would understand.

Two was that I needed to dash my own hopes with that dose of reality that I just received.

CHAPTER TWELVE

AYA LACHAT

A t least now I know that I'm not crazy.

I'm lying on my back, thinking back to that curly blond hair I found on my pillow a few months ago.

It was hers. That lousy, lying, perverted bitch.

I spent all that time beating myself up over my lack of progress in therapy. I told myself that I was acting crazy for feeling like I was being watched all the time. I was convinced that I was never going to recover from what O did to me, that I'd have to spend the rest of my life torturing myself because I wasn't strong enough to be brave and overcome my fear of him returning to finish the job he started.

But I wasn't crazy, I really *was* being watched.

I'm pacing back and forth across the room and I suddenly feel like a complete idiot, wearing this stupid sexy dress. What a clown I am, getting all dressed up for a woman who has apparently been watching me in every state of undress for nearly two years. I've got the overwhelming urge to tear the dress to pieces and I really want to do it then and there even though I know that I'm on camera. I might as well, since I know now that I don't have any privacy and I haven't had any for a long time.

That realization doesn't stop me from storming into the bathroom to tear the dress off, though. I really have no reason to believe that Elodie was being honest about disabling the bathroom cameras, but I don't have a lot of options here. I know for sure that the bedroom cameras are still on. At least I *maybe* have some privacy in the bathroom.

I peel the dress off and pull on it, trying to destroy it. It's a lot more solid than it looks and I only succeed in stretching out the stitching at the seams. I don't even ever want to see it again so I stuff it in the small trashcan next to the toilet.

Next I turn on the shower, as hot as the water will go. I sit on the edge of the tub as the mirror and window fog up. I feel like I'm covered in a layer of grime that will never wash off. I have to burn it off. I step into the shower and my skin goes red like a lobster.

I let the water run over my head and down my face and my back, purifying me. The heat and the wine I had earlier make me dizzy and I have to brace myself as I get back out of the shower.

I no longer care about the cameras and I stumble into my room and lie on my back on top of the comforter, staring at the ceiling. My skin feels burned and I'm lightheaded. I wish that I had some ice water but I'm too stubborn to risk seeing Elodie again if I go get some, so I go without.

I wonder what almost happened to me.

How much control does Elodie have over her bloodlust?

Maybe I came close to being one of those bodies that some unfortunate person finds charred up in an incinerator. It's obvious to me now that Elodie has been obsessed with me for a long, long time. Did she ever consider tasting me? Did she ever come close?

She could have crept into my room while I was sleeping and ended it all with a single bite. I wouldn't have even known what was happening to me and it all would have been over in moments.

She also could have come in and taken advantage of me. She could have come in my window, stuffed a gag in my mouth, and tied my wrists to my headboard. I imagine that she might have taken her time, kissing my body gently all over before giving small nips here and there, drinking a drop of blood from my hip bone and then another drop from my inner thigh. Maybe she would have put my legs up over her shoulders and then pierced my outer labia with her sharp teeth, mixing my blood with the wetness of my pussy.

I close my eyes and slip my fingers down my body. My fantasy morphs; I'm no longer just tied to my bed. Now I'm fully restrained, in an elaborate set of knots. My arms are behind my back, fixed together at the elbows, and I'm on my knees. My wrists are tied to my ankles and that rope snakes around my throat. Another pair of ropes runs around my throat and down the center of my body, between my breasts, then between the lips my pussy and the cheeks of my ass.

We're in some kind of dark space where I can't see the walls. Elodie is fully nude before me, her breasts swaying gently just inches from my face. I'm no longer wearing a gag. I strain against my ropes and that only causes the rope between my legs to rub against my clit, which makes me whimper.

Elodie gets closer and rubs the tip of her hard, pink nipple over my cheek and lips. I try to turn my head but I can't because of my restraints. She grabs the back of my hair and tilts my head back, which causes the rope around my throat to tighten. My lips part and she pushes her bud into my mouth. I feel her smooth, cool skin gliding back and forth across my tongue and my eyes water.

"You look so pretty, Aya," she gasps, "with my tit in your mouth."

She forces more of her breast into my mouth and I can taste something that's rich and dark sliding down my throat as the rope rubs back and forth against my clit with the motion. I wiggle and strive against the ropes but the more I move the more the friction increases until I find myself whimpering and struggling to increase the sensation.

I bring myself to orgasm before my imagination can carry this fantasy any further. My back throws itself into an arch and I can hear myself squeal involuntarily.

Great.

Now Elodie's admitted that she's spent the last two years spying on my so I've reacted by putting on a little show for her. I just heard that she was watching me, then immediately ran up to my room to give her something good to watch. What could she possibly be thinking right now? She probably is convinced that I'm happy that she's been stalking me for all this time.

I'm too tired to care.

I get up to flick off the light and then crawl back into bed and pull the sheet up to my chin. What the hell has gotten into me?

Now I'm masturbating to a weird stalker? Who kills people? Who is also not human?

I guess I really am sick, just not the way I thought.

I wasn't paranoid, but maybe I was too fixated on being someone's victim. I'm struggling with the thought that maybe, somehow, I enjoyed feeling like I was the center of someone's world. Even though that someone was deadly.

Of course now that I'm lying here in bed trying to figure out what's wrong with me, I can't sleep. I'd give anything now to be able to just drift off and simply not have to deal with being conscious for a few hours. I don't want to think about Olsen, I don't want to think about Elodie, and I certainly don't want to think about what the future holds in store for me.

Instead I'm here, lying in this bed, staring at the ceiling, trying to will myself to sleep. I toss and I turn.

Why would Elodie even tell me what she had done?

Was that supposed to make me feel like I could trust her, since she had finally decided to be honest? Or was it supposed to alleviate her guilt?

I finally settle onto my side and I'm drifting off when I hear it: the door gently opening.

I don't move. I pretend to be asleep. I don't want to have another argument. Maybe if she sees me sleeping she'll just leave me alone.

Nope.

She sits on the edge of my bed as I try to keep my breath steady. I'm so nervous and I don't know what I'm most afraid of, that she's going to kiss me or that she's going to kill me.

She doesn't do either of those things.

Instead she strokes the hair on my head and covers my bare shoulders with the sheet. I can't tell if she knows that I'm awake, but if she does, she doesn't say anything.

I wonder how many times she's done this very thing.

I find that it's a comfort to me to have her there, as if my body somehow recognizes that this is something normal and safe, even if my mind doesn't. I allow her to soothe me into a dreamless sleep.

CHAPTER THIRTEEN

ELODIE GLASS

I can't say that I'm truly surprised when I find Aya in my training room the following evening. She keeps throwing me curveballs but this I almost expected.

She must have been here for quite a while already. Her clothing is soaked through with her sweat, the scent of which roused me from my slumber at sundown in the basement. I woke up dripping with desire, something that hadn't happened to me since I'd been alive. Her sweat intoxicates me with its sweet but slightly tangy scent. I can detect the vanilla of her body wash mixed with the smokey chipotle chiles that I'd used as my secret ingredient to season her dinner the previous night. I can also smell her cunt, stone fruit and warm butter, mingling with the sweat from her thighs. I'd like to lick it from her skin, then allow the salt to flow with her blood, just a little bit. In my fantasies I'm able to control myself, draw out her pleasure and my own. Drink her slowly until she moans and then screams and begs me to give her what she needs.

God knows that's nothing like what would probably happen in real life if I actually took a drop of her precious blood, judging by my recent total lack of self-control she'd probably be dead within minutes.

I can't taste her, so I watch her.

She can't hear my approach and she hasn't realized that I'm standing in the shadows of the doorway. Aya is wearing nothing but a pair of lemony yellow cotton shorts and a thin lace-trimmed camisole, pajamas, and I make a mental note to get her some workout clothes. Her cotton pajamas are soaked with sweat and she's got her hair in a messy bun.

Around she goes, oblivious to my presence, jogging at about the same speed that she usually walks. A smile creeps onto my face when she stops halfway around the training room to catch her breath, her hands on her knees, her little pink tongue panting.

I think about it for a moment... I don't think I've ever seen her run aside from the time she ran from me. Aya's not exactly a fitness fanatic. Sometimes she'll start a yoga routine in her apartment but she never leaves unless she has to and I guess she just didn't have much room for any other kind of workout.

I never would have guessed that she had any interest in sports, but here she is, trying to run a lap around my training room. If I had known that it was only her fear keeping her so sedentary in her previous life, I could have turned the first floor of her building into a gym.

As it stands, she can make it about fifty meters before she runs out of energy. She made it a bit further than that when she was running for her life, but now she's barely caught her breath and she resumes her jog only to quit almost immediately and transition to a brisk walk. Then another three meters or so of running, then back to a brisk walk.

"You know, that's pretty rude of you to stand there laughing at me," she pants, without turning to face me. I've got my eyes on the two perfectly round apples of her ass cheeks; the way they jiggled when she picked up a jog was killing me. Those shorts are so short that they're literally causing me physical pain. I wouldn't even have to pull them down, I could just slide them to the side...

The smile falls from my face and I stand up straight like I've just been caught misbehaving by a strict school mistress.

"I wasn't laughing at you," I lie.

"You know you're not invisible, right?" she turns to ask me with her hands on her hips. "If you cast some kind of invisibility spell on yourself, it's not working. I can see you standing there with your little smirk."

My eyebrows jump. None of my Aya-dreams have ever involved her dressing me down, but now that it's happening I'm surprised by how much her scolding turns me on.

"I don't have an invisibility spell," I put my hands up and show her my palms, as if that gesture is supposed to prove my innocence.

She stares at me for a second, her lips pursed. I'm struggling not to break into a full blown grin. I don't know what's gotten into me but I'm dying to provoke her into continuing her admonishment. I don't even know exactly what I want her to do. Spank me?

I'd definitely be down if that's what she wanted.

"So what kind of spells do you have?" she glares at me.

"I don't have any spells," I pretend not to understand the question.

"So what do you have?"

A tongue that will make you feel like you're being split in two like an atom.

I don't say that out loud.

I don't want to insult her.

I just want to have a little bit of fun with her.

"Are you asking me what I'm capable of?" *I'm sure you don't want to know, sweetheart,* I laugh to myself.

"I guess you can probably run faster than me," she says quietly as she approaches. My breath catches in my throat; she smells so good.

"Honey I'm pretty sure that I can walk faster than you can run. And that was also true *before* I was turned." I tilt her head up toward mine with the knuckle of my index finger and I can see that she's suppressing a grin now too.

Can she tell what she's doing to me?

Brat, I think she can. And now she's standing so close to me that I've got to blink to try to clear my head.

"Oh yeah?" she says softly. "You want to race?"

"Race?"

She can't be serious.

"Yeah. Race. I run and you walk. From here to the wall on the other side of the room. First to touch that wall wins."

"What do I win?"

"You haven't won anything yet."

My lips part and I can taste her breath on my tongue. She's definitely flirting with me.

"Okay," I slip my arm around her waist and pull her close. "So what does the winner get?"

"Loser has to make dinner for the winner," she suggests with a glint in her eye.

"You want to feed me, sweetheart?" Aya doesn't understand what she's getting herself into. There's no way she can, and I'm both surprised and flattered that she's trusting me like this. She shouldn't. I'm about to feed on her before the race even starts.

"Only if you win OKAY GO!"

That cheater pulls from my arms and takes off in the direction of the wall. Even with her head start I could easily catch and pass her, but I let her win. Just barely.

"See!" she shrieks with glee as she slaps the wall and I know that I've made the right decision, though I made it because I didn't think I was capable of feeding from her without hurting her. "I'm not so slow after all, old lady!"

"Damn," I grimace, putting my hands on the small of my back like I really am feeling the effects of my hundred-plus years. "I guess I'm on the hook for dinner. I've got an idea. How about we have a picnic outside tonight? It's hot out but there's a nice breeze. You want to have your victory meal in the garden?"

"Outside?" she considers what I'm suggesting. "Okay. Yeah, that would be nice."

There's something different about her. Aya is so bold tonight, staring me directly in the eye and challenging me. Even her body language is brazen and provocative. She's pressed her body up against mine and I'm sure that she can feel the swell of my quad against the tender flesh of her vulva. In fact, I think she's rubbing herself up against it ever so slightly on purpose.

She'd better be careful or I'm going to give her exactly what she's asking for.

Or maybe that's what needs to happen? Maybe she wants me and she can't bring herself to just tell me?

I shake the thoughts from my head.

I'm just letting my wishful thinking get away from me again. I don't know what Aya is getting at, but I'm pretty sure that she hasn't just suddenly changed her mind and fallen in love with me.

"Okay," I say quietly, pressing myself up against her so that now there's no question whether she can feel that she's turning me on. I breathe in deeply again, taking in her little animal scent. I can smell that she wants me but I can also feel her muscles tighten slightly, recoiling at my advance. "I'll make our picnic. You go get yourself in the bath. You stink."

I wink at her and leave her with a pout on her lips, right where my labia should be.

❧

CHAPTER FOURTEEN

AYA LACHAT

W hat an asshole, my God.

I mean, besides the psycho killer kidnapping thing.

Who does Elodie think she is?

You can't just come on to someone like that and then tell them that they need to take a bath because they stink.

I mean, it's true. I do stink.

But it was still rude to say.

I make my way back to my room to get cleaned up, which obviously I was going to do anyway without being told. In fact, I'm almost considering NOT bathing now just out of spite. If Elodie doesn't want to deal with the way I smell, she could always just let me go. It's not like I *want* to be here anyway.

I can't do it though. I feel too gross.

I woke at sunset and I've been in the training room working out since then. First I did a bunch of yoga poses that I vaguely remembered from videos I'd tried at home. I want to build strength and endurance. That little run I took from Elodie the other night showed me just how out of shape I really was. I have no chance of ever escaping if I can't even outrun an ordinary middle aged man like Lou, let alone a supernatural creature like Elodie. After my yoga, I was trying to improve my running when I got so rudely interrupted.

Even though I didn't finish my planned workout, I'm still covered with a layer of sweat that has now dried on my skin. It's itchy and I don't want my skin to break out, so once I get to my room I turn on the hot water in the tub and throw in a bath bomb. I peel my improvised workout wear off and I'm about to toss it into a hamper in the bedroom when I remember that the bedroom cameras are still on.

I'm feeling bold, but not that bold.

I crack the door to the bathroom and toss my laundry onto the bedroom floor. I can pick it up later.

Rose petals are unfolding from the bath bomb and the room fills with the heady scent of an English garden. The petals are blood red and they unfurl in the hot water like salacious little bits of flesh, drifting amongst little bubbles of oil. I'm immediately annoyed at Elodie for what seems like an obviously vulgar suggestion at first, but then I can't figure out what that suggestion is supposed to be.

I know that she said that she doesn't know any spells but I'm sure that she's cast one on me. I can't stop thinking about what it would be like if she were to just take me. I mean, I don't want her. She's a monster. But my dirty mind keeps going to the same place over and over and I can't get her body out of my mind.

Suddenly I'm struck with an idea.

I wrap a fluffy white towel around myself and head back into the bedroom.

This room is identical to my room at home. It has the same furniture (albeit in a higher quality version), the same decorations, and even the same knick knacks.

I get down on my knees in front of the bed and look to find out just how detail-oriented Elodie was when she made this copy-room. At home, I've got a box under my bed where I like to hide things. My secret box has photos of my family and a few personal items that belonged to them, my sister's Scrunchie, my brother's spare glasses, you know. That sort of thing.

It's also where I keep my vibrator.

I get down and peek under my bed.

There's nothing down there but Yeti, who meows like I've interrupted his private time.

"Sorry," I apologize quietly, not bothering to conceal my disappointment.

Well, it was worth a shot.

I return to the bathroom, dejected, but not for long. This fancy bathtub has a detachable shower head! With multiple settings, ranging in tempo and intensity for people who want to get really, um, clean.

The water turns my skin pink as soon as I slip in. I've made it a bit too hot, but that's okay. I rub my arms and dunk my head, loosening the grime from my earlier activities. Bath oils run in rivulets down my skin and I rub them in, cleaning myself while I soak, massaging the floral scent into my limbs.

My hands travel down to my breasts and I close my eyes.

What if Elodie had won that race?

I should have let her win.

I imagine her ripping open my camisole and lifting me up, pressing me against the wall so that she can bite my nipples. I pinch them myself and twist them gently, imagining them bleeding tiny drops that she laps up with her tongue. She'd feed from the blood at my breasts and then hold me with one arm around my waist as the other hand traveled into my shorts, into the waistband.

I would be completely helpless, pressed against the wall as her fingers explored my sex, first sliding gently up and down my labia majora, then forcing their way inside, first one, then two.

My own hand had found its way to my lips and my middle finger worked my clit in circles as I fantasized about Elodie working my pussy as she stole drops of my blood.

I could feel warmth emanating from her own sex earlier, pressed against my stomach. I slide my butt down in the tub and turn the water back on so that the stream is pulsing on my clit, working my fingers in and out as I dream about Elodie losing all self control and plunging her fingers into me.

She'd hold me against that wall and fuck me hard and fast and...

Does she even come? I was about to imagine what I would do to her, but I don't know if her body still works like that.

I had assumed that she could orgasm but I actually have no idea. I don't even know if she can get wet.

I decide for the purposes of my fantasy that she can, and she does, and I do too. I had meant to take my time but the orgasm came so fast and so strong that I knew that it was badly needed.

Once my body stops quivering I am hopeful that at our picnic she won't seem quite so interesting to me anymore. At least not in *that* way.

I get out of the tub and dry myself, rubbing the towel over my hair even though I know it's going to make it frizzy. I wrap myself in the towel even though it's damp and I leave the bathroom, glancing around the bedroom to see if I can see any cameras.

I haven't been able to find any yet. They must be tiny, very high tech. I want to stare at one to let Elodie know that I'm looking back at her, but I can't.

There's nothing to do about that so I choose a floral sundress, this one black with deep red roses growing on a thorny vine. It suits my mood and I take my time getting ready for the picnic even though I'm now starving.

By the time I get to the backdoor where I'm supposed to meet Elodie, she's already standing there holding a huge, wicker picnic basket. Did she already own that thing? I didn't think that picnic baskets really existed outside of romance movies.

"You're looking like you're feeling better," she smirks at me.

I stop in my tracks.

"Were you spying on me?" I demand, pretty sure that she just watched me get myself off in my bathroom.

"No. No more than usual. If you're asking me if the bathroom is still off limits, the answer is yes. I wasn't watching you."

Then how does she know what I was doing? Because I'm sure by that look on her face that she knows.

"I took a bath."

"I can see," she's still got that smart ass look on her mug. "Your skin's still all flushed. It must have been a good one."

"I made the water too hot," I can feel myself blushing.

"Maybe you'd like to have a drink?" she raises her eyebrows. "I've got a nice white wine chilled here."

"Yes," I stare at the door. "I'm actually very thirsty. Thank you."

I resolve not to look at her again. I'm just going to stand there and watch her open the door.

She fiddles with a black screen next to the door and I can hear a lock release.

"Biometrics," I say out loud, more to myself than to her. "So I guess I'll need either your hand or your eye to get out?"

She flinches like I cut her. "Well you'd better be fast," she admits, opening the door to let me out. "Any drop in temperature will alert the house that it's been compromised and it will go into full lockdown."

"So this isn't full lockdown?" I'm crestfallen. "It gets worse than this? What is full lockdown then?"

"I'll show you," Elodie promises. "But not until after you eat."

CHAPTER FIFTEEN

ELODIE GLASS

"Hold this and I'll give you a lift," I hand the picnic basket over to Aya and I can see that it's heavy for her but as soon as she has it I lift her into my arms.

I shouldn't hold her so close like this while I can smell the orgasm on her, but she doesn't have any shoes and her feet are still a little fucked up from her last getaway attempt. I'll at least carry her over the gravel to the soft grass before I put her down and let her walk.

Once I get to the grass of course I can't bring myself to let her go so I carry her to the spot that I meant to have our picnic, in the middle of a little enclave surrounded by overgrown rose bushes. I set her down and take the basket from her, laying out a big blanket for us to sit on before I unpack the wine and mezze that I've prepared for us.

I can feel my phone buzzing in my pocket and I wish that I had just 'forgotten' it in the house but I don't want to risk Adrienne just showing up. I've been able to keep my sisters at bay thus far but I know that they're beginning to get suspicious about my little 'project' that I'm working on. I wish that I had come up with a better explanation than just I wanted to renovate an old farmhouse, but I can't lie to them convincingly.

They know me too well.

"Wow," Aya is already helping herself to a little plate of pita bread and assorted dips. "This stuff smells really good. Isn't it gross for you, though, all this garlic?"

"Not at all."

Actually I had specifically chosen these dishes to cover Aya's scent so that I wouldn't be driven insane with temptation yet again. And so far at least that little plan was working.

"Um," Aya sips her wine, "are you gonna get that?"

"Sorry," I pull my phone from my pocket. It's Jayden. I decline the call and see that I have several missed calls from them. "Fuck," I say under my breath.

"Is everything okay?" Aya looks concerned.

This is messing up our date.

"Yeah, it's just my little sister. Let me text them and make sure they're alright."

I'm actually a little worried myself because Jayden usually isn't one to ride anyone's ass. I hope that there isn't any kind of actual emergency.

What's up?, I text them. *I'm kind of in the middle of something*

I can see the three little dots that signify that they're texting back.

Dude what are you doing? Adrienne keeps asking Aravella and me and I don't know what to tell her

I sigh and run my fingers through my hair. I knew that I couldn't keep Aya here a secret forever but I need more time to come up with a way to introduce her.

"What is it?" Aya has stopped eating, which is not doing anything to calm my nerves.

"It's must my older sister," I try to assuage her fears. "She can be kind of a pain in my ass sometimes."

I'm working on this house, I text back, hoping that is the end of this conversation.

Why are you so obsessed with that house?

It's just a thing I'm doing

This is not going well.

Then I get a text from Adrienne, the one I've been dreading.

We're holding our meeting at your new place tomorrow night since you apparently have decided to move out

Fuckfuckfuck.

It's not done, I try to dissuade her.

We'll be there at midnight, is the only response I get, to my absolute lack of surprise.

I know that there's no use arguing with her. Trying to argue with Adrienne is like trying to argue with a wall. When she makes a decision, that decision is always final. I'm going to have to figure out what the hell to do with Aya.

"I guess I never really imagined that people like you use cell phones," Aya is saying, and I realize that I've been ignoring her in my panic.

"Sorry?"

"You know," Aya looks at me. "Like you. I guess that I never pictured people with... your condition... using the phone."

This gets a laugh out of me, for which I'm grateful. I don't want to spend the entire night together worrying about my sisters. "Yeah all of my carrier pigeons are currently disposed."

"Well I didn't mean it like that," Aya rolls her eyes.

"Jesus Aya I'm not *that* old."

"Well how old are you?"

"Not *that* old. But actually, my sister Aravella *does* hate cell phones. My other sister Adrienne practically forced her to get one."

"How many sisters do you have?"

"Three. Two older and one younger."

"So you were all turned by the same parent?"

"What?" for a moment I'm not sure what she means. "Oh, no."

"Oh, you were sisters before you turned?"

"Nope."

"So what makes you sisters?"

"We formed a coven. I guess that you could say it's my chosen family. Some immortals stay with the one who turned them and others form their own family groups. Some prefer to live alone."

"How did it happen?" she asks quietly, sipping her wine.

I take a deep breath and look at the stars above her.

"It's not a very nice story, Aya," I warn her. It's not that I want to keep secrets from her. It's just that I'm loathe to ruin our evening.

"I want to know," she says gently, not taking her eyes off of me.

"Well, I'll tell you. But it was a long time ago. Over a hundred years. I don't know if you remember this from our group meetings, but my mother — my birth mother — struggled her entire life with addiction, mostly to alcohol but also to any vice that she could get her hands on. Gambling, men, you name it and she had to have it."

"What about your father?"

"I never met him and I'm not sure that she even knew for sure which man left her pregnant. Things were different then, women didn't have many opportunities to live independently. So she ended up with a series of shitty boyfriends who managed to make her life even more difficult than it already was. She needed money and her preferred method for raising that money was selling herself. But when there were no buyers left, when her body was too broken, she turned to selling me."

Aya gasps softly but I continue.

"This went on for years until she ended up with a guy so deep in debt to my dark father — the man who eventually turned me — that she sold me to him as a thrall."

"What's a thrall?"

"Sometimes people like me will keep a human companion, or even sometimes several human companions, to serve them. Especially to help with things that need to be done during daylight hours. It wasn't alway so easy to conduct all of one's business after the sun went down."

"Am I your thrall?"

Now it's my turn to gasp. "Never," I'm shocked by the suggestion but I can kind of understand why she might ask. "Never, Aya. You're not my property."

Aya looks skeptical.

"So your dark father bought you from your mother and enslaved you?"

"No. Yes. Sort of. I call him my dark father because that's the term we use but my time with him was actually the best time of my entire human life. His name was Sonny, ironic because he hadn't seen the sun in hundreds of years, it was short for Santiago, and my mother and her boyfriend disgusted him. He was very, very old, from Italy, and he practically worshipped his own mother. He couldn't imagine a mother being as depraved as mine."

"So he rescued you?"

"He destroyed my mother and her boyfriend in front of me."

I almost mention that it's something we have in common, that a vampire killed our families in front of us as children, but I stop myself just in time. Aya doesn't know that I know all about Olsen Leonard and her family.

"That's terrible."

"I don't know, was it?"

We're both quiet for a moment.

"He taught me everything, long before he turned me." I want to be completely honest with Aya about myself even though it pains me. "I was a monster long before I was immortal."

"You're not a monster," Aya replies softly.

I glance down from the night sky and catch her staring at me. Her eyes are glassy and she's rapt, listening to my story.

I don't know how I've managed to mislead her so badly.

"Aya," I rasp, "you have to know. I'm a beast. I don't deserve your pity or your sympathy or whatever it is that you're trying to give me right now. My dark father didn't turn me until long after he knew that a lust for blood was part of my innate nature. I haven't always been an immortal, but I have *always* been a demon."

CHAPTER SIXTEEN

AYA LACHAT

"If you want to know, Aya, just ask." Elodie interrupts my thoughts.

I glance over at her, almost surprised to see that she's still there. I begin to say something, then I can't quite figure out what it is that I want to say. My tongue is as twisted as my thoughts.

"I can see that you have something on your mind."

I have a lot on my mind, she's right. I'm just not sure how much of it I want to share. I'm struggling to organize my own ideas and questions and my mind is racing.

Elodie is sitting just a breath away from me and if she had blood coursing through her veins I'd be close enough to feel the heat from her body. And I want to feel her, so badly. I want to reach out and touch her marble skin, skin that hasn't changed in a hundred years according to what she just told me.

But Elodie is rarely so candid and my instincts are screaming at me to seize this opportunity.

"How old were you when you became a…"

"Thrall?" she reminds me. I've never heard the word before.

"Yeah."

"Almost eleven?"

"And your mother just…? She sold you?"

"My mother sold me over and over and over. When she sold me to my dark father it was just the final time."

"Did she think that she would just get you back again? When she handed you over to the man who turned you? Did she know what he was?"

"She didn't know what Sonny was but she knew that she wasn't getting me back that time. The debt her boyfriend owed was an unfathomable sum of money to her and she'd heard that Sonny would pay for little girls. And I wasn't worth much to her anymore anyways. I was getting too old."

I'm not about to say this out loud, but I agree with Sonny. I can't even fathom a mother being willing to sell her own child. My stomach flip flops. I know what it's like to lose everything I love but I don't know what it's like to be betrayed by the very people who are supposed to love you. That kind of pain is foreign to me.

"Do you hate her?"

"My mother? No. Addiction is a disease and an addict will do anything to relieve her craving, a craving that causes her physical pain and can even kill her. And now I know what it's like, to need something so bad that you're willing to implode your entire life to have it. No, I don't hate my mother."

Elodie's eyes flash at me as she speaks, blue and silver. I realize that she must be talking about blood. I want to offer her mine, I want to present my wrist to her and feed her, nurture her the way her mother couldn't.

But I remain still.

"Did your dark father hurt you?"

I immediately flinch at how stupid that question was. Of course he hurt her, he fucking killed her.

"No," Elodie smiles at my obvious look of surprise. "Never."

"I don't get it. Why was he buying little girls? Just so that he could turn them? Like to make his own army or something?"

Elodie takes a deep breath and twists a blade of grass between her thumb and forefinger. "No. Many of us take thralls to serve us during the day while we sleep. Sometimes for practical reasons, like running errands or security. Sometimes for companionship. Maybe you've noticed that I don't go out when the sun is up?"

"Because you can't?"

"Oh I can," Elodie surprises me again. "I just don't."

"Why not?"

She considers the question. "It's complicated."

I stare at her and wait for her to continue, long after it becomes clear that she has no intention of explaining.

"Plus," she changes the subject, "we don't turn many people, at least not without serious consideration beforehand."

"Is it against your laws?"

"My laws?" she laughs. "More like our customs. An overpopulation would be bad for us all. We survive by staying in the shadows."

I focus my gaze on a white rose just beside me. It's in full bloom, so fragrant, and it's nearly sickeningly sweet. It's probably hours away from rotting and dying.

"Have you ever turned anyone?" I ask quietly, not looking up.

"Me?" now it's Elodie's turn to be surprised. "No," she shakes her blond curls and makes a face like the question was insane.

I don't know why, but for some reason that answer is a great relief to me. It's not because I'm afraid of her turning me, I'm not. I can't stand the idea of her sharing that experience with someone else though.

"Why did your dark father turn you?"

"I was dying, I had an injury from a job that he'd sent me on. It was more than that, though, I think that he knew that he was nearing the end of his time and he wanted... I'm not sure exactly what. A replacement? A way to provide for me?"

"How could he be nearing the end of his time? I thought you were immortal."

"He ended his own existence. He was weary of the world's cruelties, they're relentless."

"Was he like you? I mean, committed to fighting evil?"

Elodie laughs. "Not officially. But he had a deeply ingrained sense of right and wrong, one that sometimes made sense only to him. He trained me to kill long before he made me a natural killer. Evil people, people who didn't repay debts, people who offended his sense of honor, I slaughtered them and I loved it. It's how Sonny knew that I'd make a good monster. I was already monstrous, I don't know if it was because of what happened to me or I was born bad, but the transition was easy."

"You aren't bad," I say softly. My eyes drift over her lips and I want to crawl into her lap and take her face in my hands. The evening breeze is dancing over my skin and I imagine it's her fingertips.

"You want to see the house in lockdown mode?" Elodie derails my reverie.

"What?"

"You aren't eating and I promised you."

"Oh," I smooth my dress out and get my head out of the evening clouds. "Okay. Yeah."

Elodie stands up and reaches her hand down to me. She pulls me to my feet and I begin to collect the remains of our meal.

"Just leave it," she tells me. "I can grab it later. Come on."

She leads me back into the house, through the backdoor, and the sight of the small security panel breaks the spell. She's all business now, tapping on it with her fingertips, and I can't figure out how it works.

It's only a few moments before an alarm sounds, jolting me from my spot, and heavy steel shutters that I never even knew existed are dropping down over the doors and windows. The lights cut and I stumble, completely disoriented from the sudden change.

Elodie catches me so I don't fall to my knees and she supports my elbow gently but the sudden and complete loss of vision has made me feel like we're outside of time and space.

I snake my hand up her chest and around her neck and pull her face toward mine. Or, rather, I pull myself up to her.

My lips find hers in the dark and a guttural sound escapes from her throat as she pushes her tongue into my mouth, searching for my own and kissing me deeply. My body crushes against hers and I pull her shirt from the waistband of her pants, sliding my hand up over her cool skin and her ribcage. My fingers are grasping at her, trying to pull her even closer, and my short fingernails are digging into her back.

I push my tongue past her lips and into her mouth and search for her teeth. I can feel them there, sharp as razors and she gives a small moan warning me not to go any further but I can't stop.

I want to feel her weight on me. I want her to hold me down and push my legs up over her shoulders and force her fingers and her tongue inside of me, but she's so gentle and so restrained.

She's driving me insane.

My other hand searches for the button on her pants and I'm fiddling with it when the lights go back on.

I jump back, feeling like a bucket of ice water has been dumped on my head. Seeing her standing there with her shirt half untucked and her lips parted is a shock to my system. Had I really just done that? To the woman who was my captor?

"It's a test cycle," Elodie explains, tucking her shirt back into her pants.

She wipes his mouth on the back of her hand and I catch a glimpse of her fangs behind her pink tongue.

I probably nearly just ended my own life.

"Interesting," I say, a little bit too loud. "Anyhow thanks for dinner, that was good. I'm feeling a bit tired, I think I'm going to go up to my room."

I walk away from her without another glance, pretending like nothing just happened.

CHAPTER SEVENTEEN

ELODIE GLASS

S he's so wild, my Aya, when she wants something.

That kiss was absolutely nothing like I had imagined in all of my fantasies. Aya was so fragile and innocent, as pure as the freshly fallen snow. In my dreams, she'd be fearful and vulnerable when I made love to her. Sometimes I'd imagine that I was devouring her, tearing her apart and consuming her. Sometimes I'd imagine that I'd be slow and gentle; I'd teach her how to fuck and then promise her that it would only hurt a little bit when I pierced her with my fangs.

I never imagined that she'd be the one ravishing me, but here we are.

I just keep going over that kiss in my mind. The lights went out. I know that I should have warned her that it would happen, but part of me wanted to catch her by surprise and it worked. The look of alarm on her face was so precious, she obviously couldn't see a thing judging by the way she flailed her arms around.

I can see as well in the dark as I can in the light and I only let her stumble for a moment before I caught her and offered her my support. My initial idea had been that she'd have to hold on to my elbow until the lights went back on.

But then things went so much better.

The look on her face changed.

I'd seen a glimpse of that hunger in her before, but never like this. Blinding her hadn't made her helpless. Instead it made her bold, washed away her anxieties and insecurities. Her tongue darted out and licked at her lips and before even I, with my catlike inhuman reflexes, could see what she was doing she was on me like it was *her* who needed *my* blood to live.

My God it was so hot.

I had meant to clean up after our picnic but instead I retire to my room. I have to take care of myself or I'm never going to get anything done, and I desperately need to clear my head because I need to figure out what the fuck I am going to do with Aya before my sisters show up tomorrow night.

I have no reason to think that Aya is going to join me but just in case this really is my lucky night, I leave the bedroom door open behind me so that I can see her closed door. I collapse onto my back on top of the comforter and fumble with the button on my pants for a moment before it just pops off, launches across the room, and hits a mirror that won't show me a clear reflection of myself. My zipper goes down and then my pants and boxer-briefs follow. I'm already still semi-aroused from the kiss.

I bet she'd like a blindfold.

I could go into her room right now and tear one of those silk dresses into strips, maybe the green one she wore the other night. I'd tear it up and then tie her hands behind her back, make her get on her knees on her bed, and tie her ankles together and then tie her wrists to her ankles.

Then I'd use one last strip to blindfold her.

She be so ripe and eager for me, with her lips and her knees spread. I'd kiss her again, slowly, teasing her, letting her bite my bottom lip before my fingers travelled down to check how wet she already was.

I slide my fingers up and down slowly, varying the pressure from hard to soft to hard again, taking my time. I'm thinking about how warm she feels, and how warm I'd feel if I wrapped myself around her. She smells so good when she gets horny. I want to get my fingers tangled in her pubic hair and I want to feel her struggling to rub herself against my hand.

I spit in my hand and get it nice and wet so I can work myself a little faster. I wouldn't let her come just yet. I'd stand up in front of her and press her face into my own white curls. Would she accept me right away? I imagine it both ways, first that she parts her lips and stretches out her little pink tongue, eager to taste me, then that she struggles a bit before giving my mound some demure licks and then finally loosening her jaw so that she can eat me properly.

I can smell something and it's not the pussy I want.

"Can you please fuck off?" I ask the cat, who has now joined me on the bed. "I'm busy."

The cat meows at me and doesn't move. I squeeze my eyes shut and try to get back on track but the moment is lost. The cat gets louder and I stroke myself hard and fast so that I come, dripping juices onto the comforter so that I have to make a mental note to toss it into the laundry so that it's fresh when Aya really does join me one night.

"You happy?" I ask the cat, shooting him a dirty look. I've never really had a pet before, but if I was going to choose one, it wouldn't be a cat. I don't quite see the appeal. They aren't fun like horses or loyal like dogs.

"What are you even doing out here, shouldn't you be in bed with your mistress?"

The cat meows and it occurs to me, first, that Aya must have also forgotten about him and accidentally shut him out of her room, and second, I'm not sure he's been fed.

We got distracted earlier.

"Okay, come on," I gesture to him and the cat and I seem to have reached an understanding. He follows me downstairs and into the kitchen, where I prepare him a bowl of tuna and goat's milk.

I watch him eat and make a mental note to get him some cat food. He likes the gourmet treatment but Aya says that it's not good for him. I'm not entirely sure she's right about that because I'm pretty sure that the majority of cats in the world live off of whatever they can scavenge from the trash, but if she wants to feed Yeti the equivalent of meat cereal, then I'll get her some meat cereal.

I also have to stop by her place and grab the box she keeps under her bed. I saw her on camera looking for it the other day and I'm not sure if she wanted her sentimental items or her vibrator. Either way, what my Queen wants, my Queen gets.

The Notes application on my phone illuminates the kitchen and I'm making myself an errand list when I get a couple texts from Aravella.

That's weird because, out of all my sisters, Aravella is the least likely to contact me. First, because she hates modern technology. Second, I love the girl but we're not very close. Aravella is secretive, volatile, and quick to anger. She comes from a long line of immortals who don't share our compassion for mankind and she hasn't completely untangled herself from her previous connections. I'm not saying that I don't trust the woman, but she's not exactly my go-to confidante and I'm pretty sure that she feels the same way about me.

I open my message app and immediately notice that this is the first series of texts I've received from her in several months.

Hey

Adrienne has some kind of wild hair up her ass about your new place

If something weird is going on you better get it cleaned up before tomorrow night

x

I glance up from my phone and out the window.

I still haven't figured out what I'm going to do about Aya, and Adrienne must be dead set on figuring out what's going on if now even Aravella is warning me about her.

I shift my weight back and forth from foot to foot before settling on a countertop. I don't think that my sisters would hurt her, but what I've done could be the only thing imaginable that might get me shunned from our coven. We're supposed to protect the innocent, not abduct them.

I didn't have a choice, though. It was like from the moment I first saw Aya, I knew that we were destined for one another. I could never let anyone else hurt her, and I can no longer protect her from afar.

I have no reason to continue existing without Aya.

She's my purpose.

I don't want to lose my only family though. My sisters mean the world to me and it was never my intention to betray them like this or keep secrets from them. I just have to figure out a way to buy some time until I can make my sisters understand that I have to have Aya.

My phone lights up again and this time it's a notification from the house. Aya is up out of bed and pacing around her room. I watch her stomp back and forth on the video feed and I can see that she's even more frustrated than I am.

Once she settles back into her bed I head upstairs to put her to sleep.

CHAPTER EIGHTEEN

AYA LACHAT

M y door unlocks with a click from the outside. I screw my eyes shut and stay perfectly still.

I feel something soft drop onto the bed with me and then a little weight makes it's way across the comforter before dropping into the crook behind my knees.

Yeti! I forgot about him!

In my mind I silently thank Elodie for bringing him to bed. I hope that she remembered to feed him too, I got so caught up in our... exchange earlier that I forgot all about my poor kitty.

I'm lying on my side and I can feel Elodie lay down beside me. She's on her back and I'm one-hundred percent committed to pretending that I'm asleep.

I can't deal with her right now.

I don't know what happened earlier and I need time to process my own behavior. It was like the light switch went off and a switch inside of me went on. I've never actually pursued any kind of intimacy before and if that light hadn't come back on I'm not sure how far I would have taken things.

Neither of us move. Even Yeti is perfectly still.

It's surprisingly difficult to pretend to be asleep. My side starts to ache and I want to flip onto my back but I can't do that without alerting Elodie. Then I start to feel a sneeze coming on. I trace the tip of my tongue on the roof of my mouth in an effort to suppress it.

I'm not entirely sure why Elodie is in my bed right now. If she was an ordinary woman, I'd assume that she's here trying to pick up where we left off in the dark earlier.

But Elodie isn't an ordinary woman.

Hell, she's not technically a woman at all.

I know that sometimes she comes into my room and sits with me. I fell asleep with her beside me yesterday, and I'm pretty sure that it wasn't the first time that she'd kept me company while I slept.

But still.

What if she wants to talk about what happened?

My God, I think I'd die of embarrassment.

I'm thinking up my strategy, how I'll respond. At the moment, denying that I was the first one to make a move sounds like my only viable choice.

"Was your girlhood sweet, Aya?" Elodie asks suddenly.

I'm still frozen but now my eyes are open.

She knows I'm not asleep.

"Or was it something you don't want to remember?"

I roll onto my back and sneeze.

"It was magical," I reply, staring at the ceiling. "I had every-thing. Well, not like every single toy I ever wanted. I wanted a white pony and I never got one of those either," I laugh, remembering the time I convinced myself that I really was going to get a pony for Christmas. "But I had so, so much."

Elodie flips onto her side and I notice that she's not wearing a shirt, just a sports bra. It is kind of warm in the house that evening. I wonder if dead people get uncomfortable when they're too hot.

My eyes travel over her body. She's just so beautiful. Her skin is gleaming in the moonlight and she's absolutely flawless, she looks like she's cut from marble. I absentmindedly reach a finger out and trace her abs and the swells of her chest. She's so cold and I can feel her tense under my fingers but otherwise she doesn't move, she just lets me touch her.

"Do you have siblings?" she asks, her arm stretched above her head, resting behind her curls.

"Three, actually, just like you. Had," I quickly correct myself without explaining. "An older sister, an older brother, and a younger brother. Nala, Gabe, and Hugh."

"Did you guys get along?"

"No. Yes. Sometimes. I was closest to my sister, she was two years older than me. Nala was a piano prodigy, she played beautifully. She was an artist, super talented but she was also temperamental. And my parents were one hundred percent committed to helping her launch a professional career, so that meant lots of travel for concerts and lessons and auditions. Sometimes we had to scrimp and save to pay for Nala's music, skip vacations or whatever. We never got to go to Disneyland, which I always wanted to do. Back before. But going to her concerts was fun too. I know a lot about music thanks to her, it was kind of a requirement for being a member of our family. You know, it's weird, I hadn't noticed it before, but you kind of resemble her. Like a leaner, grown-up version. Just a little bit."

"Huh," Elodie considers my response. "Do you play an instrument?"

The question is so absurd that I snort with laughter, then cover my face, embarrassed by the noise I just made.

"No," I assure her. "I don't have a musical bone in my body. The opposite, in fact, I'm totally tone deaf."

She smiles. "What were you into?"

"Like for a hobby?"

"Yeah. What was your passion when you were a little girl?"

I have to think about the question for a long time. I don't think anyone has ever asked me about my talents. Probably because I have none.

"I guess my passion was just being completely ordinary," I admit. "Being the world's most plain girl."

Now it's Elodie's turn to look stunned.

"You're not plain," she says softly. "Nothing like plain. You're exquisite."

I blush at her absurd flattery but her brows furrow. Is she being serious?

"Well, you are the only person on Earth who has ever thought that."

"That can't be true."

"I was happy though," I argue. "I *liked* being plain. I never had any desire to be the world's best anything. I liked my life. I loved my family. I was proud of Nala and my brothers were very loving, kind boys. Gabe was going to be an architect and Hughey, he changed his mind about what he wanted to be when he grew up every week. If it were up to him, he would have been a firefighting paleontologist who moonlighted as an astronaut. And he was so clever, maybe he could have done it."

"What about your parents? What were they like?"

"They were just totally normal, middle class parents. My dad worked for the city, he was an accountant, and my mom was a receptionist at the elementary school. They loved road trips and we used to drive all over the country in our station wagon to Nala's music things. Once we drove all the way to Washington D.C. That was our biggest trip ever. We did the whole tourist thing there, visited the museums and the memorials and then Nala played a concert and we all got dressed up and sat in the front row. We ate dinner in a restaurant, which we almost never did because it was so expensive for six people, and I was even allowed to order dessert. I can remember what I had, tiramisu. I felt like a princess, I had this amazing blue velvet dress with a puffy skirt."

I'm so caught up in my memory that I haven't noticed that Elodie has managed to slide much closer to me, or else I slid closer to her when I rolled on to my side to face her. Now I can feel her cool breath on my lips and my hand is resting on her stomach.

It's so easy to love her when we're alone together in the dark.

When I forget what she is and what she's done.

When we're just two bodies drawn to one another.

I have to remind myself that this woman has imprisoned me in this sick house, decorated in pastels and shuttered in steel. And didn't I watch this woman tear a grown man to shreds with her bare teeth? She's not my lover, she's my captor.

But that all seems so far when she's so close. I want to keep touching her and I want her to undress me but we're both still. Whatever demon had possessed me earlier was gone and I no longer have that nerve.

I try to cut myself some slack. There's no denying that Elodie Glass is a beautiful woman. Inhumanly beautiful, probably because she's not human. And she can be so sensitive too, even though she's a monster. It hasn't escaped my notice that Elodie isn't asking me directly about why I'm referring to my entire family in the past tense. I'm grateful for her tact; I have zero interest in going over their final moments with her.

And the several months I endured in captivity after they were ripped from me.

I don't want to think about any of that right now, and I certainly don't want to explain it to her.

I want to ask her more about her life but my eyelids are getting heavy.

"Are you tired, Aya?" she asks, her voice low and intimate. Her arm slips around my waist and pulls me even closer to her so that my face is buried in her soft, cool chest.

Kiss me, Elodie, I try to will her via telepathy. *Do it.*

"Close your eyes."

I'm fighting sleep now and I don't even know why anymore. I let my eyelids shut and I drift off into another deep, nightmare-free sleep in Elodie's arms.

CHAPTER NINETEEN

ELODIE GLASS

My Aya isn't in the training room when I rise the following evening. She's also not in her bedroom, the kitchen, or the living room. I'm alone with her cat, and if I hadn't designed the house's security system myself then I'd be afraid that she's figured out how to disable it and escape.

I know that it's impossible though. She needs my eye to even access the control panels, and since both of my eyes are still in my head I know that she must be around here somewhere.

She's playing hide and seek with me, but that's okay. Every time I take one step forward with her, I push her too far and she takes two steps back. This time I'm going to show her that I've learned my lesson and give her some space.

Maybe if I give her some time to think about her options, she'll realize that I'm the best thing that ever happened to her. Maybe she'll be able to see things more clearly from a distance, maybe she's farsighted. Maybe she'll be able to admit to herself that I adore her and would do anything to make her happy.

Maybe she'll accept that she wants me just as bad as I want her.

She can be so stubborn. Sometimes I think that she's resisting me — us — just because she can't bear to be wrong about her belief that no one could love her.

"I don't know what you did to make her like you so much," I tell the cat, scratching him behind the ears. We're sitting on the sofa together, apparently having a conversation about the woman we both love.

The cat mews at me, butting me with his head and rubbing his face along my flank.

"I guess you can be pretty charming, for a cat," I continue scratching as he jumps into my lap, purring like an engine.

"Is it because you're aloof? I can be aloof. If that's what she's into."

The truth is that I'm not making a serious effort to find Aya because I need the space just as much as she does at the moment.

I've worshipped Aya for years, but now that I'm finally getting to know her, all of her little quirks and dreams and habits, I'm growing to truly love her. She's a constant surprise to me, the way she can be so strong but so naïve sometimes, but she's never a disappointment.

My mind drifts back the kiss, the fierceness of it and the hunger. My unliving blood flow responds to my new train of thought immediately, springing to action that isn't really taking place. I want to let Aya use me, to hold me down and take whatever pleasure she can find from my body, but I also want to overpower her and force her to come for me.

I run my tongue over my fangs and flinch. I need to cool down before I lose control over myself. I've been a beast for a hundred years and I've got my cravings pretty much under control but I've been spending so much time at home with Aya that I haven't fed in weeks and I know that I'm entering dangerous territory with such sweet temptation right in front of me.

I don't want to lose control of myself and seriously hurt Aya. I don't even want to force her to do anything, I want her to love me.

I'm not going to keep checking the video feed on my phone for her. I'm going to go over my to-do list and see if there's anything I can cross off before my sisters arrive for our meeting.

I tap my phone to life and immediately break my promise to myself not to look for Aya.

I slide through all the camera feeds and she's not on any of them. Has she figured out where they are? That seems impossible, they're so small, but I can't see her anywhere. The only other possible explanation is that she's been in her bathroom for hours.

I just need to make sure that she's in her room before my sisters arrive. My best and only plan is to lock her in and hope that Adri isn't expecting a tour of the whole entire house. I really don't have any other options, unless I want to lock her into the coffin where I sleep, and I don't think she'd go for that. Even though it would be our safest bet.

I've got a couple hours until my sisters arrive so I run out and grab Aya's special box from under her bed. Her apartment has been empty for weeks and it's unchanged. I throw out some rotten food from the fridge and on the way home, I grab a pint of that ice cream that she likes.

Keeping busy is the best way to avoid anxiety, so when I get home I putter about tidying things and checking my security system to kill the time.

"Should I get Aya a horse?" I ask the cat, who has been right at my heels all evening. I think he's beginning to like me too. "She said that she wanted a white pony when she was a little girl, you think she still wants one? Or is that dumb?"

Yeti considers the matter and doesn't reply.

"You're right, it's probably a bad idea. I'd have to let her outside all the time to ride it around, and then what if she tried to use it to escape? Plus I don't think you can have just one, I think they need to live in groups. Maybe something to consider for the future when she doesn't want to leave anymore."

Is the cat giving me a skeptical look?

No, I must be imagining things.

Midnight is approaching and I need to lock up Aya. Adrienne has a tendency to show up fifteen minutes early for everything so I want to be prepared when she arrives.

She's still missing in action but now I have to find her.

"Aya?" I enter her room and it's empty. "Aya are you in here? You have to stay in here when my sisters are here for your own safety."

No response, so I try the bathroom door. It's locked.

"Aya are you in there?" I knock. Still no response. "Are you okay?"

Silence.

"Aya, look, I'm sorry but I have to lock you in here. Please try to stay quiet when my sisters are here so we don't have any trouble. I'll come let you out when they leave, okay?"

Is she mad at me? Or is she hurt? I no longer have the time to try to figure out what's going on and I don't want to break the bathroom door down. I'm going to have to talk to her about this later.

I leave Aya's room and lock the door behind me just in time. My phone is lighting up with a text from Adrienne, she's at the front door with Jayden and Aravella.

"Hey," I open the door and gesture for them to come in. "We can sit at the dining room table. I've got wine if anyone wants some."

I can tell by the expression on Adrienne's face that she thinks that I've lost my mind. Her eyes are drifting over the floral sofa and the watercolor paintings on the wall.

I guess this place does look pretty different from our home.

"Did you get a cat?" Jayden half asks, half exclaims.

I forgot about the cat.

"Yeah," I try to act casual. "He belonged to that nonce I slaughtered downtown. I felt bad leaving him to starve."

"Oh, he's friendly!" Jayden picks up Yeti. "He's not afraid of me!"

"Yeah, weird, right?" I'm not surprised that Jayden is a cat person. "Here, sit down."

Everyone settles around my table and I've barely taken a seat before Adrienne is grilling me.

"You gonna tell us what the fuck is going on?" she asks, her thick arms crossed across her chest.

"Elodie, you have the same taste as my granny," Aravella adds, glancing around at the floral arrangements I picked for Aya.

"Cut the shit," Adrienne interrupts her, "I can smell a girl."

I fold my hands on the table and meet Adri's gaze. "There were a couple hippies squatting here before I moved in."

Just then my phone flashes with a notification.

Fuck.

It's the cameras.

Aya isn't in her bathroom, she's creeping around just outside the door to the dining room. My lifeless heart drops. I know that Adrienne can see my jaw flinch. Her eyes dart from me to the door and I can see her ears prick.

Before I can come up with something to say, she flies out of her seat.

Adri is much older than me, and thus much faster and stronger. She's so quick that she's got Aya pinned to the stairs already before I can even get over the table.

CHAPTER TWENTY

AYA LACHAT

I shriek and buck but it's like she's made of steel and not flesh.

This woman — this immortal goddess — is much bigger than Elodie and she has me crushed between her heavily muscled body and the stairs. Her eyes are flashing amber and gold and I can see she has much longer fangs than Elodie has too.

She's going to kill me.

Everything is happening so fast but I feel like I'm underwater. I can barely make out what's going on and I can hear my own screams but it's like I'm hearing them from a great distance.

Something tackles my assailant and in the scuffle my head slams into the bannister. Now there's a young man — no, actually, this time a boyish girl my age — holding me and checking my head. She's telling me that everything is going to be alright but she's got her arms wrapped tightly around me and she's much, much stronger than she looks. I just want to run but I'm trapped.

My vision focuses and I can see Elodie wrestling on the ground with a much smaller woman wearing two pieces of a three piece suit. This woman looks like some kind of early twentieth century gangster.

"Who the fuck is this," the gangster demands, panting and pointing at me. "Elodie, you fucking asshole, WHO THE FUCK IS THIS?"

"She kidnapped me!" I blurt out. "She's got me locked up in this stupid house and I want to go home!"

Elodie said that she and her sisters protect and rescue innocent people. I'm innocent. That means that I'm entitled to their protection.

"No," the girl holding me says quietly, her eyes wide.

She's very cute, she's tall and slender with freckles and strawberry blonde hair. She's the only one wearing jeans and a T-shirt instead of a suit but this close I can tell from her cold skin that she's a vampire too.

"It's true!" I tell her directly, since she seems like the most sympathetic of the bunch.

"You took a thrall?" gangster smiles sardonically with her arms crossed across her chest. "Elodie! Naughty bitch. I never would have guessed that you had it in you."

This one looks a little sleazy and I've got the distinct impression that she's even more of a threat to me than the giantess on the floor.

"No!" Elodie wipes her face on the back of her hand. "She's not a slave. She's my other half."

The big one groans and rubs the bridge of her nose with her thumb and forefinger.

"I wouldn't expect you to understand," Elodie sneers. "I found her at the PTSD victims' group meeting. I've been watching her for years, taking care of her."

"Why didn't you ever say anything?" the young one asks.

"It wasn't supposed to turn out like this," Elodie looks grieved. She gets up from the floor and the girl holding on to me hands me over. Elodie picks me up in her arms and nestles her face into my neck, taking a deep breath.

"I was only going to protect her from a distance," she begins to explain as they all return to the dining room table and everyone takes a seat except me. I'm still cradled in Elodie's arms.

"I've been watching her and keeping her safe. She's been hurt very, very bad."

"So why didn't you just put her tormentor on our list so we could neutralize him and she could continue to live a normal life?"

Elodie doesn't answer right away, she just stares at the ceiling. Her sisters wait silently for her to continue.

"He's one of us," she finally answers. "He's rogue, he's not taking thralls, he's catching women and torturing them to death slowly."

Now it's my turn to gasp.

I can't believe I was so stupid.

I never put two and two together, but now it makes perfect sense. Of course Olsen Leonard is a literal monster.

Visions of him tearing my little brother apart with his teeth flash through my head. Images of him cutting up Nala while he forced her to play piano for him. Memories of his inhuman strength and speed.

I glance up at Elodie.

I never told her specific details about Olsen. She's never explicitly said to me that she has no idea what happened, but she's also never indicated that she actually knew even more than I did about the events that led to my agony.

"Who is he?" now the big one has calmed down a bit. She seems interested in Elodie's story. Hell, I'm interested too. Interested and also furious.

"Olsen Leonard is his name."

The other women shake their heads. None of them has ever heard of him.

"Could be a fake name," Elodie suggests. "I've been trying to gather intel on him but so far I haven't found a thing. It's like he's a ghost."

"So you decided to just keep her locked up just to be safe?" the sleazy one grins.

"No," Elodie grimaces. "Another asshole attacked her, just a random rapist. I couldn't let him hurt her and she saw everything. I had to take her."

"She knows what we are?" the big one's eyes flash again.

This leads to a round of groans at the table.

"So what are you going to do with it?" the sleazy one ask.

"*It*," Elodie repeats sarcastically. "She has a name. It's Aya."

"Aya, I'm Aravella," the woman who just referred to me as 'It' introduces herself.

"Sorry Aya," Elodie says. "This asshole is Aravella, and that gal who I almost had to kill is Adrienne, and they are Jayden. These are my sisters."

Adrienne and Aravella don't look at me but Jayden gives me a smile. This might be the closest I've ever come to having a friend since Olsen Leonard destroyed my life.

"Don't worry," I find my voice. "I won't tell anyone about you guys. You can let me just go, I don't even know anyone anyways and I'm pretty sure that I'd be the one getting locked up if I tried to tell the police or someone that I found a coven of vampires."

I wasn't joking, but everyone at the table thinks this is hilarious.

"That's basically what you guys are, right?" I've never heard Elodie refer to herself as a vampire but she feeds on people and can live indefinitely. Plus she won't go out in the sun, which she still hasn't explained to me.

"Elodie I'm glad you're enjoying yourself, but you can't just take whatever you want. Aya is a person and she had a right to live her own life. And you made a vow to us, you know that we don't take innocent women for our own amusement."

"She's not an amusement!" Elodie roars and even I'm surprised by the passion in her response. "You don't understand. It's like she's part of my body, I can't exist without her. There is no more me without her."

"Elodie she's not safe with us," Jayden says softly. "She's human, her body is so fragile."

"I'll keep her safe," she argues without looking up from the table.

"You're an even bigger threat to her than the rest of us," Aravella sneers. "Look at you! You've lost your mind."

"Aravella," Adrienne warns.

"Look," Elodie tears her gaze from the tabletop and glances around at all of her sisters. "I know this is wrong. I know that I've betrayed you and our family's values by bringing Aya here. I swear to you and her that I never meant for this to happen. I just wanted to guarantee her safety. But now she's here and there's nothing I can do to reverse the course of time. I'll do whatever is necessary to keep her and you safe. I won't allow any harm to come to her and I won't allow her to expose you. I can understand if you no longer trust me, but I'm sorry, this is something that I had to do. I can't even explain it. It's like Aya is a piece of me that has been missing my entire life and afterlife. I have to do this. I'll understand if you're no longer able to trust me."

Everyone at the table is quiet for a moment. I can tell from the grimaces on everyones' faces that my very existence is a major wrench in these gals' plans.

"Look," I break the ice, "no one even asked me if I wanted to stay here. Just let me go and this can all be over."

"Elodie can you please secure her while we try to figure out what to do?" Adrienne glares at me. "I can't think with her squeaking at us like that."

"Hey!" I cry as Elodie carries me from the table upstairs. "Hey what the hell! You guys are just going to talk about what to do with me without even hearing what I want? No way. Put me down. I have a right to participate in this conversation!"

Elodie doesn't respond, she just steps into my room and tosses me onto the bed from the doorway before stepping out and slamming the door behind her.

I'm alone again without even Yeti to hear me out.

CHAPTER TWENTY-ONE

ELODIE GLASS

"Elodie, what happened?" Jayden asks quietly as soon as I sit back down.

I open a bottle of Pinot Noir and pour everyone a glass.

"I don't know," I admit after taking a sip. "Nothing like this has ever happened to me before."

"Elodie, you know, you can have sex without enslaving a woman? It's not like things were when you were alive, it's easy these days. Things have changed. You can just go to a lesbian bar now and behave with a modicum of civility and plenty of women will be willing to bring you home for a night."

"Fuck you, Aravella. It's not a sex thing. I've never touched her, not like that."

'You've got to be fucking kidding me," Aravella runs her hands through her black hair. "Something is wrong with you."

"Yeah I fucking know that something is wrong with me. I'm obsessed with her. I have been for years. I built this for her," I gesture at the house.

"You built her a prison," Adrienne replies, glancing around. "Hanging wallpaper in it doesn't make it any less of a prison."

"I know," I sigh. "Believe me, I know. This isn't how I wanted it."

"How did you want it?"

"I don't know. I guess I just watch her from afar for the rest of her life? Like a guardian angel?"

"You'd watch her age or get sick or injured and die?" Adrienne prods.

"Yes. No. I don't know. This isn't a logical thing for me, it's an instinct. One that I couldn't ignore."

"You can't change her," Adrienne admonishes.

"I had no intention of changing her!"

I actually hadn't even considered it. Adri has a good point though, would I be able to watch Aya decay and die? I don't think I would. But I also can't imagine myself turning her.

"I've heard of this happening before," she replies quietly. "It's like a mid-life crisis for immortals. They get fixated on a human and convince themselves that they won't be alone anymore if they sire a new immortal. But Elodie, there are reasons we don't do this."

"It's not a mid-life crisis," I reply, knowing very well that I sound like a petulant teenager. *It's not a phase, Mom*!

"I just don't understand why you never said anything about her," Jayden leans back in their chair. "Like if she was so important to you, why wouldn't you mention her to us?"

"I don't know," I shake my head. "Maybe I knew that I was doing something wrong. Maybe I didn't want to share her."

"I wouldn't mind taking a taste," Aravella interjects and I want to strangle her.

"We need to figure out what we're going to do with her now," Adrienne interrupts before there's another fight. "She's seen us all and she knows what we are."

"We can't hurt her," Jayden immediately replies.

They're right. I wouldn't allow anyone to hurt her. I don't want to be forced to choose between Aya and my sisters. I don't know what I'd do.

"Of course we're not going to hurt her," Adrienne answers. "Or at least we're going to do everything in our power not to hurt her."

"But we can't just let her go," Aravella objects. "Man you bitches have been away from women for too long. There's no way she doesn't go running her mouth to someone."

I'm about to say that she doesn't have anyone to listen, but I also don't want to let Aya go so I hold my tongue. The four of us sit at the table staring at our hands for a while. No one has any ideas.

"Well I guess you have to keep her here," Adrienne finally concedes. "Or you can bring her back to our place but then she'd have to stay in the dungeon."

"I'm not bringing her to our place," I immediately reply.

"We could clean it up," Jayden suggests.

"Just no. No. I can keep her here. I've already got it outfitted for her security anyways, she'll have more space and she won't get under anyone's toes."

I don't mention this but the bachelorette-pad condition of our house is not the only thing making me hesitant to bring Aya home. Lately it seems like she's really warming up to me, but if she has my sisters around all the time, what if she prefers one of them?

I'd rather just avoid that possibility entirely.

"I guess that makes the most sense, though Elodie this entire situation is a complete shitshow. You've really fucked up here."

"I know, Adri, believe me."

"And your girl, she doesn't seem too thrilled with your plan. Man, if you're going to keep her here you *have* to get her under control. What were you thinking letting her creep around like that without warning us? She could have been killed, even just by accident, sneaking up on us like that."

"I know man, I'm sorry. I'll rein her in. It won't happen again."

"Elodie, look, you clearly have no idea what you're doing," Aravella scoffs. "She doesn't respect you as her Mistress."

"Aravella I'm not her Mistress."

"Well you'd better become her Mistress if you want her to behave. You're going to have to break her in, like a wild filly.

That's pretty much what she is right now. Then she might become a pretty sweet ride."

"What the hell are you even talking about?"

"You have to take her in hand and show her that you'll be the one making her decisions from here on out. And you have to show her that there are consequences for disobeying you."

"What like ground her? She's already locked in this house all day and all night."

"You know that's not what I mean."

"What do you mean, exactly?"

"Take this little stunt that she just pulled, for example," Aravella leans back in her chair and folds her hands in front of her chest. "That was outrageous and you can't let her walk all over you like that. What are you going to do now, scold her? That will just show her that you have no idea what you're doing and she has no reason to respect you. You have to punish her, severely. Take her over your knee and spank her until she can't sit down for a week, until her little ass is as red as a pair of apples and she's crying and apologizing and begging for another chance to be a good girl."

"Aravella, Jesus."

"I'm serious, I can promise you that both you and her will be a lot happier if you show her that you're capable of guiding her. Show her that you're taking responsibility for her. And from her. Women like structure, especially when they're spiraling like that one. But never punish her too severely; there always has to be an escalation at hand if you need it."

"Aravella I'm not going to spank her, she's a grown woman."

My pearl-clutching at Aravella's suggestion is entirely feigned. The thought of having Aya completely submissive to me is exhilarating. I'd love to spank her ass until she was whimpering and compliant. Then I'd keep her over my knees and run my fingers over her pussy to see if the spanking got her wet.

Something tells me that it would.

I'd slide my fingers up and down her lips until she was slicked up and then wiggle my thumb into her tight little asshole, where I'd keep it while my middle finger worked her clit. Then I'd work her until she was shaking and promising me what a good girl she'd be for me—

"Elodie? ELODIE!"

"Sorry, what?"

"Maybe the two of you can continue this conversation privately so that Jayden and I don't have to hear it?"

"Sorry, there's nothing to talk about. Aravella, thanks for the advice, but I think I'll just try keeping her locked up for now, until we figure out a better plan."

"Your loss," Aravella shrugs.

"Gentlewomen," Adrienne interrupts with her most authoritative voice, "I think this meeting has reached its conclusion for the night. We'll have to schedule another one to go over our current projects, I don't want to be subjected to any more intimate details of Elodie's relationship with her new girlfriend. I'm leaving."

I get up to walk my sisters to the door but Jayden hangs back.

"El? Hey, El?" They looks worried.

I raise my eyebrows and wait for them to continue.

"I'm not trying to say that Aravella is right or had a good idea, but you have to make sure she's under control, okay?"

"Of course, Jay, she's locked down tight."

"Man I feel bad for her but if she gets out I'm afraid that Adrienne will decide that we have to neutralize her. I don't want to do that, that's the antithesis of what I'm trying to do with my afterlife now."

"I understand, Jayden, don't worry. I would never let anyone hurt her or you."

"Thanks, dude."

I give Jayden a brief one-armed hug before they disappears into the night.

CHAPTER TWENTY-TWO

AYA LACHAT

"Are you here to kill me?"

"What? No. Why aren't you sleeping?"

"How am I supposed to sleep now after what just happened?"

Elodie sighs like I'm the one who's being exasperating. "Aya, my love, I'd do anything to protect you but you have to cooperate with me. Sneaking up like that, that could have gotten you killed. And now that my sisters know about you, you can't ever run off. If you escape then they'll kill you to protect themselves."

The air is still for a moment and I consider what she's saying.

"That doesn't seem like a thing that the good guys would do."

"We aren't the good guys."

Elodie is, I can feel it in my heart, but her sisters…

I'm not so sure.

"Come to bed," I order her, not wanting to discuss the matter any further that evening.

Elodie seems confused for a moment, but then takes off her shirt and her trousers. Once she's in her boxer briefs and sports bra she slides under the covers with me, where I'm wearing nothing but a thin cotton camisole and a pair of matching blue panties.

She strokes my hair and neither of us says a word. I'm tired and I'm not in the mood for an argument. I place my head on her chest and I'm so drowsy, I can't keep my eyes open.

A moment later something wakes me up and it's not Elodie in my arms, it's Olsen. He's grinning at me with his disgusting yellow teeth.

"See, Princess," he hisses, his tongue flicking like a snake. "I know what's best for you. You were born for a cage."

"Whoa, whoa, Aya, wake up! It's just a dream!"

I can feel someone's arms around me and my legs are tangled in the sheets. I'm covered in sweat and I feel like I have to throw up.

"Aya you were having a bad dream."

I gather my bearings and I can see that it's Elodie in my bed, not Olsen.

I take a deep breath and drop my head back on my pillow.

"I dreamt it was him, keeping me here," I explain. "I know that you're not the same but this situation you've got me in…"

Elodie's face is grief-stricken but she has to know.

"Elodie, I was held in captivity by another vampire, the one who killed my family. For months—"

"I know," Elodie interrupts.

"No, Elodie, you don't know. You have no idea what it was like. I was locked in a concrete cell with no bedding and no light for months and raped on a daily basis. It would have been worse, but my pretty, talented older sister bore the brunt of this sick fuck's attentions. I had to watch as he cut her up and licked up her blood while he forced her to play piano, twisting the one thing that she used to love the most into her most dreaded torture. And every day I'd hope that this happened, because when he was torturing Nala he mostly ignored me. Then I watched as he cut Nala's throat and I was able to make a run for it but I had to leave my sister to die. You have no idea what it was like."

Elodie is silent for a moment. "I'm sorry," she finally replies, "you're absolutely right. I had no idea."

"And this fuck is still out there somewhere. He's never been caught; the police never even had any leads. I've spent my entire adult life looking over my shoulder and waiting for him to catch up to me."

It's been a long time since I've allowed myself to get so worked up over Olsen. It's something that I've been working on at my therapy for years, concentrating on not triggering myself. It had to come out though. Elodie has to know where I've been.

"Elodie," an idea suddenly comes to me, "this is the kind of man you kill, right?"

"Exactly the kind of man we end," she agrees.

"And I think you said that sometimes you guys go after other vampires, right?"

"Correct. Sometimes we destroy other immortals. I'm already on it, Aya, I'm going to find this creature and make him pay for what he did to you."

"No, Elodie, you don't understand. That's not what I want."

"Sorry?" Elodie furrows her brows and props her head up on her elbow.

"I want you to teach me how to kill him. I want to kill him myself."

"Oh, Aya," Elodie embraces me, "I understand. But that's impossible. I don't know how old this thing is but even Jayden, who's barely turned, is far, far stronger than a human woman."

"But there's a way to kill him and I want to do it."

"Aya that would be extremely complicated and dangerous. I can't let you do that."

"Please," I beg, throwing the sheet off my body. "I'll give you whatever you want. I'll let you do whatever you want to me in exchange. I *need* to do this."

Elodie scrambles from the bed and falls on the floor, then immediately stands up.

"Aya stop, you don't have to 'pay' me for anything. If it's that important to you, then fine, I'll do it. I'll train you and help you find him. There is no cost."

"Oh," now I stand up on the bed and throw my arms around Elodie's neck. I jump with such force that I crash into her and wrap my legs around her waist. "Thank you, Elodie. This is what I want. I'm sure."

I place my lips on her and push my tongue into her mouth.

She turns her head to the side to get away from me. "Aya, stop. I told you. You don't have to 'pay' me anything."

"I'm not paying you," I pull her face back toward mine and bite her lower lip. "This is what I want too. Don't say no to me."

This is too much for her. Elodie groans and throws me on my back on the bed. For a moment it looks like she's considering walking out the door again, but not this time. Instead she kneels between my legs and rips my camisole open, exposing my breasts to the cool air.

"Are you sure?" she asks, her fangs down and her eyes gleaming with flecks of ice blue and silver.

I respond by wiggling out of my panties.

I don't have to say anything more. Elodie wrestles off her own bra underwear and I get my first brief glimpse of her magnificent body before she's got her face buried in my pussy.

My fingers snake into her tangled curls and my back arches. Her tongue is long and she's got my knees pushed up so that I'm totally exposed to her. She slips her tongue up and down my lips and flicks it at my clit while I writhe and pant.

"Elodie," I gasp her name. She's not giving me any chance to warm up, she's just relentless and it's making me feel like I'm going to jump out of my skin. Her fingers are dug into the flesh of my thighs and she's tasting every inch of me.

She lets one of my legs go and slides a finger into my pussy and this sends me completely over the edge. She's gently stroking my G-spot while her tongue teases my clit and I can't help but scream as the orgasm rips through me. I'm buckling and my head is spinning and I don't care anymore that Elodie is keeping me locked in this stupid house.

She's still got a finger or two inside of me, but now I feel a brief, sharp pain. I can feel her lips on me and my entire body feels warm and tingly.

I realize that she bit me.

She must have some kind of venom, like a snake, but instead of hurting this kind of venom makes you feel really, *really* good. I'm still sensitive from the orgasm I just had and now Elodie is licking up all of my pussy juice along with the blood she drew. I glance down at her and I can see her eyes flashing like they are glowing.

"Elodie," I hiss at her, "let me taste you too."

She picks up her head and she's got my blood on her chin. For a moment I'm afraid that she's going to kill me, but that's not what happens.

Instead she drops my knees to the mattress and straddles me, her stomach tense and rippled with anticipation and her breasts swaying over me gently. I reach my own fingers down and find her sex, wet and swollen with desire. I've never seen another woman like this, let alone touched one, and for one brief second I'm afraid that I won't know what to do and I'll make a fool of myself.

It doesn't take but a second to see that my fears are misplaced. I stroke her gently and she throws her head back and cries out before placing the plump, ripe fruit of her vulva on my lips. My tongue instinctively darts out and, for the first time in my life, I taste another woman.

There's something so familiar about the way Elodie tastes, but at the same time I've never had anything like it. She's rich and creamy but I can also detect salt and just a little bit of stone fruit. I lap at her, my tongue searching for the tight little pearl of her clit, as she rides my face.

She's getting so rough with me, with her fingers in my hair, pulling me closer to her. I claw my fingers into the flesh of her ass and she rides me fast and hard, grinding away and making me feel like I'm barely breathing, mostly out of excitement. I imagine that I can taste my own blood and juices on her lips and I've still got that warm, hazy feeling from when she bit me and was sucking on my cunt.

She lets out a sound that falls somewhere between a groan and a roar and pushes herself one final time onto me, closer than ever before. I can feel her legs trembling for several moments before she releases my hair and slides off of me and collapses, her fingers finding their way back into the tangle of my wet pubic hair.

HOUSE OF GLASS: SHATTERED

CHAPTER ONE

ELODIE GLASS

"**S**quare your shoulders."

"Like this?"

I adjust Aya's body so that she's perfectly perpendicular to the wooden dummy five meters in front of her.

"There. Now remember, he can move fast but you have to wait until he's in range before you throw. Otherwise the axe won't hit him with enough force to do any serious damage and you're dead. Once you can see the whites of his eyes, you have to be ready. That's your chance."

Today we're working on increasing Aya's speed. She's got good reflexes and she's quick, but not inhumanly fast.

She braces her weapon with both hands, then draws her left back over her shoulder and makes her throw. She nails it; the head of the axe is buried directly in the dummy's face.

"Good!" I'm genuinely impressed. "See what I mean about the wrist? You have to throw your whole upper body into the throw, propelled through your hips, but then the real edge, the speed, comes from that last little flick of the wrist."

"Yeah, I get what you mean. It's all in the technique. Can we try again?"

We've already been throwing the axe for nearly two hours but I don't get tired and she's so proud of herself that I won't deny her. And she deserves to be proud. She's a quick learner and she seems to have a natural talent for melee weapons. Her smile lights up her face and I don't think I've ever seen her so happy.

But then again, I don't think she's ever had the chance to feel this way before.

I've known for years that Aya's trauma turned her into a shell of the person she could have been, hiding alone in the safety of her little den, afraid to pursue any possible interests because she's had to constantly look over her shoulder.

The more I get to know her, though, the more I can see that her deep insecurities were planted long before Olsen Leonard ravaged her life.

She barely ever talks about herself unless I ask her specific questions, but I've heard all about her perfect older sister. Nala was more talented, Nala was prettier, Nala was smarter, Nala was just superior in every possible way. And then Nala was martyred to save her 'worthless' little sister's life.

That's the way Aya sees things at least.

I never knew Nala. Maybe it's all true, maybe Nala was a legendary beauty who was on the brink of giving Chopin a run for his money.

But there's no way that she could have held a candle to the light of my Aya.

It's simply not possible.

I just wish that I could make her see herself through my eyes. I wish that I could show her how magical she really is, but she's not making it easy for me. Whenever I tell her how I feel about her she tends to react by disparaging herself and it breaks my frozen heart.

"You think I'm improving?" she interrupts my thoughts, looking up at me with her bright eyes, face covered in a thin layer of sweat.

"I think you're a natural," I admit. "But we still have a lot of work to do. You need to build strength, that way you can throw further. And soon I'm going to start you on a moving target. You won't have the luxury of Leonard standing still for you while you aim."

"I know that," Aya laughs. "I just wanted to know how bad of a lost cause I am with this thing."

"Aya, I'm serious. I'm not trying to flatter you; you really are a very quick learner."

She scoffs at my compliment and I don't press the matter, because when I do she gets even harder on herself.

Aya rests the axe on a table and stretches her arms over her head, exposing her pale white belly.

"Hey we're not done here yet," she jokes, catching me taking a peek at her. "I was still gonna run my laps too, don't get yourself too excited yet." A wicked little grin spreads across her face. "Unless you wanna take a little break?"

She slithers up to me and snakes her arm around my waist. She's not tall enough to kiss me unless I lean down into her and she usually pulls me down by the hair on the back of my head. Now she's standing on tippy toe giving me her most mischievous smirk, her eyes narrowed and her tongue darting out to wet her lips.

"Is that it?" she purrs. "You want to be pre-paid for today's lesson."

"Aya! Come on, we've talked about this. You don't have to pay for anything! And you certainly don't owe me—"

She covers my hand with her mouth and narrows her brows. I could keep admonishing her but she's grinding her sweaty body up against me now and I can never control myself when she gets like this.

Aya's body is the only thing in the world that I want but I don't like to feel like she's offering it to me in payment. Every single time I fuck her I end up feeling ashamed of myself. I think she likes it, she's always the one to initiate, but would she still want me if she was free to leave? Will she still want me after Olsen Leonard is exterminated?

"Let's take these off," she's working at my jogging pants and of course I don't stop her. My pussy is wet and my fangs are out. I keep telling myself that I'm going to gain control of myself and gently make love to her, but that's never how it happens.

"Aya," I'm struggling to stand still I want her so bad, "aren't you still sore from when we woke up? You said—"

"I'll live," she slips her hand into the waistband of my pants.

Oh God she's getting on her knees.

I hate it when she does this, by which I mean to say that I love it. Her tongue darts out and gives the split of my vulva a few dainty licks. She's gazing up at me with her devious grin and I'm sure that she can see exactly how much I'm struggling not to throw her on her back, plunge my teeth directly into her, and open a vein so I can drink her dry.

Her lips draw back and she shows me her little white teeth. I think Aya likes to pretend that she's an immortal too sometimes, which is so charmingly naïve of her. She lets out a little growl and I have to lean back against the wall behind me and grasp the brackets of a shelf over my head and pretend that I'm in restraints.

"Stop teasing me," I growl back, "or you're going to get exactly what you're asking for…"

"Oh," she purrs while sliding her middle finger up and down the lips of my cunt, stroking them so gently it feels like I'm being teased with a feather. She's shockingly adept at this for someone with so little practical experience. "And what's that?"

Now she's pushing her tongue further into me, which is doing absolutely nothing to relieve the cravings I have. It's only serving to make me feel even less in control of myself, which is a feeling that I haven't experienced in a long, long time.

Aya moans and whimpers a little bit as she tries to get her tongue all the way to my clit and my eyes roll into the back of my head. I'm gripping the shelf bracket so hard that I pull it loose from the wall and now I find myself in the position of having to hold the shelf up lest it fall on one side and drop the books it holds.

"Aya," I groan and she licks me harder and deeper. I start to warn her that she's going to make me come, but then I stop. I want to fill her mouth with my juices.

She gives me a surprised little squeak that puts a smile on my face as I come, and she doesn't pull away. She grips tightly to my thighs as the earthquake of my orgasm passes through me and then when I'm spent she looks up at me with the cutest little red drip slinking down from the corner of her mouth.

"Here," I hand her a towel to clean herself up.

"Oh!" she exclaims when she sees that the liquid on her face is red. "I guess for some reason I assumed that you couldn't get a period."

"I can't."

"Are you hurt?"

"No," I stroke her hair. She's still on her knees before me and the concerned expression on her face is making me feel like maybe she really does care about me. "It's normal for me."

"Hmm," she's curious, I can tell. "It doesn't taste like blood."

"It's not, exactly. Not human blood at least."

"Does this mean that I'm a vampire now?"

I can't help but laugh. I'm still holding the shelf up and now a couple of the books drop off, which makes her laugh too.

"No," I try to fix it, at least temporarily. "Sorry."

"But you could turn me, right? If I drank enough?"

"In theory, yes," I don't like where this conversation is heading.

"But, like, how many times would I need to eat your pussy before I turned into a vampire?"

"I don't know, Aya, I've never turned anyone." I know that she would need to drain me almost completely, cycle her blood through mine and drink it back. I haven't done the math but I know that it would probably add up to a lot of oral sex if she was hoping to change by drinking me one mouthful of pussy juice at a time. "I guess this is like the Tootsie Pop question. You're just going to have to test it yourself to find out."

"Interesting…"

I genuinely can't tell whether she's joking or not.

CHAPTER TWO

AYA LACHAT

"**O**kay. There's plenty of food in the fridge and I've brought a few bottles of wine up from the cellar if you feel like having a drink. You're all set with everything you need? Soap, cat food, whatever?"

"Yes, but I just don't understand why I can't come with you?"

"Aya, my love, it's just going to be for a few days. I have to return to our den, I haven't been pulling my weight. We've got a lot of business to catch up to."

"So I'll just come with and stay out of your way."

"I don't think that's a very good idea."

"Why not?"

Elodie looks at me like I'm being deliberately obtuse, which I am.

"You know that my sisters aren't thrilled with this situation," she explains to me for the zillionth time. She keeps calling it *our situation*, which is just making me even more angry. Like this isn't entirely her fault and responsibility. *Our situation* is that she's holding me prisoner and I'm not free to leave. And now I'm going to be locked up alone.

"I know but why can't they just mind their own business?"

"Believe me, they're trying," Elodie continues to shove clothes in her travel bag. "But my business *is* their business."

"Then why can't they accept me?"

"They're coming around, I think."

I can tell from Elodie's voice that even she's unsure about how much 'coming around' they're actually doing.

"Do you think they'd hurt me? Is that what the problem is?"

"I would never allow anyone to hurt you," Elodie stops what she's doing and looks me in the eye. "Never."

"I noticed that you didn't answer whether or not you think that they'd *try* to hurt me."

I can see that I'm annoying her and I don't care. She zips her bag closed and makes her way to the door.

"So I'm just going to be locked in here? What if there's a fire?"

She doesn't answer, she just keeps walking, down the stairs and toward the front door.

"I'd just burn! You'd just let me burn here!"

Now I know I'm being melodramatic but I'm running out of ideas to stop her. I even tried to come on to her but she just fucked me quickly on the kitchen counter and then continued with her packing.

"Aya, my love, you'll be fine and I'll be back in a few days. I promise."

Elodie leans in for a kiss but if she thinks that she's getting a kiss back she's crazy. I turn my head so her lips land on my cheek and cross my arms over my chest. I won't even look at her as she leaves.

"Can you believe this asshole?" I ask Yeti, who's in lockdown with me.

Yeti meows back. He *can* believe this asshole.

I'm so frustrated and I've got so much pent up energy. I guess I could go to the training room and work it off, but I'm not in the mood to do something healthy or productive. I want to fuck something up, and I don't mean a wooden dummy.

I'm pacing through the house without an idea of where I'm going. I need to get outside. I'm not even sure that I still want to run away, but I *need* to be outdoors right now.

"How does this thing work?" I ask the cat, staring at the blank black screen next to the door. I know that it controls the house's security system; I've seen Elodie use it a million times.

I'm pretty sure that she unlocks it with her eye but I wonder if there's some way to override the system. I tap it and swipe it several times with my finger but it doesn't respond at all.

I have another idea.

I head into the training room and grab my axe. Well, technically it's Elodie's, but I've been training with it for weeks. I bring it with me to the front door, perfect my stance, and slam the edge into the control panel.

Nothing.

Not even a scratch.

"God damn," I say out loud, half frustrated and half impressed.

Well, if that doesn't work, maybe I'll just have to create my own escape route. I try the axe on the windows, the doors, and even eventually the walls. I do some damage to the decor, the wallpaper is fucked — which at least offers me a tiny bit of satisfaction — but otherwise I don't even make a dent.

Now the blade on my axe needs to be sharpened, which Elodie also taught me how to do. I bring it back to the training room and grind the blade on the whetstone until it's sharp again, then hang it back up on the wall.

I'm not so angry anymore, I guess my little tantrum helped me to work out some frustrations. I need to gather my thoughts.

I should be tired, but I'm not. The sun is rising and it occurs to me that I haven't really seen daylight in weeks. I gaze out of one of the windows in the living room and the light hurts my eyes. I've got to squint but the colors in the garden are so vivid, I can't look away.

I haven't thought about leaving and returning to my normal life ever since I started my training. I know very well that I didn't have much to return to, but I also don't want to spend the rest of my life locked in this house.

I flip onto my back on the couch and stare at the ceiling. Sometimes it's so hard to figure out what you want, or even what your options might be. I know for sure that I want to kill Olsen. That's my only goal in life actually, to kill him, preferably painfully though I don't know if that's really a possibility. Due to his very nature it will probably have to be quick, which I guess I think of as a compromise.

But after?

If I kill Olsen, I don't have to be afraid of him anymore. And if I don't successfully kill him, then presumably he will have killed me. So I also don't have to be afraid anymore.

Without my fear, though, I don't know how to live. Am I just supposed to transition into being a normal person? Maybe go to school in person and one day get a job where I have to leave the house and interact with other people all day?

I don't know how to do that.

I'm telling myself that I'm reluctant to leave the house because I wouldn't know what to do once I was out, but in my heart I know that there's another reason I'm no longer eager to leave.

It's that monster who brought me here.

My monster.

The start of my training wasn't the only thing that changed between us that made me forget about escaping. I'm still so angry at Elodie for leaving me locked in the house, but visions of her body are creeping into my subconscious thoughts and turning me on.

I've never had a relationship with a woman before, and Elodie isn't even a woman. She's something much, much more than that and it's like she's poisoned my mind and my body. I can't choose not to want her, it's like her body is my true calling. I want to kill Olsen, but not as bad as I want to keep fucking Elodie.

I can't sleep while she's gone.

She told me that she'll be returning in 'a few days' but three pass and there's no sign of her. I drift between continuing my training alone, trying to figure out how to disable the security system, and lying around listlessly on the sofa.

I can't sleep at all so I'm awake in my bed when she sneaks into my room on the fourth night. It's early for her, the sun just went down a few hours ago, but my internal clock is completely fucked I'm up and down randomly all day and all night now.

I know that I must look like shit. My eyes are puffy and I haven't eaten a proper meal the entire time she's been gone. I'm still angry at her and she knows that I'm awake but neither of us says a word.

She just takes off her clothes and slips into bed with me. She turns me onto my back and buries her face in my stomach, then kisses me all over.

I try not to respond to her, but soon my body is reacting to her touch instinctively, rising up to meet her kisses. I don't want to look at her because I'm still hurt so I turn my head to the side and her reply is to flip me over onto my stomach and pull me onto my knees. Her fingers enter me from behind, slowly at first, and then more forcefully. She fucks me until I can hear myself moaning in pleasure and then I drift off to sleep before she can even pull them out.

CHAPTER THREE

ELODIE GLASS

"**I** brought you some stuff." I'm hoping that the tactical gear that I got for Aya makes her forget that she's mad at me. "And we have big plans today."

She looks over the boots and pants and vests and so on and I encourage her to try her new clothing on. I can tell by the expression on her face that these things excite her, even though she's still trying to show me that she hasn't forgiven me.

"You can't really hunt an immortal in a sundress," I say in way of explanation. Which is true, I guess unless you are a creature even more powerful, which Aya is not despite all of her hard work. I watch as she squeezes into her new black pants and jumps up and down in her lace up boots.

She looks adorable, my murderous little nympho.

My meeting didn't go well, but I don't tell her. Well, that's not entirely true. Adrienne went over all of our current hits and

Jayden told us all about some computer program that they wrote that made absolutely no sense to me though I'm sure it's brilliant.

I had intended on sharing my promise that I made to Aya, that I'd help her kill Olsen Leonard, but I didn't get the chance. I need to have my sisters' help if we're going to pull this off, but they're still so sure that her very existence will spell disaster for us all, Adrienne and Aravella especially.

At least I was able to recruit Jayden's help. They're going to hack the police databases to find this Leonard. I've got a suspicion that the police weren't just stumped, they were deliberately covering for someone. Someone powerful. It's just too convenient, the way that they gave up their investigation into the slaughter of an entire family so quickly.

If the police have any info at all on this guy, they'll have it stored in their database. Jayden will be able to dig it out and then hopefully cross reference that info with news articles and so on, hopefully until we get a lead.

I don't mention any of this to Aya because I don't want to get her hopes up before they find anything. This could take months, especially since I'm not sure that Jayden thinks that this is a great idea. They weren't happy when I asked them not to mention this search to Adrienne.

"Are you ready?" I ask Aya after she's suited up. "Grab your axe."

"We're going outside?"

I feel a twinge of guilt when she seems to be so thrilled with the prospect of being outdoors. I wish that I had thought of some way to build her a secured outdoor space.

I lead her to the stables where I've trapped a buck. The poor thing is pacing and pawing at the ground, locked into one of the stalls.

"Whoa," Aya walks up to the bars on the stall. "I've never seen one so up close like this. He's beautiful."

"Careful," I warn her. "Those points on his antlers are dangerous. Stand back. I'm going to let him out."

I move her to the side for safety and spring the door on the stall. The buck stands there, confused for just a moment before he launches out of the stall and through the stable doors.

"Bye Rudy," Aya waves at the empty door.

"Rudy?"

"Yeah, like Rudolph. The most famous reindeer of all?"

"Aya don't name him. We're going to hunt him."

"What? That's not fair. We just had him locked up."

"I'm going to teach you how to track him and stalk him in the woods. Come on."

Once again, Aya is an eager student. She's got so much more endurance now, she's been training so hard. She jogs alongside me as I show her how to follow the animal's tracks in the meadow.

"Look," I show her some broken branches when we reach the edge of the copse. "See the damage here? It means he ran through."

"I see it!"

"Shh. He can hear much better than you." But not better than me, I think. I can hear the buck and I know that he's at least 200 meters away but I want to teach Aya to stalk quietly. "You'll scare him away," I whisper, my finger on my lips.

"Oh right," she nods and whispers back, her eyes as big as saucers. She glances around the woods and I have to show her the trail at first. It's so dark and I know that she can't see at night like I can.

Once her eyes adjust, though, she's very eager to find the trail herself. I give her time and space and it takes her several minutes but she succeeds.

"Look!" she whispers, her voice charged with excitement. "He's this way!"

She's right. I teach her how to creep through the woods, making the least amount of noise possible, and I show her the birds and small animals that she wouldn't have noticed until I taught her how to spot them. She's excitedly pointing out a raccoon to me when I hush her.

"Aya," I whisper, "look."

I gesture slowly with my finger.

"Oh!" her eyes go wide again, "I see him!"

We both sit perfectly still for a while and watch the buck drift through the trees and nibble on bushes.

"Okay," I say when the time is right. "Now's your chance. Line up your throw."

"What?" Aya says loud enough to alert the buck. He bolts into the trees and I groan. I know that it will take us probably at least another hour to find him again. Realistically more than an hour.

"I'm not going to kill that deer," Aya looks at me like I'm crazy.

"Aya, sweetheart, you'll never be able to kill something that looks like a human being — something that could potentially beg you for its life — if you can't kill an animal."

"No," she protests and I can tell she's unsettled. "That's wrong."

"I told you that you shouldn't have named him."

"It has nothing to do with naming him," she argues back. "That deer didn't do anything wrong. He's completely inno-cent, but Olsen Leonard isn't. I'm not just going to kill a random thing, I'm going to kill the man who slaughtered my family. How can you not understand that? You yourself restrict yourself to killing only predators."

I can't argue with that. I concede that she's right and killing the buck was a stupid idea. It's not the same thing.

"Anyhow how are we going to find Olsen?" she asks, and my heart tingles at the way she says 'we.' "I'm assuming that we're not going to be able to just track him through this forest like a deer."

"Jayden's working on it," I tell her. "They can work magic with computers, any information that exists, that dude can find it."

"What's their deal?" Aya asks as we walk back to the garden.

Jayden's 'deal' is as dark as mine but it's not my place to go sharing it with people. All of my sisters have dark, ugly secrets and I love Aya but those secrets aren't mine to tell.

"They're younger than you, right? In both ways?"

"What do you mean in both ways?"

"Well they look younger than you and they also haven't been a vampire for as long? Is that right?"

"Yep. They're older than they look, but not by much."

"They seem different from the rest of you. I don't know what I mean. I guess they just seem not very vampire-y. How did they change?"

"You'd have to ask them," I suggest.

"Oh is it, like, private?"

"Something like that."

"Well what did you girls do at your meeting? Did you kill someone?"

"No we just talked. Went over our recent work."

"Which was?"

"Adrienne took out a crooked cop... oh I know! Something interesting did happen. Aravella killed a woman. That almost never happens."

"Really?" Aya looks shocked. "Why did she do that?"

"She was trafficking women and children from Vietnam in shipping containers and enslaving them."

"Oh wow. Good job, Aravella. What will happen to the women and children now? Are they going to some kind of a women's shelter or rescue organization?"

"Unfortunately we don't know. Aravella freed them but they scattered into the night, scared out of their minds. They might be afraid of getting arrested and deported."

"Hmm," Aya nods, hopping over a fallen log. "I guess a situation like that is complicated."

"Absolutely. We can destroy evil but setting the victims up for success in their new lives isn't really our thing."

"Actually," Aya stops and turns to me. "I kind of wanted to talk to you about that. My new life. I had an idea."

My instincts tell me that I'm not going to like this idea and I'm right.

"Here it is: I kill Olsen Leonard and you record proof of me doing it. Then you'll have evidence against me if I ever try to tell a soul about you and your sisters. Kind of like an insurance policy. And I'll be able to leave and you girls will have peace of mind."

"Peace of mind," I reply back to her, staring at the trees above her head. "And you can just leave. You want to leave?"

I pull her pants down to her knees, pick her up, shove her knees against her chest, and slam her against a tree.

"You want to leave me?" I hiss at her as I work my hand between us and past her crumpled pants. I reach her curled hair and soft skin and work my fingers into her. I'm not giving her any chance to warm up to me this time, I know I'm hurting her but I want to teach her a lesson. "You want to leave?" I ask her again. "Say it. Say you want to leave now."

She doesn't answer. Her little pink mouth is hanging open and she's grimacing, both in pleasure and pain.

"You're mine, Aya. I'll never let you go."

❧

CHAPTER FOUR

AYA LACHAT

I watch as tiny pieces of tree bark swirl down the drain of my shower. I'm a little scratched up on my shoulders and the hot water stings, but I'd rather not get an infection so I'm wincing as the dirt from the tree rinses off of my skin into the tub.

I'm sore all over, but in a good way. My pussy aches from the thrashing it received just now from Elodie's fingers. The feeling is completely new to me and I catch myself grinning at the memory of how wicked she was, how hungry and unhinged.

What the hell is wrong with me?

Since when is 'unhinged' an attractive quality in a partner?

I guess part of it may be that it's still so unbelievable that anyone wants *me* that bad, boring, scaredy-cat, dull me. Even before I fell apart at Olsen's hands I never really had much to offer the world. I certainly wasn't a beautiful genius like

Nala, but I also wasn't clever like Gabe. I wasn't even cute like Hughey. I was kind of always just... there.

Now, though, things are different. I am actually, physically different. My training has transformed my body from the kind of cold spaghetti noodle that used to best describe my physique to this catlike, spring-loaded machine that I am now. My energy levels are way up and I can run for nearly an hour before I need to take a break. I'm also much stronger; I can lift and throw my axe with one arm — either arm, actually — with no trouble at all, whereas when I started I needed two hands. I feel like a new person, and I look like a new person.

I can see myself reflected in the hunger in Elodie's eyes when she looks at me and I know that it's not just because she's literally hungry. It's *me*. She actually, truly wants me.

I've never felt good about myself like this before and the feeling is addictive.

I get an idea: I'm going to take her on a date.

Okay, obviously I'm not going to take her anywhere because she has me locked inside of this house. But I'm going to prepare a date night for her. I check the window; it's still early in the night. I've learned to tell the time from the position of the moon in the sky, and tonight it's full and still low on the horizon. I've got time.

I turn off the shower and fill the tub with hot water, pouring in half a bottle of creme brûlée scented bath milk. The ingredients on the label include honey and nutmeg, both of which are natural antiseptics. I'm hoping that the soak will treat the wounds on my back.

The water is silky-soft and the tub is deep enough for me to sink in all the way up to my neck. I've got my hair tied up since I already washed it and I let the temperature ease the aches in muscles while the milk bath does its work on me.

It's funny how easy it is to get used to this kind of luxury. One minute you're removing the jalapeños from your online grocery cart so that your debit card doesn't get declined again, and the next you're soaking in a tub full of liquid that cost more than a week's worth of your rent. And you don't think a thing of pulling the plug and letting it disappear down the drain when you start to get bored.

I get out of the tub and dry myself off on a fluffy, clean towel. I feel sexy and I want to wear something sexy, but the stuff that Elodie picked out for me tends to be more feminine. I don't want to wear the green velvet again, so instead I go for a paper-thin, featherweight black silk chiffon sundress. It's not exactly sophisticated or sultry, but it is sexy in a subtle kind of way. If the light catches it just right, it's completely transparent. I slip it over my shoulders, skipping a bra, and pull on a pair of clean panties.

The kitchen is empty. I don't know where Elodie or Yeti are, maybe showering too or sometimes Elodie has some kind of paperwork she does in her office. I think she's keeping records of something, but I don't know what. The fridge and the cupboards are full of food. Elodie is constantly bringing home more stuff, way more than I can eat.

I pull out a selection of meats, cheeses, fruits, nuts, preserves, and chocolates. The house is full of snack food like this and here's my plan: i'm going to make it into a fancy charcuterie board.

I know that Elodie can eat but not much or it makes her uncomfortable. But she does enjoy taking little tastes of things, so what better date activity than a board full of little bites of highly flavored delicacies? I'm arranging little rosettes of prosciutto and salami, interspersed with hunks of sheep's milk cheese and dollops of fig jam.

I've never tried to make a charcuterie board before, but when I'm done I must say that i'm pretty impressed with my work. This former cutting board now looks like something someone would photograph for their social media.

I'm excited to show Elodie what I've done, so instead of leaving the board unattended where Yeti might wreak havoc, I try out the house's intercom system. There's one in every room and Elodie has never used it, but it's self-explanatory. I push a button next to a speaker that says 'intercom.'

"Um, Elodie?" I lean in too close to the speaker and I can barely make out my own voice through the static. "Elodie?" I try again from further away. This time my voice is as clear as a bell. "Elodie Glass, please report to the dining room?" I giggle and can hear my laughter ring throughout the house. "Please report to the dining room at once for an important briefing?"

I can hear the uncertainty and nerves in my own voice, each statement ending in an upward lilt like a question, but I'm having fun and the entire premise is a bit ludicrous to me.

She doesn't appear so I guess I better go find her. She's not in the living room, though Yeti is, napping on the sofa. She's not in her room or her office either.

I finally locate her in the training room, half dressed. I'm about to tell her that I'd like to try something different for the rest of the night when I see what she's doing.

A hiss escapes from my lips and I run toward her.

"What is this?" I gasp. "What the hell are you doing?"

She flinches away from me but doesn't drop her hand. She's got my dagger up against her breast, where she's made a long cut that's dripping blood down between her breasts and into her underwear.

"It's okay, Aya," she holds me at arm's length. "This is just something I have to do sometimes."

"What do you mean 'something you have to do?'" I demand. "Are you trying to kill yourself?"

"No, and this wouldn't work if I was."

"So are you going to explain this or what, because this looks pretty fucking bad."

"It's complicated."

"Oh my God, Elodie, that is not an explanation."

"I'm trying to regain control of myself."

"What do you even mean by that?" she's being so stubborn right now, so frustrating. I hit her chest with the side of my fist.

"Okay," she finally drops the dagger. "You know how some stuff like alcohol or steroids or even an increase in testosterone can make people feel more aggressive?"

"Yeah I guess I've heard about stuff like that," I don't get her point.

"Well when I drink blood, it makes me stronger but it also makes me more animalistic. More violent, more hungry. Especially if I drink a lot at one time, I end up struggling to control my own behavior. Ever since we've been together and I've been drinking off you, I've been indulging way more frequently than I normally do. I have to bleed out a bit once in a while to rein myself back in. I just cut myself a little bit like this and it makes me feel calmer."

I shake my head and examine the cut in her chest, which is already healing. "Really?" I ask, uncertain but also having no actual idea how these things work. "But does it hurt?"

"Not at all," Elodie strokes my hair with her free hand. "Actually it feels good, like I'm draining away my anger and frustration. Plus, even if it did hurt, I'd have to do this. Otherwise you'd be in danger. I can't just keep taking little sips from you like this all the time. If I don't bloodlet then eventually I'll lose control of myself and take it all. You wouldn't be safe with me."

CHAPTER FIVE

ELODIE GLASS

"So," I can see the wheels turning in Aya's pretty head, "you *have* to cut yourself so you don't… what? What is the big danger here?"

I didn't want to have to explain this to her. She wasn't supposed to see me doing this, I'm sure it looks bad from her perspective. It didn't even occur to me that she'd be afraid that I'd end myself and leave her to starve, locked in this house like a tomb.

"Aya, I just don't want to lose control of myself and hurt you. You don't understand what your blood does to me and… I can already see that I'm drinking too much. I'm afraid that I won't be able to stop myself and I'll drink it all."

"What? What do you mean that you can *see* that you drink too much?"

That wasn't supposed to be the detail that upset her. "You're so pale now," I say in way of explanation, almost like an apology.

"Maybe that's because you don't allow me to go outside."

"Aya, I can tell. You're anemic."

"I don't feel anemic."

"I just want you to be strong."

"So then why don't you just drink it all?" Now she's raising her voice and I'm taken aback by her anger.

"Aya, I can't."

"Why not?" she demands, pushing against my already sealed chest. I stumble back into the wall behind me.

"You know why not! I would never hurt you!"

"You hurt me every day! Why won't you change me? It's the only thing that makes sense! You wouldn't be tempted to hurt me anymore and I wouldn't be so vulnerable. Your sisters would be forced to accept me. Plus, how is that not the *obvious* answer to how I can become strong enough to face Olsen? Really," she spat with disdain I'd never seen in her before, "I'm supposed to somehow kill a creature even more powerful than you? Do you feel like I could kill you right now?"

She certainly could if looks could kill.

"Love, I get your point, but you don't know what you're asking."

"What? To be made your equal? Wouldn't want that, now, would we?" she sneers and I can see that she's tearing up.

"Aya, no. It's not like you think. You'd never see the sun again!"

"I don't see it anymore anyways, since you have me locked up in this house. Just do it! Turn me!"

I'm trying to reason with her but she makes a grab for the dagger I just put down and I have to tackle her before she's cutting herself. My arms wrap around her in a bear hug and she kicks and shrieks as I drag her up the stairs to her room.

I have to throw her on the bed and lock her up. There's nothing in there she could use to hurt herself and I need to get the hell out of this house before either of us does something we regret.

I don't even bother using the door, I just shift to smoke and then I'm outside in the warm summer night air, drifting along with the breeze. I'm spiraling and I don't know what else to do so I go home. Not the home I've built with Aya, but my actual home, the one where my sisters are waiting for me.

It's empty when I arrive and I retreat to the library to try to occupy my mind with some distraction while I wait for someone else to show up.

I don't have any exit strategy for this situation with Aya. In my dreams we just exist in an eternal present, I don't have to change her but she never changes. She never gets sick or old, and eventually she chooses never to leave the house. She never wants to be alone again and she's satisfied living her tiny life within the bounds of the estate with me.

It's not a surprise to me that real life isn't quite working out that way, but it's becoming increasingly clear that I need to come up with some kind of plan. Wishful thinking isn't cutting it anymore, not when Aya is threatening to hurt herself.

She's not happy.

I couldn't make her happy.

"You get tired of playing house?"

I was so distracted that I didn't hear Aravella approach.

"Something like that," I mutter back, not looking at her. "You know where Adrienne is?"

"Just downtown. She went to go check out a rumor that there's a nurse at the hospital who's playing grim reaper, poisoning her own patients. Should be back before dawn."

"Thanks."

I don't invite Aravella, but she takes a seat next to me on the Chesterfield anyway.

"She must be brave," she starts, looking at the fireplace across from us. "I can see what you see in her."

I glance up at her. What is she getting at? It isn't like Aravella to be kind or try to empathize with anyone, not even her sisters.

"She reminds me of someone I used to know," she grimaces before getting up to leave me alone again.

Strange.

She's right, though, I don't have to wait long for Adrienne. And I'm not surprised at all when Adri isn't happy to see me.

"What happened?" she demands immediately, collapsing onto the sofa next to me. She's dressed in a pair of jeans and a fitted black T-shirt, which looks strange on her since she usually wears either a suit or her tactical gear. She must have been trying to not stand out when she was visiting the hospital. "You let her go? Is that it?"

She studies my expression when I don't answer immediately.

"Or you kill her?" she asks, her voice more quiet.

"No," I throw my hands up. "No, nothing like that. She's fine. I'm fine. She's locked in her room."

Adrienne's eyebrows go up, prompting me to continue.

"I'm just looking at our options here. What options do we have to return her to her life?"

It pains me to ask and I wonder if Adrienne is perceptive enough to hear the crack in my voice.

She sighs and leans back against the sofa, spreading her arms wide. Even stretched out like this, she isn't close enough to touch me. The sofa is big enough for us both.

"Options?" she chuckles quietly. "None? I don't see any? You really screwed us here, Elodie, the girl too. I'm not going to keep riding your ass about this because I can see you're fucked up over it but I'm not going to blow sunshine up your ass either."

"Hey," I make my move, "she has an idea. What about this: she suggested that *she* take out Leonard and we get it on video so we have proof that she did it. Then if she ever sings we can just turn over this video of her committing a murder and she'll end up right back in the mental institution, this time for life."

Adrienne's eyes flare. I can tell that she's a bit shocked by Aya's plan. "How the hell is this little girl going to take out an immortal?"

"I'll make it happen," I promise.

She considers the proposition. "Yeah," she says finally, "I think it could work. I read this girl's medical files and the state psych who was seeing her already thinks she's a nutter. Wrote down that she was suffering from *severe paranoid delusions*, always thought someone was following her."

Adrienne gives me a look and I find it totally unnecessary, I'm already deeply ashamed of what I've put her through.

"So we're in agreement?" I get the conversation back on track. I'm perfectly capable of beating myself up over Aya; I don't need Adri's help.

"If you think you can make this happen," Adrienne agrees. "But Elodie — we can't just hand this girl over to Olsen. If you're wrong about what she's capable of and you can't teach her to end him, you have to let him kill her before you end him. None of us want to see her get hurt, especially not after what she's been through, but we can't have her running around, telling people stories."

"I understand," I concede. And it's true; if I can't help Aya to put an end to Olsen Leonard, I'm going to let him put an end to all of this. For both of us.

"And just to be clear," Adrienne adds before she leaves me alone, "I think this is an absolutely terrible idea. And I also think that this is a terrible thing you've done to this girl. It's not the kind of thing the Elodie I thought I knew would have done."

"I know," I reply, not having anything else to add to this conversation.

So there it is, the end. Either Aya destroys her torturer and walks out of my afterlife forever, or Aya's torturer ends the both of us for eternity.

We haven't got much time left together, or possibly at all, so I'm eager to get back to the house. I don't want to torture myself with her presence but I also can't bring myself to just stay away.

CHAPTER SIX

AYA LACHAT

"**W**hat's wrong with you?"

Elodie is teaching me to grapple, in particular with someone much bigger and stronger than myself. Unlike in our usual hand-to-hand lessons, though, she won't let me kiss her. Every time I try, she turns her cheek and tells me that we need to concentrate on our work.

"I'm just trying to take this seriously," she answers without even looking me in the eye.

I go at her again and twist my body so that she has to hug me against her chest and can't reach me with her teeth.

"Remember," she growls, "Leonard is much, much stronger than you. You want to avoid getting caught like this because he can crush you, break your ribs. This is better than getting bit, but if he can hurt you bad enough he'll be able to get to you easily."

I'm paying attention to my lesson and I'm still trying my hardest, destroying Olsen Leonard is still my highest priority, but I've got a lot on my mind.

For the first time in weeks, Elodie didn't come to join me in bed at the end of the night last night.

I know that we were fighting, if you can even call it that, but I wasn't expecting her to just leave me alone like that and it stung. I was up for hours, just lying on my back and staring at the ceiling, waiting for her to join me like usual. I know that she came home because she slid food under the door, but I wasn't released until after the sun went down this evening.

Elodie shows me a few more evasive moves and I wipe my forehead on my sleeve. Sweat is dripping into my eyes. Usually she likes the way I smell when I'm working out, but today she's clearly trying to avoid me, taking a step back whenever we aren't in the middle of a move.

"Should we call it a night?" she asks, only forty minutes after we get started.

"What? I'm not tired yet."

"Well I need to shower. I didn't get a chance last night. You can go for a run if you want to keep training."

It hasn't escaped my notice that all the weapons are locked up now. I think it's safe to assume that the knives from the kitchen are gone too. I haven't looked but I know that I came on too strong yesterday.

She walks away without waiting for an answer and I watch as her tall frame disappears in the doorway. I'm still kicking myself over what happened.

I've been thinking about it a long time, and I've already convinced myself. I want to change.

I can't go back to my previous life. I was living in terror, afraid to even visit a supermarket. I had no friends and no job. And I have a good reason to be afraid! A monster killed my family and he's still on the loose.

At the same time, I don't want to be Elodie's prisoner forever. I'm not Yeti; I won't ever be happy locked up in a single house with no freedom, no matter how many luxuries Elodie brings home.

I'm falling in love with Elodie but that's not enough for me.

I don't want to spend the next seventy years locked in this house, getting old while Elodie comes and goes at her leisure, never changing.

If she turned me, all of our problems would be solved. I'd be strong enough to protect myself, plus she'd no longer have to worry about me sharing her secret because it would be my secret too. I'd stay young forever like her and I could even join her family. I think that I'd enjoy that work. I certainly enjoy the training and the prospect of bringing men like Olsen to justice when the police can't or won't.

I shouldn't have just blurted it out like that though. It was too much of a shock for her. I guess to her it just seemed like I was asking her to kill me, which technically I was. I should have strategized more, introduced the idea slowly.

At least tried to figure out what the special rules are that she and her sisters have for changing someone.

I know that Jayden isn't that old. I can tell by the way that they don't have the same kind of familiarity with the past that their sisters have. They weren't alive yet to witness things like horse drawn carriages or men carrying swords in public or whatever. Plus they once mentioned watching television when they were a kid.

They must have turned Jayden recently, and if they could turn Jayden, then why can't Elodie turn me?

I'm going to have to revisit the subject after Elodie calms down.

For the time being, I have an idea about how to get back into her good graces. I follow her out of the training room and up the stairs, then pull off my sweaty gym clothes and slip into her shower behind her.

Her skin is uncharacteristically warm from the hot water and I let my fingers slide around the ripples of her abs. She doesn't stop me this time, but she also doesn't tense up like she usually does when I touch her this way.

Instead, she turns around and wraps her arms around me. She pulls me tight and nestles her face into my hair. I snake my arms around her and hold her for several minutes, then rub her back up and down. Her shoulders are slumped and her entire body language just looks so defeated it's breaking my heart.

"I'm so full of rage, Aya," she says quietly and I just listen to her. "I don't have to feel it often but it's like it builds up inside of me. It's one of the gifts that comes with immortality. All of my physical senses are heightened, but my emotions are dulled. In the cold, dark night I know, logically, when something is wrong but I don't feel sad or angry — either for the people I hurt or for the people I protect."

"During the night?" Something about the way she said that made me think that the specificity was important.

"It's why we don't go out during the day. If we enter the sunlight, we're confronted with all of the sorrow and terror and rage that's built up over our existences, the feelings that are blunted at night. We feel things the same way we would have when we were alive. It's bad enough to drive an immortal insane, or to drive one to end her existence. We call it The Grief, what we experience in the sun. A hundred years of guilty conscience and loss. We remember our feelings for everyone we've ever lost and we're faced with the reality of an existence that means losing everything eventually. Continuing on when everything around you — people, cities, entire cultures — eventually collapses."

I don't answer but I think to myself that it actually must be very nice, to be able to choose whether or not you feel your feelings. Or how much you have to feel them.

"So," something occurs to me, "you don't feel anything now? Like toward me?"

"No," Elodie looks down at me. "It's the only thing I feel. Maybe that's why it's so hard to regulate, I don't have the constant input or distractions that humans have. I only feel my need for you. I'm sorry, Aya. I'm sorry for everything that I've done to you and I'm sorry for putting you in this situation now."

I don't answer. I want to alleviate her guilt, but I also feel like she owes me an apology.

Instead I just hold her and comfort her.

"I've still got all of this anger bubbling underneath the surface about what happened to me. It's a dull anger, but it's there. The bloodletting drains it a bit, keeps it at bay. Prevents me from going totally feral."

I keep holding Elodie and listening. She seems to be relaxing into my arms. I wonder if this is another kind of bloodletting for her? An emotional bloodletting. It seems to be hurting her a lot more than the literal bloodletting.

"I'm sorry, you must be freezing," she turns to shut off the cold water that's now spraying on us. The hot water ran out several minutes ago, and she's right. I catch myself shivering.

She offers me a fluffy towel and I dry off and lead her by the hand to her own bed, the one where she never sleeps.

We crawl under the covers and stay silent in one another's arms.

It's not fair.

It's not fair what happened to her when she was a girl and it's not fair what happened to me, but here we are, two broken shells of humans, clinging to each others' naked bodies in the dark, trying to figure out where we can go from here.

CHAPTER SEVEN

ELODIE GLASS

I don't make it a habit to share my vulnerabilities with anyone.

Objectively, it's dangerous to reveal my Achilles' heels. I'm nearly invincible to most mortals and the more my kind run our mouths about our few weaknesses, the more exposed that leaves us. Not that I'm afraid that Aya would hurt me, though she'd certainly be well within her rights to do so at this point, but it's our habit and custom not to list the ways I can be tortured — or destroyed — physically.

I glance over at my Aya sleeping and regret my limitations. I'd like to wrap my body around hers and stay by her side for several more hours. The sun will be up soon though and I have to leave her alone, return to my crypt in the basement, and slumber.

I'd rather be sleeping with her, like a mortal lover. It's not like sleep, my slumber, it's like what I assume death is like.

I'm perfectly still. I don't dream and I don't ever wake randomly in the middle of the day. The world just doesn't exist anymore when I'm underground, and neither do I.

I'm not about to take any foolish and unnecessary risks, though. I've only experienced The Grief once, and that's only because I wanted to see for myself what it was like. It had all been explained to me in detail of course, Sonny was a good dark father and he never left me to try to figure out things on my own. I've always been the type to need to learn everything the hard way, though, so I thought that I knew better. I thought that he was underestimating my fortitude, that it couldn't be *that* bad to be faced with the emotional consequences of living on while everything around you eventually fell to the ravages of time.

I can tell you right now that I was dead wrong.

I slip out of the bed without waking Aya and make my way down to my crypt. The entrance is hidden in the pantry and protected by a locked, iron door. I don't want Aya to find it and freak out, and I don't think it's likely that anyone else will get into this house but I would't want any potential though unlikely strangers to find it either.

My coffin rests upon a stone altar, the lid slightly askew. I don't actually have to rest in a coffin and sometimes I feel like it's a bit kitschy, but it makes sense. If someone does somehow find it, hopefully that curious person will immediately identify it as something that should't be touched. Plus I need a place to slumber that won't leak light or damage my body if it somehow gets moved about.

My eyes close. My eyes open and I feel like it's been just a moment, a blink, but I know that at least twelve hours have passed. I get up and stretch and make my way into the kitchen, where I assume that I'll find my Aya fixing herself something to eat.

I'm surprised to find that she's still asleep, and I feel a twinge of guilt, like that emotional and verbal diarrhea that I unloaded on her yesterday must have exhausted her.

It's not just the threat that keeps me from sharing. I've never felt comfortable telling anyone about any weakness of mine, probably because a revelation like that when I was young would have been immediately turned against me and used to torture me.

Aya is different though. I have complete faith in the belief that she would never, ever use my vulnerabilities as weapons. That talk might have exhausted her, but it's put a spring in my step. I want to do something nice for her in way of thanks.

Breakfast in bed seems like just the thing. I slink back downstairs and just hope that she doesn't get up while I make her pancakes and bacon.

"Here," I pour a little of the bacon grease over the cat's dry kibble. "Don't tell anyone I let you have that."

I start to open a bottle of white wine, but then get a better idea. I pop a bottle of champagne and fill a pair of glasses two thirds, then top them off with grapefruit juice.

"What's this?" she asks, sleep still in her eyes when I enter the room.

"I made breakfast," I set the tray down on the bed. "Don't get up! That's the whole point, you get to eat without even getting up."

"Did you make mimosas? Oh! It's grapefruit juice! I love grapefruit."

"I know."

I'm pleased with this reaction. Aya is impressed with my offering and she's already crunching on a piece of bacon.

"I woke up in the middle of the day," she explains. "I got up and did some training, then showered, then just went back to bed. The light bothers me now."

I take a sip of my drink and pretend that something on the wall has my interest. I don't want to get into another conversation about why I can't turn her.

"Thank you for this," she catches my drift. "It was delicious."

She moves the tray to the night stand and puts down her drink, then kisses me deeply.

"Slow down," I ask her as she works at the buttons on my clothes. I'm trying to remain in control of myself but it's not easy for me, not around her. I don't want to deny her but I also don't want to lose myself.

"Wait," she smiles. "I had an idea. Lie down."

I'm not sure about this but I follow her orders. She lays me on my back, then tears a couple strips from the bedsheet and ties my wrists to the headboard.

"Aya—" I start.

She shushes me. I was going to tell her that these sheets can't hold me, but she probably already knows that.

Okay, if she wants to play a game, we'll play. I've decided to just pretend that the ties can hold me. It will be a good exercise for me, trying to control myself.

Next she surprises me again by tearing off another strip of sheet and tying it over my eyes as a blindfold.

"Are you okay?" she asks as she mounts me and I can feel that she's removed her clothing.

I grunt in the affirmative. I'm actually not entirely sure that I'm okay but I also don't want her to stop so I'm doing my best here.

Then I hear it. Glass shatters. I immediately suspect that she accidentally knocked a glass off the nightstand, but a moment later, I feel it.

"Aya," I gasp.

"Do I need to gag you too?"

"Under my heart. You have to cut under my heart."

Not every part of my body will bleed for her. She understands what I'm saying though and she cuts me just under my breast, just like she saw me do to myself yesterday. I can feel her little pink tongue lapping at me and I can smell her pussy getting wet. My blood is a natural aphrodisiac (or I guess a supernatural aphrodisiac) and I think my Aya... she likes to be in control. It turns her on, which is no surprise for a girl who is so used to having all control taken from her.

I let her drink me and just when I'm about to break the restraints that she put on me so that I can force her onto her back, she stops teasing me. She turns around and slides her body up over my face and I can taste her wet lips before she sits gently down, allowing me to draw my tongue over her slowly, centimeter by centimeter.

I buck my hips under her and she cuts me again, deeper, this time right next to my own sex. She's drinking me as she rides me and I can feel the blood that she doesn't catch dripping down the side of my thigh as she fucks me.

I want her to ride me harder and faster but she's drawing it out, her body rubbing against mine, sliding slowly back and forth, getting hotter and slicker. She's driving me insane and this is like nothing I've ever done before.

If she hadn't cut me I wouldn't have been able to stand it. I would have torn my wrists from the frame, flipped her onto her back, and devoured her mercilessly.

Between the release from the cut and the restriction of my vision, though, I'm able to restrain myself and let her fuck me the way she wants to be fucked. She rides me slowly until I can hear her gasping and feel her trembling on top of me. Then, before I finish, she slides off and I'm alone for a second before I feel her mouth on me.

She licks me deep and long and sucks hard on my clit. I don't last much longer; I wouldn't have even if she wasn't working me so hard. I cry out as I fill her mouth with sweat and blood and desire and she swallows everything I have.

CHAPTER EIGHT

AYA LACHAT

"**W**as it still okay for you? Or did that make it less... something?"

Elodie shakes out her curls and sits up in the bed. Her breast has already healed and her inner thigh is still slick with our mingling fluids. I've removed her blindfold and untied her.

"It wasn't less," she answers after a moment. "It was... different. Aya," she looks at me, "why did you do that?"

I have to think for a minute before I answer.

"I guess that I was just mostly acting on instinct," I answer truthfully. "You said that you need it sometimes. That you're struggling. It felt wrong but it also felt so good. I think it's something in your blood, it does something to me. And usually you're so aggressive; it was nice for me to get the chance to take charge for once."

She looks concerned and I'm afraid that I've made a mistake, overstepped some unspoken boundary.

"I'm sorry," I apologize. I should have asked, but she seemed to like it when it was happening. "Do you want to drink from me now? Would that make you feel better?"

"What? No, Aya, don't offer that. You don't ever have to offer me that."

"I want to give it to you."

We're at an impasse. Elodie is uncomfortable but she's not talking.

"Did it hurt?" I ask quietly. I just want to know her better but sometimes she makes everything so hard.

"No," she finally cracks a smile.

"Can you feel pain?"

"Yes, but my tolerance is high. A cut like that just stings a little. In a good way, actually, it feels pleasantly sharp."

"Interesting," I nod. "So... would you say it turns you on?"

"Well," Elodie considers the question, "I've never thought of it that way before, but I guess yes. Not the same way as when I drink. A different way."

"It turns you on when you drink?"

"Yes. It's like alcohol, but way more intense. And the more I drink, the more I want."

"Just with me? Or when you drink from anyone?"

"I don't fixate on other blood like I do yours, but all blood is arousing to me. To different degrees. I can't help it. It's almost like me and my body are two discreet entities. You turn me on. Blood turns my body on."

"Does it turn you on to kill people?"

"Yes. I always get wet when I drink. But that doesn't mean that I'm attracted to the person I'm feeding on. It's more of a physiological stimulation. Like I could probably get wet if I ground myself against this pillow, but that doesn't mean that I think the pillow is hot."

The mental image of Elodie mooning over the pillow is too much for me and I giggle.

"But what if it was, like, a really nice pillow? Like one of those memory foam ones?" I tease her and she hits me with the pillow.

"But for real," I continue, "have you ever been attracted to anyone that you killed?"

"Never. I was never on my own, trying to find myself. Not like Adrienne. I worked for Sonny, then he turned me into what I am and his family doesn't kill at random. Then when he left me I joined up with Adrienne and Aravella, who had already found each other. I enjoy killing, but I've never killed exclusively for pleasure."

"Who have you killed?" I want to know.

"Total?" she looks at me like I'm crazy.

"I guess it's a lot of people."

"It is, but actually now that I'm thinking about it, Jayden could probably tell you most of them because Adrienne keeps very detailed records of all the work we've ever done."

"How do you decide who to kill?"

"We have a couple different ways to find our prey. We have an informant in the police, a guy we trust who tips us off when they're unable to stop someone for whatever reason."

"Why would they be unable to stop someone?"

"Sometimes they can't find someone, sometimes that someone is too clever and hasn't left enough evidence to convict, sometimes that someone is well connected. Sometimes someone is rich enough to get a slap on the wrist. All kinds of reasons."

"I wonder if Olsen is one of those someones."

"Probably, yes. That's what Jayden has been thinking, at least, and they've been working nonstop trying to hunt this guy down."

"How else do you find people?"

"I helped a lot of people at our group meeting."

"Oh!" I'm surprised that this hasn't occurred to me yet. "Is that why you were there?"

"Mostly, but everything I shared there was true."

"You barely shared anything."

"But the things I did share were all real. I was there primarily to find people who needed help now. Like that one poor woman, Melissa MacLean. I helped her."

"The lady with the ex husband?"

"Yeah. She was right to be afraid of him; he was even worse than she already knew. He was into some real sick shit."

"What kind of shit?"

"Kids."

My stomach turns.

"Did you stop him?"

"Oh yeah," Elodie laughs. "I stopped him alright. And I took my time, made him squeal like a little pig, that fucking fuck. That's his cat in your kitchen right now, by the way, I felt bad leaving him."

"Yeti!" I laugh. "You stole Yeti from a child abuser."

"I rescued Yeti. Judging by some of the stuff this guy was checking out, even Yeti wasn't safe."

"So," I want to know more but I don't want to push my luck, "what did you do to him?"

Elodie gives me a suspicious side eye.

"Don't worry," I assure her, "I won't tell anyone."

She laughs again and explains it all. The break in, the torture, and eventually the kill. I'm surprised to find that the more detail she gives, the more turned on I get.

"Are they all perverts?" I ask her. "Everyone that you kill?"

"They're all sadists," Elodie explains. "But they aren't all just hurting people for fun. Some of them are also doing it to enrich themselves."

"Like how?"

"Well," Elodie thinks, "I've killed people who were committing benefits fraud."

"Benefits fraud? Really?"

"Not 'benefits fraud' like they were lying on their unemployment applications. Sometimes people will take in foster kids or disabled people or elderly people and then apply for benefits on their behalf while not caring for them. Like they'll fill a house up with old people, starve them, get rid of the bodies, and keep on collecting social security while they look for more victims."

"Oh my God," I had never even thought about that happening before. I guess that I had been so occupied with my own victimhood that I hadn't really been aware of the myriad ways other people were being tortured. "I can't even imagine how horrifying that must be, to be completely helpless and then get trapped by someone like that after you thought that they were going to help you."

The more I thought about it, the angrier I got. I flipped from my back onto my side and then back onto my back. I wanted to say something — to do something! — but I didn't know what.

"Did you hurt the people?" I narrowed my brows. "The ones who were doing that?"

"I killed them," Elodie admitted. "But I don't always take my time. I usually just do the job quickly and get out."

"Well if it had been me I would have taken my time. I would have handcuffed the guy to his own bed and then starved him to death. And then eaten him."

My imagination is getting away from me and Elodie is listening to me with a bemused expression on her face.

"What?" I demand, indignant. I'm not angry at her, I'm just angry at the world, but she's the only person here to hear me out. "You think I couldn't do it?"

"Oh the more I get to know you the more sure I become that you could do it," Elodie answers, pulling me close.

"What kinds of other guys do you catch?" I want to know. I've been so laser focused on Olsen that I haven't thought much about the other kinds of scum that inhabit our city. "Do you only work here or do you travel all around catching them?"

"We travel occasionally, but most of our work is only here. Unfortunately there are so many here that we don't have to leave to constantly have a never-ending supply of work. Everywhere is like this, though, here is only slightly worse than average."

I make Elodie spend the entire night telling me all about her work, the people she stops and the people she saves. She describes her jobs to me in detail and I imagine myself at her side, avenging the helpless and innocent.

I'd slaughter them all, the people who think that the world is theirs to victimize. And I wish that I was like Elodie so that I could devour them too.

I understand why Elodie gets wet when she hurts these people. I'm getting wet and it's not a physiological thing at all.

CHAPTER NINE

ELODIE GLASS

"**H**ey," I answer my phone, having just excused myself from training with Aya.

"Hey," Jayden answers back.

"What's up?"

"I think I got your man."

I should have been expecting this, Jayden's a genius when it comes to tracking people online, but I'm still a bit taken aback. It seems so soon; I wasn't expecting things to move *this* quickly. If Jayden's found this Leonard, that means that soon I'll have to give Aya the chance to kill him. Soon all of this — the house, the relationship, everything we have — will be over. I'll have to let her go.

Of course, it hasn't been that fast. It's been several weeks that we've been waiting for this information. I should have known that this call was coming but I still feel blindsided.

"Yeah?" I try to sound casual but I can hear my own voice tremble.

"Yeah I'm ninety nine percent certain it's him anyway. He's based here but lives in D.C. half of the time. He's got some kind of family connection to the automotive industry, lots of published op eds, lobbying for total lack of regulation over factories, union-busting, all kinds of shit, he's very well connected, but get this… there aren't any pictures of him or videos anywhere to be found. Looks like he's rubbing elbows at all kinds of events but his picture somehow never makes it into the paper or onto the internet."

"Maybe this guy's just into privacy? I would be if it was my job to be a total asshole."

"Could be, but wait, there's more," Jayden says like I've just won a game show. "I cross referenced this guy's schedule and it looks like he was spending a lot of time here, then suddenly appeared back in D.C. the day your girlie was picked up by the police. And, get this, he was definitely at the sister's piano performance. He won tickets by dumping an extraordinary amount of cash into some kind of charity raffle and gave a quote about the show to the paper afterward."

I groan. It's sounding more and more like this is our guy.

"Babe? Everything okay? Anyhow I'm not surprised that the Feds didn't look at this guy very hard. He's loaded, like money from way back in the day loaded. Actually that's something else I've been working on. Trying to find out how old this guy is. I'm pretty sure that he's at least two hundred and fifty; that's how long his 'family' which seems to exist exclusively of one single man at a time has been at this local house. It's just one man who suddenly has a surprise heir going all the way back, never a wife or mother mentioned. Or other siblings. If this guy isn't immortal I'll eat... I don't know, I guess I'll eat an entire wheel of Parmesan."

Jayden proceeds to give me all of this guy's information, including the address of his local home which in an ironic twist of fate isn't very far from my farmhouse, and the address of the place where he's staying in D.C. They also give me the name he's currently living under: it's Orrin DeLeone.

"Hey," Aya looks up at me from a mat on the ground, her ponytail swinging. "Everything okay?"

"I've got good news for you," I reply, though my voice belies my own lack of enthusiasm. "Jayden found your guy."

"Olsen? Really? You found Olsen?"

"His name is Orrin now, DeLeone. God only knows what his original name was, probably neither of those. But yes, he's got a place near here."

Aya springs to her feet and grabs her axe. "Let's go," she makes for the door without even looking at me.

"Wait," I grab her arm.

"Wait? Are you crazy? I've been waiting for the past several years. I'm not going to wait another second!"

"You're going to have to, I'm afraid." I've really got to grip her tightly now. She's fighting me with everything she's got. "He's got another place in Washington D.C. where he stays, he's there now."

"D.C.," Aya narrows her eyes.

"That's how Jayden made the connection," I explain. I hope that I haven't just ruined her most favorite memory with her family. "This guy, he was at your sister's show."

"You think that's where he first saw her?"

"Possibly. Or possibly he attended the show specifically to see her, like he already knew her. We don't know for sure, but Jayden connected a lot of dots, too many to be a series of coincidences. I think it's him."

"Can I see a picture of him? I'd like to see if I recognize him. His face is so blurry in my memory."

"That's one of the dots. There are no pictures of him. That's called a glamour, immortals can't be photographed or filmed, we won't ever appear in focus. And we can do the same thing to people's memories or impressions of us."

"Have you done that?" Aya eyes me suspiciously.

"Not to you."

"Okay. So what do we do now? What's my next step?"

I take a deep breath. "Sweetheart. Aya, my love. You're where you need to be. We haven't confirmed this yet, but Jayden believes that this Leonard or DeLeone or whatever the hell his name is could be at least two hundred and fifty years old. That means that we both need to be at the top of our game before we try anything. That's much older than I am, and I'm pretty sure that this guy hasn't been restricting his feeding. We need to train."

She's deep in thought, probably thinking of how she's going to word whatever protest she's about to unleash.

"I didn't think that anyone could be stronger than you," she finally admits.

"Thank you. I'd like to believe that too, but that's sadly just not the truth. Even my two older sisters are stronger than me."

"So what are we going to do?" Aya asks quietly. "Do you think he's going to kill us? Because I'm not capable of turning back now. Either we kill him or he kills us. But if he's so powerful… Do we stand a chance?"

"More good news," this time it really is good news. "We've got backup. All three of my sisters will be with us. Hopefully DeLeone doesn't also have a coven, then we'll probably die. Jayden thinks he's working alone though. None of the publicly available information about him indicates that he has any close relationships with, well, anyone."

"Really?" Aya's eyes brighten. "They're willing to help me?"

"No," I reply honestly, "they're willing to help me. But you're a part of me now so here we are."

"Well I'm going to thank them anyways. But when will we be ready? If O is really as strong as you say, what difference will a few weeks of training make? Or even a few years?"

"Very little," I admit. "But there are still a few things that I want to show you. One month. That's how long we have. But Aya, we need to discuss something else."

She raises her eyebrows.

"We need to travel to Washington D.C. to catch him. There's no way we'd stand a chance against him in his ancestral home, even with my sisters' help."

"Okay," Aya agrees. "I've been to D.C. before, remember? I don't have a problem with traveling there."

"Aya, I need you to give me your word. Can I take you out in public? Will you be able to travel across the country without betraying me? If not, I'll have to go alone and then send you the proof."

And that would mean, my Aya, that you remain my prisoner for the rest of your life.

I don't say that last part out loud, we both know it's true. This is the moment that she has to make her decision, though. Either she trusts me and stays quietly by my side as we navigate life in public, or she stays locked up forever.

"No running, no screaming, no trying to pass the TSA a note," I want to make sure that we're absolutely clear in our expectations for one another.

"You have my word," Aya promises. "There is absolutely nothing in the world more important to me than getting my chance to destroy Olsen. I would never do anything to forfeit that chance, not now that I'm so close. I don't have a life to return to as long as he still walks the Earth. I promise you. I'll behave."

I believe her. I'd already convinced myself that there was no way that Aya would stab me in the back, she doesn't have that kind of treachery in her. Plus, I can see it in her eyes when she talks about DeLeone; she needs to get her revenge, for herself and for her loved ones.

"Okay, Aya," I pull her close to me. "I'll book our tickets then."

CHAPTER TEN

AYA LACHAT

"ID and boarding pass. ID and boarding pass. Ma'am? MA'AM? ID AND BOARDING PASS?"

"Oh," I shake the thoughts from my head and reach into the side pocket of my tote bag. "Sorry. Here you go."

I hand over my documents and the officer barely glances at them before she shoves them back to me and sets her eyes on the next person in line.

"You okay?" Elodie asks quietly as we queue for the security check. She's guiding me by the elbow and I'm not sure whether it's because she's afraid I'll run or she's afraid I'll get lost. Both seem possible to me at the moment.

"Yeah," I glance around at the mayhem surrounding us. "I just haven't been through an airport in a while."

I don't remember airports being *this* chaotic, though the last time I was in one was... I guess I've only been in an airport once before and it was when I was a kid so maybe my memories aren't entirely accurate. When I was little I would have found all this hustle and bustle exciting rather than nerve wracking.

Now, though... It's just *so loud*. There are people everywhere, someone is making announcements that are so staticky that I doubt anyone can understand them over a loudspeaker, and machines are beeping and buzzing all around us. It's constant sensory input, amplified by the fact that I haven't been out in public in months. I never thought about it, but the house is usually so quiet. Elodie and Yeti barely make any noise at all, so usually the only sounds I can hear are those I make myself.

"This place must be a complete zoo during the day," I observe. For some reason we are now taking off our shoes and loading them into plastic trays along with our carry ons. We're absolutely surrounded by people, both travelers and employees, and everyone is in a mad rush.

"Just think of it as a factory line," Elodie suggests. "Take it one step at a time. Tray through the X ray machine, passenger through the metal detector, just keep moving."

I try to follow her advice but there are so many distractions around us. My eyes are being drawn in every direction at once, toward a lady struggling with a crying baby, then to a man arguing with the officer manning the metal detector, then to a golf cart that's blinking and beeping as it moves in reverse. I'm reminded of that old video game, Frogger. Everyone is moving so purposefully I'm afraid that if I take a step without looking then I'll be hit by a truck or something.

Elodie and I are taking a red eye flight to D.C. The past month of training flew by and I was feeling so prepared, like I could take on anything. Until we arrived at this airport.

"Don't even think about it," Elodie growls at me under her breath.

"Think about what?" I truly have no idea what she's talking about. Then I realize that I've been staring at a TSA agent's fake nails and she probably thinks that I'm considering asking her for help.

The truth is, that the thought did briefly cross my mind. As soon as we stepped out of the big, black SUV that dropped us off at the airport and we were surrounded by cops, I thought *now's my chance*. They were everywhere, swarming likes ants, telling people that they couldn't park and helping confused passengers to find the correct terminals.

What could Elodie have done? If I had screamed or run to a cop and begged for his help. There were so many of them, not to mention all the other passengers and video cameras. Elodie surely would have just had to flee.

Of course I never considered it seriously.

If I betrayed Elodie, then I'd never get the chance to finally end things with Olsen Leonard. I'd go back to my shitty little life and then probably resume hiding in a tiny apartment, afraid to go out in public. Only now I'd have to be afraid of Olsen, Elodie, *and* Elodie's sisters. And I wouldn't even actually have a place to live because Elodie owned my old building.

No, that wouldn't do.

Not at all.

It wasn't just a matter of practicality though. I also didn't *want* to leave Elodie.

Did we have a healthy relationship?

No.

Could I imagine any kind of future for us that wasn't a tragedy?

Nope.

Was I sure that Elodie even wanted to spend the rest of her life, or I guess just my life, with me?

Also no.

Yet here I was, making one bad decision after another. It was like I was addicted to her, her body and her blood, and I wasn't willing to walk away from what we had, even if what we had was a disaster waiting to happen.

It wasn't just Elodie though.

I wasn't willing to give up the new *me*.

I didn't want to go back to being weak and terrified. I liked the new Aya, the one who could run a mile in six minutes and throw an axe accurately from five meters. The one who was brave enough to chase her dreams, even if she was trembling on the inside.

"This is us," Elodie indicates a gate. "Do you want to board now? Or last?"

"They're only boarding first class now anyways."

"That's us."

I should have known. Elodie leads me onto the plane and to my seat, letting me take the window. She's still nervous; I can tell by the way she won't let go of me. She doesn't settle down until we're up in the air, soaring through the dark on the way to meet our fate.

She's rented a car for us in D.C., another big black SUV with dark windows, but now we're one in a million. It seems like the vehicle of choice for people who live and work in this part of the world. The roads are surprisingly busy for the middle of the night and I guess the gears don't stop grinding in a place like this.

We pull up outside of a three story townhouse in a ritzy part of the city and park on the street. Elodie hops out and carries our bags for us; we had to send our weapons ahead of time via FedEx, so we're traveling with just our clothing and personal effects. She unlocks the door and I'm startled by the three figures lounging around the living room in the dark.

"Oh," my eyes adjust to the light. "I didn't know we were all sharing a place."

Elodie's sisters had made their own travel arrangements and she hadn't mentioned to me that we were all going to be staying together, but I guess it made sense, especially in a huge place like this.

"We're not," Elodie says, a little bit too loudly, and I am able to guess that this was a surprise for her too.

"We are," her biggest sister answers with a grin that I can tell has more of a smart-ass vibe than a friendly one.

"You gals couldn't find your own place?" Elodie groans, shutting the front door behind her and flicking on the lights.

"We just thought it would be better if we were all staying together," Adrienne answers. "You know, for moral support."

"Moral support," Elodie grimaces.

"Don't worry, this place is huge, you two will have plenty of privacy," Aravella pipes in. "Unless of course you *want* to—"

"Shut up," Elodie warns. "I don't want to hear it."

"We just wanted to make sure that you guys were okay here," Adrienne explains.

A-ha. That's it. They don't trust me and they're afraid that Elodie doesn't have it in her to stop me if I do something stupid.

"But we've got work to do," Adrienne continues. "If you think our city is bad you won't believe the kind of shit people do to each other here. This place is absolutely depraved. We can clean up some of this scum as long as we're here, Jayden has already identified a target for us. What do you say, Elodie, how about we bring your girlie with us? Then she can see a real assignment in action. See if she's still interested in going after DeLeone herself."

Adrienne shoots me a challenging look and I can tell that she thinks I'm going to back down. She doesn't know me at all. I'm not going to let a bully like her try to scare me away from finally achieving my life's only goal. Plus, my interest in Elodie's work has been growing by the day anyways. I'd love to come along on a real job.

"That's a great idea," I give her my brightest smile. "Some last minute training. And I bet you girls could use the extra help."

"Aya, I don't think—"

"No, El, let her come," Aravella interrupts her. "Like she said. We could probably use the extra help."

✤❧❧✤

CHAPTER ELEVEN

ELODIE GLASS

I t's too late to go out on a job, thank God. I hope that Adrienne reconsiders before tomorrow night. I don't want to start taking random needless risks now that we're far from home and so close to our goals.

I take a look at the touchpad on the wall next to the front door and click a few buttons, activating an elaborate system of shutters. I've rented this place totally outfitted for immortals and it wasn't cheap, so I'm actually not that surprised that Adrienne preferred to stay with us. Here we've got a security system that will enclose the entire house while the sun is up but just looks like regular blinds from the streets. It's perfect for us. My sisters have already chosen their rooms and I'm excited to finally be able to stay with Aya, though my excitement is tinged with nerves.

"Aya," I'm already in bed when she emerges from the shower. "I sleep during the day."

"Yes, I was aware of that," she gives me a look like I am treating her like she's dumb.

"I just wanted to warn you: I sleep very deeply."

"Okay?" she's drying her hair with a towel. I don't want to freak her out but I also want to warn her.

"Very, very deeply."

"Got it," she nods. "I won't disturb you."

"That's the thing," I start, trying to figure out how to explain this, "you can't."

"I won't."

"You can't."

"Okay, jeez."

"I mean, I won't wake up. Even if you try, I don't wake up during the day when I slumber."

"Ah," she nods back. "So would you say that you sleep like the dead?"

"Aya that's not funny."

It was a little bit funny.

She crawls into bed with me and I pull her in tight.

"You don't have to do this," I remind her one more time.

"I want to do this."

I'm beginning to fear that I've created a monster. Ironic, given the fact that I am a literal monster. Aya is visibly psyched about our job tomorrow. I'm happy that she's happy but I'm also worried that she's too enthusiastic and not being realistic enough about her abilities. I don't think that any of my sisters would let her get hurt, but this job could turn into a real mess.

By the time I wake the following night Aya is already up and dressed in her tactical gear. She's wearing head to toe black and she's got her hair in a tight bun. She even has her boots on in our bedroom.

"Are you ready to go?" she prods me as I slide out of bed, still completely naked. "We've got work to do. Come on, Jayden is already waiting in the living room."

I briefly wonder if she somehow *did* figure out a way to wake Jay from their slumber. I get dressed and join them in the living room, where they are politely listening to Aya tell them all about her axe skills.

"It sounds like you've been really busy," they reply as she goes on and on. They catch my eye and give me a half smile.

"Do you even need us to come?" Aravella asks from the door. I shoot her a look. "I mean it sounds like you probably have this situation under control yourself."

Aya just ignores her. I can tell that she doesn't like her and I don't blame her. Aravella is the kind of person you need to get to know before you can see any of her good qualities. She's an expert at keeping them hidden under a layer of asshole behavior.

"Look," Adrienne joins us last and sits down on the sofa next to Jayden. "This is our guy."

Jayden pulls up a file that has pictures of a townhouse even nicer than ours but no other images.

"He's a beast," Jayden explains.

"What has he done?" Aravella asks. "And why is it our business?"

"He turned a child," Adrienne snaps back. Aravella sucks her teeth in response.

"He's immortal?" Aya interrupts, looking over Jayden's shoulder at their laptop.

"Mm hmm," Jayden replies. "It's not allowed to turn children. Ever."

"Why did he do it? Was it his child?"

"No," Jayden fortunately has the patience to explain. "Sometimes immortals will turn a child and enslave her. Train her as a sex slave and then use her or pimp her. It's terrible for them; people and other immortals can torture them without killing them, possibly forever. They can do things that a human child wouldn't survive. And the child immortals aren't strong enough to protect themselves."

"Oh my God," Aya is shocked. She's so naive. It's one of the things I love about her but I hate to see her constantly disappointed by the world's cruelty.

Now there's no way I can convince her to stay home. She's dead set on accompanying us to this job. I'm pretty sure that she'd try to take it on herself if Adrienne would allow it, which thank God she won't. She's already got a plan; Aravella is going to enter the home as a customer and then let the rest of us in.

I drive us in the rental since there's room for us all and our equipment. Aya rides up front with me and we drop Aravella off in front like she's using a ride share service. There's nothing suspicious about any of it since the car blends in so well in that neighborhood.

I pull the truck around back and park in an alley where people have set out their trash. We slide out and split up, Aya with me and Adrienne and Jayden off to fulfill their roles.

"Look," I indicate a second floor window quietly. It's a washroom and Aravella slides the window open.

"How are we going to get up there?" Aya glances around.

I help her onto my back and scale the tree outside the window. It's just barely strong enough to hold our weight.

"How many?" I ask Aravella as soon as we get in.

"Just the one as far as I can tell. I haven't even met the girl yet."

"Stay here," I sit Aya down on the edge of the tub. "In front of the window. Otherwise they'll smell you."

I don't feel entirely comfortable leaving Aya with just a dagger but I have no choice. I slide out after Aravella and wait in a doorway as she heads back to the front of the house to make her appointment.

This needs to be quick. The faster we act, the less chance there will be that something goes sideways. I can hear voices and a nondescript man who looks to be in his mid forties but who I know is much, much older is leading Aravella though the hall, promising her that her 'date' is chained to the wall and can't get out of her room.

I don't want Aya to hear this. I step out behind them and plant the axe square in the back of this thing's head, splitting it in two.

"Jesus, Elodie, you couldn't wait until I stepped out of the way," Aravella is unhappy because she's been sprayed with black blood. I can see Aya standing in the doorway of the bathroom after I specifically told her to stay put. She's seen the whole thing and I can't quite read the expression on her face.

"Let's finish this," is all I have to say to Aravella. I didn't mean to make such a mess but I'm not apologizing either.

Aravella finds the keys to the house in the pockets of the beast I just slayed, who is already starting to decay and dry up. We have to try several doors before we find what we're looking for.

Inside there's a naked Filipina girl who looks to be about twelve years old chained to the wall with a thick iron collar. She's hissing at us and Aravella is trying to calm her.

"Just wait for Beryl," I advise her, though she doesn't listen.

"Who's Beryl?" Aya asks, looking at our victim with her mouth agape.

"An old friend of Adrienne's mother. Beryl can help girls like this," I pull Aya close.

"Are you going to hurt her?"

"No. She'll be taken away to a kind of orphanage where she'll be taught how to... I guess just how to exist. How to hide and how to eat without getting herself into trouble. It will take a long time for one like her to be able to exist independently. Maybe never."

Just then Jayden and Adrienne arrive with an older black woman wearing a dark cloak.

"Aya," I introduce them, "Beryl."

Beryl takes one look at Aya and then gives me a disapproving look. She doesn't bother responding or making small talk, she just clucks her tongue and shakes her head and sets to work trying to calm down the girl before Aravella frees her from her chains.

"I don't think she likes me," Aya says quietly as I lead her back to the car, leaving everyone else to clean up the job.

"It's not that," I try to explain, but I can't.

CHAPTER TWELVE

AYA LACHAT

"You can't let her do that. It's not safe. I don't even think she's physically capable of taking down that poor wretch we freed last night. There's no way she can face a full grown man."

"I made her a promise! And I know that I'll have to kill DeLeone myself. But she should be able to be there. Just think of what this thing has done to her. She needs this to move on."

"You're crazy, Elodie. We should just activate Plan B. Cut her loose and we can start over somewhere new. She'll be the end of us all otherwise. Come on, El, and it's not even her fault. She's not a killer. This isn't fair to her or us."

I'm sitting up in bed eavesdropping on Elodie and Jayden. I feel slightly guilty about it but not guilty enough to let them know that I'm awake and can hear them talking.

Jayden wants Elodie to dump me somewhere public, then I guess the four of them will disappear and build a new home elsewhere. And I'll never see them again. I'm not sure whether this plan includes destroying Olsen or not.

Elodie wants to honor her agreement with me, though it's news to me that she herself also does not believe that I can really kill Olsen. I thought that she believed in me, but I guess not. Oh — and she plans to dump me after I kill Olsen anyway.

I don't know what I was imagining was going to happen to me, but that doesn't stop me from being disappointed.

I thought that Elodie and I had something, but I guess people come and go from her life all the time. That must be the reality of living forever.

I still need to kill Olsen though. Even if no one believes that I can do it except me. I'm not afraid of dying and I can't live like this anymore.

"Hey," Elodie enters the room and is visibly surprised to see me sitting on the end of the bed. "I didn't know you were up. I had an idea. Let's go out on the town. Are you interested in art? The Smithsonian is having Night at the Museum. They serve cocktails and snacks and they're open late. Let me take you out?"

After overhearing that conversation about my imminent dumping I'm struggling to pretend that I'm thrilled with Elodie's date idea but I also need to get out of the house. Being cooped up with her sisters is starting to get on my nerves.

Once we're on the road I'm feeling a bit better. I roll my window down and take in the sights. Elodie gives us a little driving tour and we glide past the Lincoln Memorial and the White House. They look different than I remember, lit up at night like this.

It takes a while to find parking. The first two lots we find are full and of course there's nothing available on the street for blocks. By the time we actually find a spot we've got a bit of a hike to get back to the museum. I don't mind the walk though. I've got my boots on and it's nice to be out in public. D.C. isn't chaotic like the airport was and I'm enjoying doing a bit of people watching.

That's when it first happens, when I see her. We're walking along the sidewalk alongside the Mall and I see a woman in a black dress with a black veil with long, honey blonde hair that reaches her hips. I catch a glimpse of her out of the corner of my eye but when I look to see her, she's gone.

My stomach drops.

It's Nala.

I know that hair, and I know that walk.

I can't tell Elodie; she'll think I've lost my mind and then she won't let me go through with the assassination. My eyes dart everywhere and she's gone. Am I hallucinating her because I associate this place with her so heavily in my memories? I'm either hallucinating or she's a ghost, because she's vanished into thin air.

If vampires exist, does that mean ghosts can too?

Or am I being haunted by my own memories?

I don't know what I saw. Maybe I saw a woman in black and then my imagination connected some dots that weren't really there. Maybe I dreamed up the whole thing. I'm pretty sure that other people would be staring at someone wearing a veil in public like I thought I saw, though, that was too weird to be real.

I decide to believe that I was imagining things. I don't believe that, not in my heart, but I don't see any other good options for myself at the moment. If I mention the woman to Elodie she'll drag me back to the farmhouse and I can't very well go searching on my own. She still won't let me out of her sight, though I guess she's right to do so now seeing as I'm hallucinating and I can't even trust my own judgments.

We arrive at the museum and it's got a healthy crowd but it's not packed.

"We're underdressed," I lament immediately upon entry. We're surrounded by men in suits and women in smart dresses.

"Nah," Elodie looks around. "The website said that the dress code was casual. These people probably just got off work and didn't change."

I'm not convinced but I also don't really care. We enter and Elodie grabs a couple glasses of white wine.

"Are you hungry?" she asks. "There's food in the hall."

We wander around amongst the art and the finger foods and it's nice, being out in public in a normal place like a normal couple. Elodie knows a lot about the paintings on the wall and she shows me some of her favorites. She's been to this museum before.

"Hey, I'm just going to stop in this ladies' room," I notice a bathroom as we're walking the halls.

Elodie looks a little concerned — does she think I'm going to take off through a window? — but she holds my glass as I run off to pee.

I'm washing my hands in the sink when I see it in the mirror. At the base of one of the other stalls I can see the hem of a ragged black lace skirt. It's the same one I saw before; I'm sure of it. I freeze in place and wait for the other woman to exit the stall.

I'm standing there for several minutes not moving when Elodie calls my name through the door.

"Aya? Everything okay? You've been in there a while."

I dry my hands and exit.

"Yeah. Sorry. There was a line."

I still don't feel like I can tell her what I saw. I try to stall outside of the restroom for a while but no one in a black skirt exits. My mind must have been playing tricks on me again.

By the end of the night I think I've seen the woman twice more, but I know for sure that she's only in my imagination because no one else around me seems to see her. I'm disturbed, mostly at the prospect of losing my grip on reality just days before my long nightmare is destined to come to an end.

"Whoa," Elodie smiles as I push her onto her back on our bed at home. "I guess you liked the date."

"What? Oh yeah, it was nice." I'm removing my own clothes and unbuttoning her shirt. I need the distraction and this is the only thing that I can think of that will take my mind off of the lady in black.

I straddle Elodie and kiss her deeply, cutting my tongue on her fangs on purpose. I know that once she gets a drop of my blood she can barely control herself. She tastes me and groans, lets me rock my hips slowly back and forth on her for just a few moments before she pulls me off and puts me on my knees in front of her, facing the headboard.

From this position she grabs me roughly from behind. She's got one arm snaked under me, between my breasts and around my neck, holding me in a kind of headlock. I couldn't escape from her grasp if I wanted to. She bites deep on the back of my neck, way deeper than she usually does.

It comes as a surprised to me and I cry out. I don't want her to stop but she's scaring me. She's drinking so much that it's making me drowsy.

"Elodie," I gasp. My vision is getting blurry. She's not hurting me, at least not in a bad way, but I'm afraid that even she doesn't know what she's doing.

I don't want to die before I even get the chance to try to kill Olsen.

She seems to regain control of her senses just in time. She loosens her grip on me and drops my now limp body on the mattress.

"Aya!"

She tears at her own wrist with her teeth and lets me drink.

CHAPTER THIRTEEN

ELODIE GLASS

Everything is going off the rails.

Ever since Aya saw that poor kid who had been changed against her will, she's been pressuring me to turn her too. She thinks becoming an immortal will solve all of her problems, as though she'll be instantly cured of her PTSD and have nothing on Earth to fear. As though becoming a monster wouldn't just give her an entirely new set of problems that needed to be hidden from the world.

For the past twenty four hours she's been nagging me relentlessly. She vacillates back and forth between begging and attempting to take matters into her own hands, like she did the last time we fucked.

And my God, it nearly worked.

I nearly lost control of myself and drained her. And I'm not willing to lose her now; if she gets hurt then I'll bring her back. God help me if she figures that out, I'd have to put her on suicide watch. It wouldn't surprise me at all at this point if she purposefully hurt herself so that I'd be forced to turn her. She's completely delusional about how great it is to be undead.

I'm nervous about tomorrow night too. I want this so badly for her, to be able to avenge herself and her family. I'm ready to destroy DeLeone myself, I'd do anything to protect my Aya, but I know how badly she wants to be the one to take off his head. I can't say that I blame her.

At the moment, I'm avoiding her. I told her that I need to focus on cleaning and organizing our weapons so Jayden's babysitting her downstairs on the deck. I can hear them chatting from our bedroom window and I feel bad for Jayden but not bad enough to go relieve them of their duties.

"I guess I just think it's interesting," I can hear her ranting in an accusatory tone, "that you think that I can't handle killing Olsen Leonard because I'm too weak, and you girls *have the ability* to make me much stronger, but you won't use that ability so really it's *you* who's making *me* too weak."

"What?" I can now hear the confusion in Jayden's voice. I should have asked Aravella to watch her, she's probably more adept than anyone I've ever met when it comes to the field of 'arguing with scorned lovers.' She probably would have refused though.

"That's not what I said!" I can hear Jayden struggling. "I didn't say you were too weak!"

"Well then please explain," Aya is raising her voice now. "Why is it that you're so sure that I can't kill Olsen."

"I don't think you couldn't, I think you wouldn't."

Uh oh, wrong move Jayden.

"What the hell do you mean I wouldn't?"

"Aya," Jayden is pleading now, "you're not a killer. You're a good person, I can tell. Believe me, you don't want to be a killer."

"Don't tell me what I want!" Aya shrieks back. "You have no idea what this, *this thing* did to me. Did you know that he ate my parents and my little brother in front of me? Not drained, Jayden, *ate*. I watched him tear off pieces of my little six year old brother with his teeth, while my brother was still alive and conscious."

"I'm sorry."

"Oh and that was only the beginning. It didn't end there, oh no. It went on and on and on, he kept me locked in a concrete cell where I turned into the kind of person who prayed that my own sister would get raped just so it didn't have to be me!"

"I'm not arguing with you, Aya. We all agree that this guy has to go. I just don't think that you should do it."

"Why not?"

"Like I said, you're not a killer. Don't do this to yourself."

"I am a killer. I'm going to kill Olsen Leonard."

"You're not like us."

"Make me like you! I want to be like you."

"No, Aya, you don't. It's not just our nature now. All four of us were terrible people *before* we turned. We're more efficient killers now, but we were always killers."

"What? No you weren't. Elodie wasn't some kind of a psycho killer before she was turned."

"Elodie was an assassin for the mafia."

"Bullshit. She was sold as a child."

"And then raised in an organized crime family where she learned how to kill people for money. That was the entire point of turning her, to make her an even *more* efficient killing machine."

"That can't be right."

"Ask her."

"But she was only killing evil people."

"Yeah," Jayden laughs, "like people who borrowed money and then couldn't pay it back. Real evil."

I have to stop this before it gets even worse. I was never dishonest with Aya about my past... but I can't truly say that I gave her the whole story either.

Everything Jayden is saying is true.

Sonny was a much older immortal but he was also the head of an organized crime family that was, largely, human. He adopted me as his heir after his distant blood relatives — the ones who expected this honor — betrayed him to another family. I was raised to kill and, though I don't think I ever killed anyone who didn't deserve it, I never verified any of my hits myself. I only did what I was told.

"Aya?"

By the time I get downstairs she's stormed off.

"I'm sorry Elodie, I thought she knew. I didn't know that you were keeping it to yourself. It wasn't my place to tell her."

"It's not your fault. I should have explained everything to her crystal-clear. I guess I just liked the way she was so sure that I was inherently good. I didn't want to say anything that would make her hate me."

"Dude, I just don't think this is a good idea. Aya is a sweet girl and she's been through a lot. Is it really fair to put her through this too? Even if she thinks that's what she wants? She doesn't know what she's getting into. How do you know that this isn't just going to fuck her up even more?"

I take a deep breath and run my fingers through my hair. "Yeah, I know. Actually I don't know. I think she needs this. She definitely really wants it—"

"She *thinks* that she wants it. But she can't know what it's really like. And it's not like the kind of thing you can just take back if it turns out to be a big mistake."

"I know but I also can't keep this from her. It's not my right."

"It wasn't your right to take her either."

Jayden's correct, of course, but I don't want to have this conversation with them. Hell, I don't even want to have this conversation with myself. My jaw clenches and I stare into the nondescript backyard.

"You see which way she went?"

Jayden just indicates back inside the house.

"Look dude, I really am sorry."

"Don't worry about it. I'll talk to her."

They follow me back inside the house, hopefully not because they think that the three of us are about to have a little conversation together. I appreciate that Jayden has a point but I don't want to make this a group discussion.

It's been hard enough to convince Adrienne to let me help Aya with this execution without Jayden and Aravella throwing in their two cents. I have no doubt in my mind that Aya would be perfectly willing to argue with all three of them until they were absolutely convinced that she was unhinged and incapable of following instructions, using common sense, or maintaining any regard for her own personal well-being at all.

"Fuck," Jayden sees it before I do.

The fucking front door is open. I don't know who left it like that, possibly me because I was so sure that Aya wouldn't try to run again, but there it is, gaping open onto the street. Aya is gone and I have no idea where she thinks she's heading. *She* probably has no idea where she's heading.

The only thing that I know for sure is that she's not safe out there, and as long as she's gone no one else I care about is safe either. If Adrienne and Aravella find out that she ran they'll surely want to hunt her down and end all this.

I have to find her before they find out about this. I'll do anything to protect my Aya, even if that now means protecting her from my own sisters, my only family in this world.

"Aya!" I call, and Jayden and I are both already running to the door.

We get there just in time to see her lifeless body being dragged into the back seat of a huge black SUV, just like the one that we rented.

CHAPTER FOURTEEN

AYA LACHAT

I'm so stupid.

So fucking stupid.

Of course she's a fucking liar. She's a stalker, a kidnapper, and a murderer. She's an actual living monster. Why wouldn't she be a liar too?

It would be weirder if she wasn't.

I just don't get *why* she had to lie to me about her past. I mean, it's not like I was really laboring under any delusions regarding what a nice girl she was. She spent years stalking me, disrespecting my privacy, manipulating my life behind the scenes, and giving me *just* enough evidence of her existence to make me think that I was losing my mind. Then she murdered a man in front of me with her bare hands and abducted me, kept me locked in a freaky dollhouse maximum security version of my home, and came just to the brink of sexually assaulting me over and over without crossing that line.

Maybe that was part of her game. Maybe she wanted to manipulate me into thinking that it was *me* who wanted *her* so bad.

So now I get to be in the position of feeling like I'm so mentally ill that I threw myself at the predator who destroyed my life. The *second* predator who destroyed my life.

Ugh, I can't believe that I let her convince me that she's a victim of circumstance, just like me. I was so in love with her story, the poor little lost girl who grew into an avenging angel. I wanted to be just like her.

Well, you know what? I am going to be like her. I'm going to be more like her than she and her stupid sisters ever imagined was possible. After I kill Olsen maybe I won't stop there. Maybe I'll kill them all. Hunt down every single immortal walking the Earth and destroy them all. Stop them from ever hurting another person.

I storm right out the unlocked front door, out into the cool night air of D.C. I don't know where I'm going, but I'm definitely going somewhere. I'm not going to stay another minute in that house with my fucking Mafia girlfriend and her little mean girl sorority of assholes.

The townhouse Elodie rented is in a ritzy part of town with a lot of large, meticulously kept properties that probably cost more than I could get for selling my organs on the black market. The street is spacious and brightly lit and lined with perfectly manicured old-growth oak trees but that doesn't stop me from charging directly into another pedestrian out walking his small dog.

"Excuse me," I try to walk around him. "I'm sorry."

The little dog, a Papillon, jumps up on his hind legs and scatters a pattern of dusty white paw prints across the knees of my leggings. I'd ordinarily reach down to pet him but I'm in a hurry. I want to get as much distance as possible in between me and the house before Elodie figures out that I left.

"Victor," the man barks. "Victor, get down. My goodness, I'm sorry. Oh no, he's hurt you? Let me take a look."

"What?" I have no idea what this man is talking about. I don't think a dog this little could even hurt me if he wanted to, which he doesn't seem to anyways.

"You're crying. Are you afraid of dogs? Don't worry, he doesn't bite."

"No, I'm fine, sorry, excuse me." I try to get around the guy but he's just not letting me pass. Now I'm annoyed, first because I don't have time for this nonsense, and second because I just got caught crying in public. I hate it when people feel sorry for me, it always seems to make whatever's going on seem even worse.

"Let's get you cleaned up."

He starts to dust off the paw prints on my leggings despite my protests and I catch a scent that I haven't smelled in a very, very long time.

It's roses and rotten flesh.

First I'm seeing Nala and now I'm smelling Olsen. This can't be him though. The Olsen I remember is much, much bigger than this guy. This guy is just weird and trying to be helpful. Elodie has driven me completely insane.

"Excuse me," I try to get around him one last time before I retch from that odor and my frustrations. If I can't get away I'm just going to turn around and go the other direction, I don't care how strange and crazy I seem at this point.

"I can't just leave you out here like this," the man keeps apologizing for his little dog that didn't even do anything.

"I'm fine, really."

"You're crying."

"I'm fine. I just need to get going."

"It's dangerous out here, young lady. I know that these houses look nice but these streets are actually filled with predators. They're attracted to all these beautiful things. They like to take them and destroy them. I can't just leave you out here, helpless and alone."

"Sir, I'm fine."

Now I'm really trying to get away but the man's gripped my upper arm and isn't letting go. He's shockingly strong for such a small man and my instincts are telling me that I'm suddenly in a lot more trouble than I thought. I struggle and before I can get a scream out he's stuffing a rag in my mouth with a sickly sweet, chemical taste. My legs kick out from under me and the man has his arms wrapped around me in a bear hug, holding my own arms tightly against my sides.

He's dropped the leash of his little dog, who is following obediently behind us as the man pulls me to the street. I'm kicking with all I've got but I'm getting drowsy and struggling to keep my vision focused.

The back door of one of the many anonymous black SUVs that lines the street opens and for a moment I just see a flash of stringy blonde hair falling in cascades over a ratty black garment. The man shoves me into the car and I land with a thud on the floor. The seats must have been removed. The back of the SUV is spacious and empty, more like the back of a van, and all of the windows are completely blacked out. There's some kind of screen or a pain of dark glass in between the front seats of the truck and the empty back.

The last thing I can remember is slamming against the side of the car as it jerks forward into the night.

My vision darkens and blurs and I lose my fight against the sleep taking over.

***

When I finally do wake up, I'm not entirely sure that I *have* woken up.

It's cold and dark, so dark that I can't see a single thing. I can feel that I'm lying on a hard surface and my head is pounding. It hurts so bad, but it's a welcome pain because that pain is the only thing that's making me pretty confident that I'm still alive.

If I was dead I wouldn't be in so much agony. At least I hope I wouldn't.

My eyes are open but they might as well be closed. The only reason that I'm sure that they're open is that I can feel them drying out in the cold, arid air. I blink and take in a deep breath. The air is chill and there's no flow at all, aside from the little disturbance I create when I exhale. Am I underground?

I reach my hand out and pat the surface where I'm lying. I think it's concrete.

Next I reach around my body. I'm not restrained in any way, not tied at my hands or feet, so I can sit up and feel my way around.

Unfortunately there's not much to feel. I'm in a small space, maybe three meters by three meters by three meters. The material is exactly the same on the floor, the ceiling, and every wall. I can't find a seam anywhere, like this box has been poured into a mold rather than assembled by pieces.

Where the fuck is the door?

My mind is spinning and I'm panicking. I know, logically, that there must be an opening somewhere, because someone somehow got me in here. That thought isn't comforting me though.

I can't see anything, I can't hear anything, and I'm increasingly feeling like I can't breathe.

All of my training with Elodie has gone out of the proverbial window. I no longer feel like I can fight Olsen; I don't even feel confident that I'll survive this panic attack I'm having.

I have no way of telling where I am but my imagination keeps trying to tell me that I've been sealed alive in a tomb and I'm not ever getting out.

One of these psychotic assholes won, and I didn't even get the chance to try and fight.

I guess I always knew how this would end.

HOUSE OF GLASS:
TEMPERED

CHAPTER ONE

AYA LACHAT

I have no way to measure time.

It's always dark and nothing ever changes. Well, that's not quite true. There are no changes to my space. There are plenty of changes to my body.

I'm starving and the only thing I've had to drink is the salt water of the tears that I was able to catch falling down my cheeks. I don't know who locked me in here, but that person hasn't provided me with any of life's necessities. I haven't had food, water, a blanket, or a place to relieve myself.

At least I know that this room must have ventilation coming from somewhere. This I'm pretty sure of because I haven't suffocated yet. If this room really was completely encased in concrete, I wouldn't keep waking up.

I also know that it must be pretty well ventilated despite the lack of air flow because I've chosen one corner to pee and

I've had to go a couple times but the ammonia scent in the air is only faint.

I haven't completely resigned to my fate.

Sometimes when I'm feeling manic I search the room. I'm looking for a door that I could have missed or wherever this fresh air is coming from. I take off one boot and put it in the corner that I've designated as my sleeping corner so I know where I started and I work over the floor and the wall with my fingers. I know I've felt every square centimeter over and over and over, gliding my fingers over the concrete just in care whatever difference there might be in the surface is barely perceptible.

So far I haven't been able to find anything at all, which is leading me to believe that there must be something up on the ceiling. Which I can't reach.

Not because I haven't been trying. When I'm fueled by rage and feeling ambitious, I try jumping so that I can feel what's up there. I jump and jump and sometimes try to get higher by kicking off the wall like I'm doing Parkour. Which, of course, doesn't work at all.

That's how things go on good days, anyhow. Days when my determination to survive is renewed and I've got the energy and motivation to try to improve my circumstances. On these days I give myself little pep talks and try to organize my thoughts. I tell myself that if there's a way in, there must be a way out. I fuel my searches and my jumps with my hatred.

Unfortunately, the longer I go without food, the fewer and farther between those good days grow.

My stomach is eating itself from the inside out.

I can't actually tell how many literal days I've been in what I've come to think of as my tomb, but I know that it must be several because I've been hungry before but never like this. My teeth are covered with a kind of sickly sweet film and I'm constantly disoriented. I don't need to relieve myself anymore because I have nothing to relieve. My jaw aches and when I do get up, I have to take frequent rest breaks now.

Most of my bad days are spent sleeping. My body is shutting down and sleep is the only thing that relieves my pain. It passes time and keeps my mind from racing.

I'm afraid that I'm losing it. Sometimes, when I can't drift off to sleep, I begin to suspect that I'm actually dead. That this is what death is if you're not immortal - just nothingness, or a kind of vague awareness of your own physical suffering but no relief.

I also obsess over trying to figure out who is responsible for my current condition. Elodie, for sure. I'm not sure that she's keeping me here, but I'm also not sure that it's not her. Maybe she had this place ready for me all along, in case I tried to run. Just like she had the other, nicer house ready for me.

I mostly blame her for putting me in this predicament, though. If she hadn't pulled me from my life I wouldn't be here. I'd still be safe at home. I also wouldn't be here if I hadn't had to find out from someone else that she lied about who she was.

I've got a lot of time on my hands, and I spend a lot of that time indicting Elodie.

Not all of it though. Sometimes I'm sure that it's Olsen. I've spent my entire life preparing for the day when he came back for me, but the man who grabbed me on the street wasn't the man in my memories. I guess it's possible that Olsen has people working for him, or possibly an entire coven that I didn't know about, just like Elodie.

At other times I wonder if it wasn't a third completely random fucking psycho. I don't see why not; it was random that I encountered both Olsen and Elodie. Maybe the entire world is populated by undead men and women who are just around every corner, waiting to annihilate everything you've ever had just for their own personal entertainment.

Just when I've made peace with the fact that my life is over, everything changes again. I wake up and I'm immediately blinded. I have to squint my eyes closed because I'm no longer in the dark.

It takes several moments for my vision to adjust, but when it does I'm knocked in the gut. I'm no longer in my tomb. Instead, I'm back in the same room where Olsen kept me for months.

So now I have died, and apparently I went to hell. I'm not sure what I did to deserve this, but here I am.

"You're not dead," a voice says, one that I recognize, and I wonder if Olsen can read my mind. Why not? He has all kinds of other supernatural abilities that I didn't know about.

"Not yet at least," he continues, and I realize that he's still talking to me. "Here. Have some water."

I glance to the nightstand he's indicating and there is indeed a huge glass of ice water waiting for me, beads of condensation dotting the outside of the glass. It's so appealing that it looks unreal. I hesitate.

"What, are you afraid that after all that I've decided to poison you? Absurd. Suit yourself though. You can lead a horse to water and all that."

I do believe that Olsen is sick enough to trick me into poisoning myself after all that, but I'm also at the point where I don't actually care if this water kills me. I take a small sip at first, only because I'm afraid that if I gulp I'll just immediately throw it back up. The water tastes so sweet, it's like a magic salve on my lips and tongue. Olsen waits patiently as I drink my fill, slowly. My stomach feels bloated and sore, probably because it's shrunk over the past… however long.

"I didn't think I'd ever see you again," Olsen starts once I set the glass down. "How've you been? God, it's been, what? Five years? Longer? Time flies."

I glance up at him and wonder if he's being serious right now. It's him, the guy walking the dog on the sidewalk, and I can't believe that I've spent the last several years of my life living in terror of *this* guy.

He's just so much smaller than I remember him being. It must be that I've grown. I'm lying in a metal framed twin bed across from a wispy looking man who can't be any more than 5'6" tall.

He's absolutely nothing like Elodie and her sisters. Olsen can best be described as nondescript. He's small, he has a weak jaw, and he's got lank, dishwater colored hair. There's nothing at all remarkable about him. Maybe that's part of the reason I didn't recognize him.

Just when I begin to feel foolish for feeling so afraid of him, he reminds me that's he's not as harmless as he looks. He raises some kind of stick with two prongs on the end and applies it to my outer thigh, sending me jumping.

A cattle prod.

"Aya, I asked you a question," he says calmly, lowering the stick. "I wouldn't try me if I were you, not in your condition. I don't know how much more stress your heart can take. Now, what's the matter? You don't want to catch up? Then why were you looking for me? I didn't even know it was you until you just showed up here in D.C., with no invitation, how gauche. I knew that someone was looking for me, I monitor my online accounts, but I wasn't expecting you until you showed up here with those vigilante dykes. I never expected to see you again, you left in such a hurry the last time."

"I'm here to kill you," I'd like to smack that smarmy little smirk right off his face.

"Aya," Olsen recoils and places his hand over his heart, or I guess the place where his heart would be if he had one. "No! After all I've done for you? Well, you failed. Sorry. Can't help you with that. But I can offer you a little family reunion. Kitten!"

The door opens and the entity that I thought I had hallucinated before steps in. Long, scraggly blonde hair, and a ratty black lace dress. The only skin I can see is stretched over her skeletal white hands. She closes the door behinds her and lifts her veil and I pass out.

CHAPTER TWO

ELODIE GLASS

"Check the floorboards, he might have a cellar."

"I've already been in the cellar. There's nothing down there but wine."

"Well check for an even deeper cellar! There must be something! Where does this guy slumber?"

I know that I shouldn't take out my anxiety and frustrations on Adrienne but I'm frantic. We've broken into Olsen Leonard's townhouse and we've been ransacking it for the past two hours. Aravella is at his office downtown and Jayden is on the case online, trying to figure out where else he may have taken Aya.

"Sis, it looks like it's been a long time since anyone has been here," Adrienne drags a fingertip across the top of a shiny, well-polished dresser, revealing a thick layer of dust. "Are you sure that this is where he was living?"

"That's what Jayden found online," I run my hands through my hair in frustration. "But you're right. Looks like he hasn't been around here in a while."

Adrienne checks a window. "Look," she indicates the top of the frame. "Shutters. He could just have been sleeping in that bed."

This house is weird. It has a master bedroom that has a full-on, kitschy, red velvet, old school Dracula-style vibe. There's a huge four poster bed with velvet bedding and a canopy, plus a lot of heavy mahogany furniture. It even has candelabras with real candles.

Then there is another bedroom that's just a bare, stained mattress on the floor, plus a closet full of raggedy looking granny dresses.

"You think he meant to keep her in here?" I asked Adrienne about the sad-girl bedroom, which is a name she made up.

"I thought so, but look," she shows me the door. "No lock."

"Hmm." It is strange. "I'm just gonna go through one more time, see if we missed anything. Can you go through the office again, see if you can find any papers or info about other properties?"

"Yeah, El, I'll look but I think we'd be better off checking in with Jayden at this point. There's nothing here. It's like the place was abandoned."

"Can you please just look?"

"Hey, you don't need to get snippy. I know you're worried, girl. But don't forget, your lady Aya isn't completely helpless. She's a trained killer now; you trained her yourself."

"Not for this! There's no way she can face him at a disadvantage like this. You didn't see her; he had her out cold. All of her training is based on the assumption that she'd have the element of surprise! And that we'd be there with her! But we're not. I've failed her. She's alone and God only knows what he's doing to her."

Adrienne tries to comfort me but she knows that I'm right. Problem is, I know she's right too. There's nothing in this house.

Our best bet is to reconvene at the townhouse and see what Aravella and Jayden have for us. I'm hoping that one of them was able to at least find our next step, another address or lead.

"Maybe it wasn't him," Aravella suggests when Adrienne explains that the house seems to have been empty for a long time. "I mean, it could have been a complete stranger, someone out looking for a vulnerable young woman. We encounter these types of guys all the time; it's our job. Guys out looking for a woman to rob or rape. You saw her get pulled into a car with no plates, right?"

"Jesus, Aravella, that's worse. If it was *another* predator then we have absolutely no leads at all. We'll never find her in time. Christ she's probably getting raped right now—"

"It was him," Jayden interrupts me before I go completely off the rails panicking about what's currently happening to Aya. "I'm pretty sure."

"How do you know?" I demand, my voice sharper, more accusatory than I intended.

"I've hacked DeLeone's file in the Department of Defense databases."

"What?"

"He's in the DOD database."

"I don't know what that is."

"The Department of Defense?"

"I know what that is, Jesus Jayden I'm not senile, I mean why would they have a database with him in it and what kind of information did it have?"

"Well they keep records on all their employees and contractors."

"Employees? I thought this guy was lobbying for the automotive industry."

"He is. But apparently all those factories are making more than just cars. He's also selling military grade weapons. Some real crazy shit that isn't even available to the public. Experimental stuff."

"Shit. So you got another address?"

"Yes. A few actually. I also learned that before he was lobbying he was contracted by the National Security Administration in Computer Cryptography. This guy is older than you but he's more plugged in than me. He definitely knew that we were looking for him. He's got the skills and resources to tell whenever anyone searches him out online. He probably knew that Aya was coming for him."

"But how is that possible?"

"He's probably got notifications sent to him whenever anyone conducts a search for him or requests information on him. I'm sorry man, I should have caught some sign of his safeguards. I just wasn't expecting him to be so technologically adept. I guess I thought that I was looking for an older creature. I wasn't imagining that he could be older than you guys but more up to date on tech than I am myself."

Jayden is clearly feeling guilty but it's really not their fault. I also had no idea that this DeLeone was some kind of plugged in computer genius. Usually the older we are, the slower we are to adopt new technologies. Aravella would definitely not be carrying a phone at all if Adrienne hadn't practically forced her, and I myself generally have very little interest when Jayden tries to explain the mechanics of how their research and work functions.

"It's not your fault, dude, this guy… I've just underestimated him."

I can only hope that my own mistakes won't cost Aya her life.

"Hey babe," Adrienne pats me on the back and I appreciate the gesture but I really don't have the patience for a pep talk right now. "We'll find her. The more I hear about this guy, the more sure I am that you were right. We need to stop him. We'll do it, and we'll get her back. She's still alive, right?"

I glance up at Adrienne.

So she knows.

She knows that I've been letting Aya feed off of me and I can tell that she's alive and she's suffering. That I feel pain when she feels pain. I haven't let her feed enough to turn her but I have fed her more than enough to form a permanent bond. Just not strong enough of a bond to tell where she is right now.

"Yeah," I reply quietly. "She's still alive. Barely."

"Then we better act fast," Adrienne gives me a sad smile. "But it's dawn. We'll head out tomorrow."

I excuse myself to the room I was sharing with Aya and close the door behind me.

Her things are still scattered about the room. She's a chaotic traveller, I've learned. All of her assorted shirts and pants are unpacked from her suitcase but placed, folded, all around the room, covering every single surface. I finger the hem of the shirt she was wearing when we went to the museum. It's a soft black T-shirt, plain, and it still smells like her.

Then I remember what she was wearing when she disappeared, another black T and her old leggings. My stomach clenches when I realize that she's probably still wearing those clothes, if she's wearing anything at all.

I know that Olsen isn't taking care of her. I know that she's got a dull, consistent pain and I can tell that it's either from hunger or from some other ongoing physical discomfort like exhaustion or the lingering effects of an injury. I know that if she gets much weaker, she won't ever make a full recovery.

Now I know how she feels, though, not just physically but also emotionally. I don't think that I'll be able to let her kill DeLeone anymore, even though I promised. I don't think that will be possible because now I need to do it myself. I've never hated anyone or anything like this before, but now that this kind of hatred has taken hold of me it's consumed me like a wildfire.

I want to see this son of a bitch suffer.

For the time being, though, there's only one thing that I can do to relieve the rage that's bubbling under my skin.

I sit down in the shower and I draw Aya's dagger across my breast. I cut deep, even though I know that I ought to save some of my strength. I have to bleed like this; otherwise I won't be able to control myself any longer.

I tell myself that I should just take Jayden's info and leave, go out and face The Grief if that's what I need to do to save Aya.

Instead I watch as my own blood spins in futility down the drain.

CHAPTER THREE

AYA LACHAT

I wake up in the iron bed and my eye immediately goes to the chair where I last saw Olsen sitting.

He's gone, but I'm in for an even deeper shock.

It's Nala.

It's really her.

It doesn't look much like the Nala that I knew, but it's definitely Nala.

She's not wearing her black lace anymore, some time must have passed while I was out. Now she's in a dingy white dress. It's got long sleeves and a boat neckline and I think if she stood it would be about tea length. It kind of looks like something that a working class teenager might have gotten married in back in the 1950s. Judging by the condition of the dress, it might actually be that old.

It's not the dress that's shocking me though. The dress is hanging on her grey, skeletal frame. She's so, so thin and her skin is dull and papery. I can see bruises all over her and her cheekbones are jutting out from her face, which looks like it has aged forty years.

Her face.

I can see why she wears a veil when she leaves the house. The veil is less conspicuous than what's become of her poor face. She's got a long, dark purple scar that runs up the entire length of the left side of it. I don't know what could have happened to her, but whatever happened took her left eye. She's got an empty socket now. She's also missing all four of her canine teeth and I can still see the scar from where Olsen cut her neck when I ran away.

"Go ahead and stare," she hisses at me. "You like what you see? You did this to me."

I'm stunned silent for a moment. Nala's other lifeless eye has a vacant stare and I guess that I had assumed from her behavior and general demeanor that she was no longer mentally present. I assumed wrong, apparently, because now her one glassy grey eye is focused on me.

"Why did you come back?"

"Nala," I don't quite know what to say. I'm trying not to stare at her disfigurement but I haven't seen my sister in so long. I didn't think that it was possible that I'd ever see her again. She was dead, I was sure.

"Why did you come back?" she demands, louder this time. She's gripping the arm rests of the chair where she sits and she's started rocking back and forth, first slowly and then with increasing violence.

"Why did you come back?" she screeches, rocking hard back and forth, grasping the chair so hard that her fingertips have started to bleed.

"Nala what happened?" I beg. I don't have the wherewithal to figure out what to say to her, how to calm her. I'm so disoriented, both from my own physical ordeal and with being confronted by the fact that I abandoned my sister to… whatever this is.

And I never tried to help her.

"Why did you come back?" she's shrieking, over and over now, not even pausing to give me the chance to respond if I did somehow gather my senses and come up with an explanation.

The door opens and Olsen steps in. He puts a single finger to his lips and she's silent immediately. She resumes her still posture and her vacant stare.

The control that he clearly has over her makes me even more sick than her behavior and appearance. I can just guess what he had to put her through in order to get her to that state.

"Aya," Olsen clucks at me in admonishment, "you've upset your sister, you nasty girl. Nala is *very* sensitive. Of course she is. You don't develop a talent like hers if you aren't sensitive. But what would you know about that? You always were crass and dull. Nothing like my Kitten."

Olsen strokes Nala's chin and she doesn't respond at all, not even to glance up at him. It's like whatever spirit had possessed her just a moment ago has completely left her body.

"How is it possible?" I finally ask, "that Nala is here?"

I know how stupid that question sounds even as it's parting from my lips, but I have to know.

"Silly girl," Olsen grins at me. "I'd never give up my most prized possession. It's not every day that I find something like Nala. Nala is one of my treasures. I'll never let her go."

With that he gestures to the door and Nala scampers away, her head hung low and her dirty bare feet moving fast. Her stringy blonde hair reaches her hips and swings around her as she leaves us. I wonder if Olsen has this entire place locked down just like Elodie's house was, or whether he has Nala so well trained now that he's not afraid that she will just walk out the front door.

"Please don't upset Kitten," Olsen turns his attention completely to me now, as though I'm the person responsible for whatever has happened to my sister. "Every little distraction affects her work. And we wouldn't want to interfere with her talents, now would we? Speaking of which, have you developed any talents, or are you still completely useless like you were the last time we saw one another?"

"I can kill you about a hundred different ways now," I growl back. I actually don't feel like I could even stand up without shaking right now, but my desire to destroy Olsen slowly and painfully has returned with a vengeance.

"Oh my," Olsen pretends to clutch his pearls again. "Well I guess that just means that I'd better make sure you're secure. I wouldn't want you to… what? Can you even get out of that bed without help? What are you going to do, hurt my feelings so bad that I just wither up and die?"

Olsen's laughing at me now and I swear to God that I'm going to make him eat his words.

I have no other reason to continue living. I've lost Elodie, I never had much to start with, and I'm pretty sure that I'm not going to survive this event anyway.

I'll be damned if I don't take him down with me.

"How did Nala survive having her throat cut?" I ask. I may as well find out what the hell happened since I'm stuck here.

"She didn't."

"What?"

"You can't tell? She didn't survive. But it doesn't matter. I improved her. She was born gifted but she wasn't truly able to unlock those gifts until I gave her my gift."

"No," I cry quietly.

"You can't stand it, can you? You thought that you'd gotten rid of your perfect sister for good, but here she is, back again, better than she ever was. Better than you'll ever be."

"How is it possible? She's so weak?"

"Why don't you come see," Olsen springs from his chair and has me by the upper arm.

He drags me out of my cell, through a massive house which I don't think is the same one as the one he held us in before, and into a conservatory. The rooms are lined with towering walls full of books, an entire library's worth, and in the center stands a concert piano. Olsen drags me to a pair of chairs, one of which already has chains waiting.

I don't have the strength to fight him as he wraps them around me. Then he whistles like he's calling a dog and Nala comes running, barefoot in her ugly white dress. She knows to take her seat at the piano. Olsen takes his place directly behind her and she starts playing.

I listen to her music and it's breaking my heart. Nala's haunting notes are nothing like the joyful music that she used to play at home. It's almost like she's figured out how to make the piano weep and wail. The music is beautiful but it's also terrible, almost unbearable to me.

Then I notice. Olsen is standing behind her, cutting her. He's dragged a long fingernail across her neck and she's bleeding. She seems to be lost in some kind of reverie or state of bliss, maybe from her playing or maybe because the bloodletting does something to her. Just like Elodie.

I watch as Olsen laps up the blood that's dripping from her and she doesn't miss a note. He drinks from her as she calmly finishes her piece, then sits and allows him to drain what little energy she has.

The sight is too much for me. My stomach rumbles and I vomit bile all over myself and the carpet in front of me.

"You filthy, stinking pig!" Olsen immediately thunders over to me, seeming much bigger than before. Big like he seemed when I was a child. "How dare you?"

He takes one of the ends of the chain that has me fixed to the chair and uses it to whip me until I lose consciousness.

CHAPTER FOUR

ELODIE GLASS

"So this is what I have," Jayden spreads a huge paper map open across the dining room table.

Night's fallen and the four of us are standing around the dimly lit room, already dressed to roll out though we don't know where to start. Days have passed since Aya was lost to me and I know that she's still alive. Better than alive. Over the past twenty four hours her condition seems to have improved, both mental and physical. She must have access to food and water now and I'm feeling better about her chances for survival.

I just need to find her as soon as possible. I'm afraid that the butcher who stole her could be fattening her for slaughter.

"Here," Jayden puts a red flag sticker on the map, "is the townhouse in D.C. You guys have already checked that out and it's clear?"

"Yeah," Adrienne answers for me. "Looks like whoever lived there hasn't been around in at least a month. It's well kept but there was a layer of dust over everything. No footprints but ours, so no one has been there since it settled."

"And what about the office?" Jayden puts another red flag on the map, close to the first flag.

"It's empty," Aravella replies. "I was able to find his ledgers but they're all standard business transactions, nothing unusual or interesting. He's paying off every politician in congress, it seems, but I guess they all are. That's what lobbyists do. Nothing to indicate that he's also into kidnapping women."

"Alright," Jayden puts another flag on the map. "Moving on. Here's the mansion back home. That's where he had Aya the first time he captured her. I guess there's a chance that he brought her back home? I don't think it's likely though, since he knows that someone is on his tail."

"Yeah that wouldn't make much sense," I agree. "What else have you got?"

"Well, here," Jayden puts another flag on the map, this time in upstate New York, "he's got a lake house. Seems he usually uses it to entertain senators who are playing hard to get. And here," they add another flag down in Palm Beach Island, "he's got a beach house. God only knows what a guy like that needs with a beach house but here we are. The place is huge and it's a recent purchase, so this one I think has potential."

"Is that it?" I ask, feeling like we're missing a few pieces.

"No," Jayden shakes their head and widens their eyes. "No, we've got more. Now we get to the interesting stuff. Here," they add a flag, "is his factory. It's near his home, it's huge, it's loud, there are probably lots of places where he could have secret rooms that no one ever enters. I think the factory has a lot of potential if he's keeping her in a dungeon-type scenario."

I cringe and grind my teeth. Jayden's right. An old car factory — one that Jay already discovered is possibly producing top secret military grade weapons — would be the perfect place to stash a victim. Especially one that you wanted to keep around for a while, so you could toy with her while you drew out your sadistic fantasies.

"But get this," Jayden continues. "This is interesting too. I was able to find an offshore company registered to an Orrick DeLeone. This guy is supposedly a nephew of our guy, but I wasn't able to find any other proof that Orrick ever existed. He has no job record, no personal property or bank accounts, no legal records of any kind. I'm not one hundred percent sure about this connection, but this company owns a huge estate outside of D.C. So this one's a maybe. But — and here's where it gets interesting — the company also owns a private jet that made a flight this past week from Dulles down to Palm Beach International, according to flight records."

"Hmm," I'm looking over everything Jayden collected. We seem to have gone from having no leads to having too many leads. "Is that everything?"

"Everything so far. I can't promise you that this is a comprehensive list if this guy's got fake companies and fake identities everywhere, but it's a start."

"Thanks for finding all this, Jay, this is amazing work. I'd be lost right now without you." It's true. I really do appreciate Jayden's work. I know that they still feel guilty about what happened to Aya, so I want to reassure them that I'm not holding any grudge. None of it was their fault and I know that they tend to be hard on themself.

"No problem, dude, I wish I could have gotten more intel about his movements but he's very good at covering up his tracks online. It was only through sheer luck that I was able to dig up that offshore thing. All of this stuff, the businesses, the properties, the plane; it was all registered through the same disbarred attorney. That's the only connection I found."

"So where do we start?" Aravella asks, her eyes drifting over the now mocked up map. "I think Florida or the factory."

"If we start at the factory we can do the original house at the same time," Adrienne suggests. "On the one hand, if he wants to avoid a confrontation with us he'll probably stay away from the most obvious place to look. On the other, that's his den, where he'll be at his most powerful. So I think that still has potential as a location for her."

"But that flight," Jayden looks uncertain. "It's just too big of a coincidence, I think. And if he's down in Florida with the jet that means that he can make a fast getaway if we waste any time."

"We could split up," Aravella suggests, her voice laden with obvious uncertainty.

"I don't think that's a good idea," Adrienne counters right away. "Not with this guy. I agree that we need to take him down and hopefully we can find the girl alive but I don't want to lose any of my girls. This is a job that is going to take all four of us. I mean, Jayden says he's into some secret weapon type shit. We don't even know for sure what kind of fight we have waiting for us."

As much as I want to find Aya as fast as possible, I have to agree with Adrienne. I don't just want to track Aya, I want to rescue her, not get defeated by her abductor in front of her. This DeLeone is seeming more and more like a bigger threat than we anticipated. I need my sisters for this job.

"I'm gonna leave this up to you," Adrienne looks up at me. "She's your girl. What do you say?"

I take a deep breath and look over the map. I honestly have no idea. I don't feel truly confident about any of these places. None of them is really speaking to me.

Now I find myself wishing that I had given Aya what she wanted. If I had turned her, none of this would have happened. She'd be safe now, and if DeLeone *had* managed to grab her, I'd have a deep enough connection to her to be able to track her down.

I wish that I would have listened to her about what she wanted. Why did I think that I knew what was better for her than she herself knew? I also wish that I would have told her the complete truth about myself. If I had been honest with her about everything, who knows where we'd both be right now. Certainly not here.

I don't really have time to feel sorry for myself though. Not right now.

"Florida," I say with conviction that I don't actually feel, tapping my finger on the red flag on the map. "Let's follow that plane. See what he's got down there."

"Alright, I'll find us a flight," Jayden offers.

We don't need tickets. We can travel in our incorporeal forms short distances, so it's easy for us to get onto even private or cargo flights undetected if we aren't traveling with baggage. We just dissolve into smoke and drift. That's why none of my sisters took the flight I was on with Aya. It's easier for us to travel outside of our bodies. Plus that means that we won't appear on any passenger manifests.

It doesn't take Jayden more than a few minutes to track down a FedEx plane that's traveling from D.C. to Miami tonight. We just need to get ourselves to the airport immediately if we want to catch it. Then we'll be there in under three hours.

It's technically still possible that I recover Aya tonight, if we get lucky and find her in that house in Palm Beach. I just wish that I felt that it was likely.

CHAPTER FIVE

AYA LACHAT

"**S**tay still."

My eyes open and I can see my sister — or, rather, what remains of my sister — dabbing at my nose and then sucking the blood she collects off of the tip of her finger.

"I have to clean this up so that you don't suffocate on your blood," she explains, though she's lapping it up like she's been allowed to lick the frosting from the hand mixer.

"Are you okay?" I ask her.

I've been wondering about her condition. None of the other vampires — including Olsen, who looks weird in his own way — look sick like her. Is she like this because this was how she looked when she was changed, or is she like this for another reason?

The question only makes her laugh though.

"That's funny, Aya," she smiles.

"Are you hungry?" I venture. I'm beginning to suspect that I might have some idea about what's wrong with her.

"Of course," she looks at me like I'm crazy. "I'm always hungry now. That's what it means to continue to live... to hunger."

"Do you need to feed?" I ask quietly. "I know what you are now," I try to explain. "I met someone like you."

"Father told me you're a thrall now," Nala nods with a sad look on her face.

"I'm not a thrall," I try to argue. I also want to tell her that Olsen is not our father, but something tells me that now is not the time to argue with her.

"Okay Aya," she agrees, like a mother trying to placate her fussy toddler.

"That's it, isn't it?" I continue prodding, setting aside the question of whether or not I'm a thrall for a moment. "You're hungry. Do you want to feed? I can let you. It will make you stronger."

"I can't," Nala replies. Then she draws back her lips and shows me her teeth, what's left of them. She's got four gaping holes in her mouth where her canines used to be.

"What happened?" I ask, though I think I know.

"I got too upset," Nala looks forlorn. "Father had to take them to help me calm down. Now I'm feeling much better."

"Are you starving?"

"We all starve."

"You can't eat?"

"That's silly. I wouldn't be here talking to you if I didn't eat. Father feeds me. He knows what is best for me. If I eat too much, I get upset and make bad decisions. Then I get in big trouble. So he measures my portions for me and gives me just the right amount to help me stay calm."

I have somehow found myself in the position of being disgusted when my own undead sister tells me that she does *not* eat other human beings.

I'm not only disgusted, though. I'm also cautiously optimistic. Up until this moment, I was laboring under the impression that Olsen's control over my sister was entirely psychological. Now, though, I've got hope.

"What kind of bad decisions were you making?" I ask nonchalantly, as though I am just trying to make conversation.

"I don't remember," Nala replies absentmindedly. I'm not entirely convinced that she's telling the truth. "Really bad ones though. I had to be punished."

If Olsen is maintaining control over my sister by starving her, that means that if I can get her to eat she might still be able to resist him. Maybe she can even make a complete recovery.

"Nala, look, if you bring me something sharp I can feed you."

Nala looks up but doesn't reply.

"Do you have free run?"

"What do you mean?"

"Is he waiting just outside the door, or can you wander around the house by yourself?"

"Father allows me to be alone in the house. Sometimes he has to leave me here for a while."

"Wait, can you just leave?"

"No!" Nala looks shocked that I'd even suggest that. "I'm not allowed out alone."

"But is the door locked?"

"I don't know."

I'm not getting anywhere. I need to convince Nala to eat but she's so disoriented and easily distracted. If I was just able to cut myself, I think she'd see the blood and I'd be able to persuade her to take just a little lick. Then once she tasted it she could get a real drink. *Then* I'd be able to tell for certain whether she's still got any sanity left in there.

Unfortunately Olsen has me handcuffed to the bed. After I threw up on his carpet he nearly lost his mind with rage. He's very precious about his things, I've figured out, and nothing makes him more angry than to have one of his personal possessions damaged. And that includes Nala, apparently. The only person allowed to destroy Olsen's 'things' is Olsen.

"Nala," I try a new tack, "get me the keys to these handcuffs. I'm going to help you, but I need you to help me first."

Nala's eyes narrow, and to my utter surprise she draws back her thin right hand and slaps me across the mouth.

"How dare you?" she asks me with a sudden clarity that didn't exist just a moment ago. "How dare you ask me for help after what you did? You *left* me here. Look at what you've done to me. I owe you *nothing*. You ran away and you never looked back. You *wanted* me gone. And now here we are."

Nala sits back in her chair and a fog settles back over her face. Her muscles relax and her eye loses its focus once again. She seems to have returned to her gentle trance. I saw it though; for a moment Nala had control over her faculties. I just have to keep digging to find that Nala.

"I don't want to leave my home, Aya," she says in a quiet sing-song voice. "And soon you'll learn your place here. Either you'll learn or you'll die."

"Nala, I thought that you were dead. I didn't leave you, I swear. I saw Olsen slit your throat! We didn't know then what he could do!"

Nala flinches but she doesn't look back. She gets up, smooths out the skirt on her dress, and leaves my cell.

I don't hear a lock click behind her, but I'm not alone for very long. Olsen comes sauntering in with a big grin on his face and takes her seat, turning it around to straddle it backwards and get right in my face.

"I heard that you had some concerns about my Kitten," he purrs. "So thoughtful. You're worried that she isn't eating enough. Is it her sallow skin? It's the cheekbones, isn't it? Wow. Such a thoughtful and caring sister. Even tried to convince her to go get a knife so you could feed her."

"So it's true?" I demand, staring Olsen down from my spot on the bed. "You're starving her on purpose aren't you? So you can control her."

"Honey I don't know if you've noticed," Olsen laughs, "but your sweet sister is batshit crazy. She can't handle a full feed. Trust me, it's for her own good."

"I'm not going to trust you," my voice is dripping with scorn. "Why would I trust you?"

"You know who does trust me? Your sister. The one you abandoned. Your sister obeys with even more alacrity than my little dog. When I whistle she comes running. When I tell her to sit, she sits. She doesn't eat unless I tell her to eat. I've got her under my complete control."

"You've made her sick so she'll be compliant. She doesn't trust you."

"You think you can convince her to betray me? Go ahead. Try it. Offer her your blood. She won't take it unless I tell her to drink. But go ahead and try to break the hold I have over her. You would never understand what we have together. Your Mistress didn't find you worthy of her gift, and neither would I. You're nothing like my Kitten."

"If you're so sure that she'd remain loyal to you, then let her eat. Come on. Go ahead. Show me just how much control you have over her."

"Oh I will. I'll show you. I'll do you one better though... I'll show you how much control I have over you. Soon you'll be just as eager to obey my orders as your sister. But only if you can prove that you're worthy of my collection. You think I can't see right through you? You're desperate to be prized like Nala. Show me what you can do, Aya, and I'll keep you."

"No thanks," I scoff. "I'd rather be dead."

"You had your chance at that. You nearly were dead, Aya. Seven years ago you were so close to being culled. You didn't have a single talent; you weren't worth keeping. If you hadn't run off when you did I wouldn't have kept you around much longer. I had no reason to. This is my collection; it's not an animal shelter. I didn't harbor strays then and I won't now either. You came here claiming that you've become someone but I haven't seen any proof of that yet. Show me what you've got, Aya, if you want to keep living. Otherwise I'll just, shall we say, deaccession you."

He gets up to leave me alone with that threat but before he closes the door behind him, he leans back in for one last jab.

"Tick tock."

CHAPTER SIX

AYA LACHAT

I can't lie around here waiting in the hopes that Nala will come to her senses long enough to help me out. She might not be totally lost, but she's not all there either. And I have no idea how much time Olsen plans to give me before he decides that I'm boring and thus don't deserve to exist.

My shoulders are aching from having my wrists handcuffed to the iron bars of the bed frame over my head. I try to adjust my weigh in the bed to relieve some of the pressure on them and as soon as I move my left shoulder goes from dull ache to sharp pain. I wince but I know that things aren't going to get any easier for me as long as I'm still lying in this bed.

I crane my neck back to take a look at my restraints. The cuffs seem to be standard police issue. I try to work my wrists through them and I think I might be able to just wiggle them out. The cuffs aren't so tight that they're pressing against my skin. I spend several minutes trying to shimmy my hands out but the cuffs seem to be just tight enough to keep me in place. At least I won't be escaping without any kind of lubrication.

Then I remember.

My hair is still in the French braid that I put it in before I left the townhouse. It's messy and it probably looks like shit now, but it's still intact for the most part.

I slide my butt as far back on the bed as I can go, slowly so I don't end up making a ton of noise rattling the cuffs or the iron frame, and reach for my hair with my fingers. I can feel the grease on my scalp and I'd give anything for a hot shower. I swear to God that Olsen's little dog is probably cleaner than I am right now. I wrinkle my nose and tap my fingers on the top of my head.

Score!

I still have a bobby pin stuck in what's now probably looking very much like a rat's nest on the top of my head. I can feel it through my hair and now I'm going to be extra careful when I remove it so that I don't end up dropping it. If it slips from my hair onto the bed or behind the bed then it might as well slip into another dimension.

I feel like I'm doing a brain surgery on myself rather than just removing a hair pin. I take several deep breaths in an effort to keep my hands from shaking, but it's hard after they've been suspended over my head for so long. I shake them out a little bit to get the blood flowing to them and let them tingle before I take another deep breath and dive in.

First I run my finger gently up the length of the pin to determine which end is open. Once I'm sure, I pinch the closed end firmly between my thumb and forefinger before slowly wiggling it out.

I swear I don't even breathe until I've got that pin free from my hair, tightly gripped in my fingers. Now that I have my makeshift key, here comes the hard part. I grip the closed end of the pin in my right hand and crane my neck again so I can see the keyhole on the cuffs.

It takes me several tries to get the pin in the keyhole. It's not so easy to unlock cuffs that are on your own wrists. I have to bend my wrist at a weird angle and leverage it against the top of the bed frame.

Once I get the pin in the keyhole, though, the lock proves to be shockingly easy to unlatch. I just have to wiggle the pin around a little bit until I feel it catch on something. Then I catch it and twist.

I cannot explain how elated I am to hear that little click. There are no words for this feeling.

My hands are now free. I'm very careful to loosen them from the restraints so the handcuffs don't end up clanging against the bed or the wall, or worse, falling to the floor. I can't make a sound right now; I know that Olsen's hearing is supernatural and I don't know whether Nala can hear me too.

It feels so good to sit up straight and put my arms down by my sides. My shoulders are screaming at me now that the blood flow to them has increased and I take a moment to rub the pain out of my wrists and make big circles with my arms to stretch out.

I wish I knew where my shoes were. I take a quick peek in the nightstand and it's empty. This room doesn't have a closet or a dresser, so I guess I'm shit out of luck when it comes to footwear.

At least I'm still dressed, albeit in my T shirt and leggings that I've now been wearing for so many days that they probably need to be thrown in the garbage once I escape. Thanks to the beating Olsen gave me the night before, my shirt is crusted with blood and stuck to my drying wounds. I want to peel it off but I'm afraid that I'll open the sores and Olsen and Nala will smell the fresh blood so I stop myself.

Then I realize that I smell so bad right now that a normal human being could probably smell me from ten meters away, so there's no way that Olsen and Nala won't be able to smell me. I'll just have to hope that my scent is so strong that it's already filled the house for them. I peel the shirt off and toss it onto that God awful bed so that now I'm just wearing leggings and a black sports bra, looking like some kind of activewear ninja.

I try the door, and to my surprise it's unlocked. Olsen must have felt pretty confident in those handcuffs. I peek my head out and the coast is clear. The hallway is carpeted so it's very easy for me to move quietly along the walls. I only wish that I knew which way was out.

It's so dark in Olsen's house, partially because he likes to keep the place lit with candles. I'm moving along, looking for an exit when the idea hits me... I take one of the heavy brass candlesticks from a side table and blow out the flame. This thing probably weighs nearly ten pounds. If I run into trouble, I can use it as a weapon.

I've decided that I'm going to make a run for it, then come back with help for Nala. I'm not equipped to fight Olsen on my own like this. I keep creeping along, checking every door but they all lead to little cells identical to my own but empty.

I'm still feeling pretty optimistic when I turn a corner at the end of the hall and step into a large, brightly lit room. The room is completely empty aside from the lighting and two chairs in the center of the room. There sit Nala and Olsen with his little dog as though they were waiting for me to appear.

Olsen gives me a slow clap and stands up. I'm crouched, poised and ready with my candlestick. I didn't want to face him head on like this but I'm not going to go down without a fight.

"Nice work," Olsen gives me some kind of deranged compliment. "I like your new look. Very girl-assassin. It's hot. Oh, come on. Don't look at me like that. What's the matter? Didn't expect to see us here? What the hell were you thinking, that I just forgot to lock you in? I let you out. I wanted to see you perform."

"Fuck you."

I couldn't think of anything else to say.

"Still as vulgar as ever, I see," Olsen puts his hand on my sister's shoulder. "Anyhow, there you go. There's the door. You can leave now."

I look around the room, waiting for whatever danger I'm sure is coming. Nothing happens.

"Oh come on, don't be a coward now," Olsen whines. He marches across the room and throws the door open. It does lead outside; I can see the outlines of trees against the night sky.

"What's the catch?" I ask slowly, creeping toward the door with my back against the wall.

Olsen just grins like an ass. I'm sure this is a trap, but I'm not sure how.

"Nala, come on," I order her.

Nala sits in her seat and looks at me like I'm nuts.

"Nala, let's go! Come on!"

"I can't," Nala shakes her head "you don't understand."

"Nala, you're sick and I can help you. Come with me."

I'm nearly to the door. There it is, open in front of me. It's clear that I'm not going to be able to persuade Nala to come along. I look out at the night sky, then I look back at Nala.

I can't abandon her a second time.

"I won't go without you," I shake my head.

This sends Olsen leaping to his feet. "You think you can take her from me," he growls. "I'm everything to her. You're nothing. Worse than nothing. She'd kill you herself if I let her."

He comes at me and grabs me by my wrist. Then, to prove himself, he takes a small blade from the pocket of his shirt. He flicks it open and I shriek in agony as he uses it to take off the pinky finger on my left hand.

"There," he throws my dismembered finger on the ground. "Go get it."

The little papillon and Nala dive to the floor at the same time, but Nala beats the dog. I stare in horror as my sister roars at the dog and grabs my finger herself, devouring it like she thinks that it could be her last meal ever. It's gone in moments and she's licking off the tiny bit of blood left on her fingers.

"Now take her back to her room while I think about what to do with her," Olsen orders.

Nala does so without a word back.

I don't bother trying to reach her again.

CHAPTER SEVEN

ELODIE GLASS

I 've never been to Miami before. I guess I never really considered myself a Miami type of gal, not while I was alive and certainly not after.

The city is so hot and bright, even in the middle of the night. From the moment we drift off the FedEx plane, we're illuminated by neon lights in every color, advertising girls, booze, and fun. It probably *is* fun, if that's what you're there for.

Unfortunately for the four of us it's just humid and noisy. Everywhere we look, there are tourists coming and going, despite the late hour. There are also several planes full of passengers arriving from South America unloading at the same time. If we don't hurry, we're going to end up stuck in traffic.

We slip into the passenger arrivals terminal at the airport and set to work getting a rental car. We still have to make it up to Palm Beach Island, which is a little over an hour north. I'd like to get moving as soon as possible so that we don't end up having to find a place to spend the night before we raid DeLeone.

"Let's get a convertible," Aravella suggests while we're waiting in line at the rent-a-car.

"Let's not," Adrienne glares back.

"Come on. Why not? We need to fit in once we get to Palm Beach, right? Isn't that basically the setting for *Lifestyles of the Rich and Famous*? We *need* an ostentatious ride if we're going to blend in there."

She has a point, I think, but we don't know how much DeLeone knows about any of us. Would he recognize us on sight? Plus, what if Aya is seriously injured when we recover her? We can't drive her around in the backseat of a Cabriolet.

Adrienne's version of a compromise is to get a Lincoln Navigator, which is the same model of car she always chooses when given a choice. I can't fault her for it, though, it seats four tall women comfortably and has plenty of cargo space for equipment, abductees, and personal effects. Plus it affords us the privacy that we need and want, with its blacked out windows and high clearance.

It's a bit of a relief to slide into the front passenger seat as Adrienne drives. She turns up the air conditioning and the four of us blend back into the darkness of the truck's interior. I'm used to standing out in a crowd but not like this. I feel like I arrived in Miami from another planet and I can't even begin to imagine the steps that local undead have to take to avoid detection. I'm pretty sure that spray on tan is one of those steps though.

Adrienne drives fast and we don't talk much on the way to Palm Beach. I just look out the window and try to get a read on Aya.

Nothing.

There could be several reasons for this. The first, best case scenario, is that too much time has passed since she last fed from me. The connection weakens if it's not reinforced, at least on a living subject. Her blood cycles through her body and eventually will filter out all but the slightest trace of me if she doesn't feed again.

The second possible reason I'm not feeling anything is that she's not here. The connection should be stronger if we're closer in physical proximity. I didn't have any indication that I would find her here and now I don't know if my lack of connection is confirmation bias or real.

The third — and worst — possibility is that Aya has fed from someone else. Just the thought is driving me mad with jealousy and rage. I know that she's not dead. I would have felt that. But our connection could have been weakened by someone else. Either someone who offered her blood to heal her or someone who forced her to drink.

I'll find out soon, I hope.

It doesn't take long to get to the Island, which is way, way smaller and also less island-like than I was envisioning. It's fewer than ten square miles total, which I guess is one way the local residents keep it ultra exclusive. The entire Island is just a string of flamboyant mega-mansions, mostly in some kind of vague Mediterranean style, a small museum, and a few shops that look like they cater to old ladies.

At least parking is easy to find. We leave the Navigator behind and assume our incorporeal forms. It's necessary here; we'd stick out like sore thumbs if we just walked even though we're only a few blocks way. We're obviously not locals. None a single one of us owns a pastel linen suit.

I'm very knowledgeable about locks and security systems, both natural and supernatural. During my past life my employment required me to break into all kinds of high security homes, businesses, and facilities on a regular basis. I've kept up my studies, mostly out of personal interest these days, and I'm looking forward to seeing what kind of system DeLeone has in place.

"He's got his own jungle back here," Jayden comments once we have breached the backyard. It's true. We're surrounded by weird tropical plants that I've never encountered in person. It's hot and dark, like a real rainforest. It's really quite a contrast to all the artificial neon everywhere else. I would probably like it if I wasn't so preoccupied with saving Aya.

It was relatively easy for us to get this far. DeLeone's property is surrounded by a peach-colored wall with a giant iron gate that operates electronically and is monitored on all sides by cameras. It's probably very secure against human intruders but doesn't work to keep out women like us.

I'm not entirely surprised.

Immortals very, very rarely intrude on each other's lives. It's easy to avoid conflict when there are so few of us. It's very complicated and expensive to secure your house from the undead, and the only reason that we do it with our house is because we sometimes do get into conflicts and disputes with others of our kind.

Like right now this very moment, for example.

"I'll take a look around," I say before I leave my team behind to look for a point of entry.

I've already noticed that the windows are shuttered. It could be because they're inside. It could also be because the house is empty. Hell, for all I know, it could be a hurricane precaution.

I'm trying the entrance to the service delivery garage when I notice the front door.

It's open.

Not just unlocked, but open.

They're not here, I immediately text Adrienne. *Maybe just left though.*

How do you know? she responds just as fast.

Door's open

We should still check it out

Could be some clue where they went inside

It's settled then. I won't get Aya back tonight but I'm still holding on to the hope that either she or DeLeone have left some kind of clue for me here.

"It was just open like this?" Jayden asks, the disbelief audible in their voice.

"He's playing with us," I inform them. I'm absolutely sure I'm right. This was done on purpose. That open door was meant to infuriate me and it worked.

"This guy is a freak," Adrienne adds from behind Jayden.

We walk in and it's like we've entered a time machine to 1986. We're surrounded by white marble with gold detailing and random splashes of peach and turquoise. In the center of the large entry is a gleaming white grand piano, flanked by a pair of life sized gold statues of lions.

The place looks like Liberace married a Central Asian dictator and together they designed this love nest.

"Lions," Aravella remarks. "DeLeone. Get it?"

"Oh I get it," Jayden answers. "I just don't *get* it."

"That's a Koons," Aravella points out what seems to be a sculpture of a balloon animal dog, but also done in gold. "And look, he's got a Richard Prince," she indicates what looks like a giant ad for Marlboro cigarettes on the wall. "This guy has quite a collection."

A collection.

I don't know shit about art but Aravella is able to point out a ton of things that look ridiculous to me but are apparently quite precious to people in the know about art and other expensive stuff. It's not just art though. This house also contains millions and millions of dollars worth of: bottles of wine, instruments, designer clothing and furniture, small things like stamps and coins, and finally, exotic animals who have all died recently in their gilded cages.

"She starved," Adrienne stands next to me staring at the remains of a white tiger. I'm hit with a pang of guilt that I wasn't able to save her like I saved Yeti. I'm not even a big animal person, but this was cruel.

"Hopefully he's taking better care of Aya," Aravella adds, and for a moment I want to hit her even though I know, logically, that my anger is misdirected.

"We need to find this asshole," is my only reply. But dawn is approaching and we need to find a place to go to ground.

CHAPTER EIGHT

AYA LACHAT

I s it infected or am I in shock?

I'm shaking on my bed, sweating through the sheets and deep into the mattress. My wrists have been handcuffed to the iron rails again, this time by my own sister.

The same sister who just cannibalized me.

That scene just keeps playing in my head over and over again. Nala on all fours on the floor, snarling at that little dog like a beast. She didn't look human.

I guess she's not human.

I squeeze my eyes shut and try to wipe that image from my brain, but the more I struggle to forget it, the more insistently that memory replays in my head. Is there any semblance of my sister left in that creature? I'm doubting it right now, after seeing how she behaved just a few hours ago.

As soon as she was allowed to eat, it was like any possible relationship between us never existed. Our humanity didn't exist. There was no Nala and there was no Aya and there never had been as far as she was concerned. The only thing that was real to her was her craving, and for a brief moment some relief from that craving.

I knew that Olsen had Nala under his thumb but I don't think that the extent of his control over her was really clear to me until now. It's become evident to me that the only thing more real to her than her hunger was her fear.

What had he done to her to make her so afraid of him? I had begged Elodie to turn me because I had believed that turning would naturally increase my strength, my speed, my mental processing... everything. I thought that turning would make me way more powerful. Turning didn't seem to have made Nala stronger at all though. In fact, quite the opposite: now that Nala had been turned by Olsen she seemed to have no defenses against his influence at all.

Was Olsen's total control physical or mental? Both?

And to what extent was the damage done to Nala reversible?

I wish that Elodie was here. I desperately want to ask her opinion about my sister. I have so many questions for her about what it means to turn someone. My mind keeps going back to that young Filipina girl that we freed. Elodie and her sisters handed her over to an older woman who they said could help. Could this woman help Nala?

And what would happen to Nala if no one could help her?

I've spent my entire adult life feeling like I was being crushed under the burden of survivor's guilt, but now I know that the guilt I previously felt was nothing. I didn't survive after watching the murder of my entire family. I ran away and abandoned my sister to an existence of pure pain, never once even considering the possibility that she needed my help. And now that I've found her I'm in the position of having to think about whether the most compassionate thing for me to do would be to kill her myself. That is if she doesn't kill me first.

My finger, or at least the place where my finger used to be, has progressed from a searing pain to a sour, metallic ache that's causing the bile to rise from my stomach into my throat. My biggest and only new concern in life right now at this very moment is to not allow my hand to bump against the headboard or the wall. It's not an easy task since I feel like I'm barely holding on to my consciousness but every time my vision blurs and my head fills with dark fog, my cuffed hand brushes against an iron rail and an electric shock shoots through my body from my wound through my toes.

I'm on fire with fever and the pain has radiated from my wound throughout my entire body. My muscles ache from tension and I'm so thirsty. If things keep going this way, I'm not going to have to worry about what to do with Nala because I'm not going to make it through the night.

I'm barely aware of my surroundings when I hear the door click, and then I'm instantly brought back to my senses. I assume that it's Olsen here to rape, torture, murder, or all of the above me but it's not.

It's Nala.

She slips in and closes the door quietly behind her. My body is frozen on the bed but my eyes follow her as she walks purposefully across the small room to the chair next to my prison bed. My breath comes in short, shaky gasps. Nala is older than me but I can't recall one single time in my life before now that I've ever been afraid of her.

Sure, we fought, all sisters do. But she was always the more gentle of us two. She never had a temper and she wasn't malicious. The most danger she ever posed to me as a child was being a bit of a tattle tale.

Now things are different. Nala suddenly looks lucid and dangerous. I can tell the little bit of nourishment that she received has made a huge difference in her general condition. She doesn't look so ashy and disoriented anymore, but now I've got the distinct impression that she's here to finish the job.

Neither of us says a word. We just look at each other in the still of the night. Nala slips her hand into her pocket and pulls out a small silver key.

I'm still not sure what she intends to do when she holds it up to show me. She leans over me and I still think she might kill me when instead she slips the key into my hand.

She's still right on top of me when the door opens again.

"Nala!" I hear Olsen's words cut through the stillness. "Get down this instant. What are you doing?"

"I wanted to ask Aya why she didn't leave earlier." Disoriented Nala has returned and I wonder if it's an act or if this is just what Olsen's presence does to her. "I came to ask if she's going to behave properly now."

Nala flutters her eyelashes at Olsen, giving him sad puppy eyes, and it's so transparent that even I can see through her. But it works on Olsen.

"Little fool," he says softly, approaching her and running his hand through her hair. "Nasty Aya is trying to trick you."

"Aya is tricky," she instantly agrees.

"Don't come in here alone without my permission again," Olsen warns her. "Aya is dangerous. She isn't special like you."

"No," Nala agrees as she glides serenely out of the room, "she's not."

"Your sister," Olsen turns his attention back to me. "She's ethereal now, isn't she? She was always gifted but I've turned her into something truly unique. She's so sensitive. Her talent is unequaled but any disturbance to her routine takes such a toll on her. Too much food, too much stimulation, it's all just too much for her. She needs to be kept like an orchid; if her environment isn't perfect she withers up. She's my prized possession," Olsen hovers over me and rips my shirt open, "but she's not much fun."

Every instinct in my body is telling me to scream and fight but I have to keep control over myself. I know that my only chance for escape now is to keep that key concealed. I've got it in my good hand and I need to keep it there if I want to survive.

"She's nothing like you, Aya," Olsen continues, ripping off the rest of my worn and dirty clothing, leaving me handcuffed completely naked to this rickety iron bed. "Look at you," he comments, more to himself than to me, "you're filthy. Just like a nasty little pig. You stink, like sweat and piss and blood and rot. Imagine if your goody two shoes little Mistress could see you now."

"She'd destroy you," I can't help but spitting back.

Olsen has pulled his dick from his pants and is straddling my stomach. He's semi erect and stroking himself over my breasts.

"Not likely," Olsen laughs back. "You want to die tonight, Aya? Because that's what's going to happen if you don't suck me. You need me now, just like your sister. Your blood is infected. You'll rot alive if you don't drink from me."

"I'm not dying," I argue back, though I actually suspect that I am.

"You don't have to," Olsen teases. "Not if you don't want to. Open your mouth."

I turn my head as far as my neck will allow to the side, staring at an ugly yellow flower on the wallpaper beside my bed.

"Suck it and you'll live. But she'll know. We can smell it when our thralls have fed off someone else. She won't want you anymore. You'll be used up."

I don't know if what Olsen is saying is true. It might be, but I can't bear to unlock my jaw anyways, even if I wanted to.

"Suit yourself," Olsen huffs as he braces himself with his other hand on the wall behind my head. He jerks himself faster until he ejaculates blood on the side of my face.

I remain perfectly still, I don't want to give him the satisfaction of a reaction.

"Pig," he spits on me as he tucks himself back into his pants and leaves the room.

CHAPTER NINE

ELODIE GLASS

From the outside, DeLeone's factory looks like any other nineteenth century warehouse in our city. It's dirty red brick with a few windows that are too high up and thin for burglars to enter. There are giant steel doors in the back for shipping and receiving, and only two front doors for employees to exit and enter, remnants of a time when things like fire codes didn't exist.

"This looks promising," Aravella scans the building from the parking lot. "If I was going to keep sex slaves, I'd keep them in a place like this."

I know that she's not intentionally being an asshole but her comfort at the thought of my Aya being kept as a sex slave is getting on my last nerve. I crack my knuckles and pace around the parking lot, straining my ears to see if I can hear anything going on inside.

It's silent.

Eerily so.

"How are we going to get in?" Jayden asks.

"Girls, I think we've got to go big this time," Adrienne replies. She is the only one of us with military experience and she tends to want to do things in the boldest, most destructive manner possible. Not good for times when you're trying to sneak around undetected, but we've already pretty much concluded that DeLeone is one step ahead of us so we're not as concerned with stealth as we were in Florida.

Her plan is to blow up the hinges on one of the giant steel doors with C4. She claims that she's done this a million times and, frankly, I believe her. We're in the middle of a mostly abandoned industrial zone and loud, booming noises are par for the course here anyway.

I think the plan is good.

The rest of us stand back as she does her thing. I watch, anxious but curious, as she attaches her explosives to the hinges with some kind of green putty. The detonator is digital and she joins us at a distance and hands out ear plugs before she hits the magic button.

"Trust me," she insists as she gives us each a set of pink plugs. "Unless you want your ears to be ringing for the next three days."

We won't be injured but with our heightened senses a sound this loud can be quite uncomfortable so we all take her advice and use the plugs before she hits the button.

A flash of light and the entire door drops to the ground.

"This doesn't look like a high tech secret weapon facility," Jayden comments what we're all thinking as we enter a big, dingy place littered with trash and industrial relics.

The floor is strewn with moldy, wet cardboard boxes and the machinery doesn't look like it's been operated since... well, since this city was the center of the American automotive industry back in the mid twentieth century.

"What the fuck is this?" Adrienne asks, wandering around amongst the remains of what clearly used to be an assembly line. "Jayden I thought you said that this was some kind of secret military thing."

"That's the info I got from the Department of Defense," Jayden shrugs. "But I don't think anyone has even been in here in years."

"You think this is some kind of shell?" Aravella asks. "He's got this fake company to cover for something else?"

"Who the hell creates a fake weapons company as a *cover* for something?" Adrienne shoots back. "Aren't you supposed to have a cover *for* your arms dealing?"

"How old was that information you found in the database?" I address Jayden, examining a faded pile of fax machine paper from the 1980s."

"The entered date was back in 2013."

"So this information was entered in 2013?"

"Not necessarily. The system isn't that old. Someone would have had to import that information from the old system. Or enter it manually."

"Can you tell if it was entered manually."

"Not from my end." Jayden grimaces and rubs the bridge of their nose with their thumb and forefinger. "Fuck."

"So someone could have entered that information last week and we wouldn't know?" Aravella says what I've been thinking. "Like someone who wanted to make up a bunch of bullshit to waste our time?"

"Easily," Jayden admits.

"God damn it," I kick a collapsed metal shelving unit and a rat the size of a cat scampers into the shadows.

"Shit," Adrienne moans. "So what the fuck are we going to do now? Do we go to the lake house? Or one of the other dozen places listed? We don't even know if he actually owns all these places."

"We can't just go on a wild goose chase," I shake my head. "Some of those places weren't even in the country. What are we going to do? Fly around the world like we're hunting for Carmen Sandiego? Aya will be dead before we find her."

"Hey," Aravella interjects. "What about this lawyer? Jayden said that they were able to get all of these addresses because they were all registered by the same lawyer. Does this guy really exist?"

"Hold on," Jayden pulls out their phone and begins tapping away. "Todd Price. He's not a lawyer anymore, but he seems to be a real person. And he lives locally. I can get his address because — get this — he's on the sex offender registry. That's why he got disbarred too."

"He might know something," Aravella suggests. "And if he doesn't then at least we didn't spend hours or days trying to find him."

"Where is he?" I ask Jayden.

Jayden has already worked their research magic and has an address in the suburbs between the city and DeLeone's estate.

"Are you sure that's right?" I ask as we're already underway. This address is in a rough part of town. I've been there for work and it certainly doesn't seem like the kind of place a lawyer would live, even an ex-lawyer. We drive through neighborhoods filled with homes that have been abandoned for at least a decade interspersed with homes where people are still trying to live, probably mostly the remains of families who lost their income when the factories closed.

We're even more surprised when we actually locate Price's address. It's in a trailer park that isn't even the nicest trailer park in town. Not even one of the nicer ones in fact.

At least this makes our job easy. It takes no effort at all to break his door down and once we're inside everything is perfectly clear.

Price is a thin, bald man in his early forties with yellowing skin and the mannerisms of someone who wasn't raised in the kind of poverty in which he now lives. His trailer is absolutely repugnant; we could smell it before we even entered the trailer park. With all of these decomposing remains scattered about, it's a wonder that his human neighbors haven't complained. Or maybe they had and no one cared.

It's obvious by these living conditions that Price is DeLeone's thrall. It looks like he was responsible for legal affairs and illegal affairs, like dumping bodies. Judging by the condition of his trailer, he was better at the legal parts of his job.

"Where is he?" I demand, holding the weak and sickly thrall by his throat. "Where is your Master? And where has he taken the girl?"

Price chokes out a laugh and manages to get a fleck of his disgusting spittle on my face. "He won't let you take her. She's Master's prized possession. His treasure. She's his."

"She's mine," I growl back, shaking Price until Aravella has to stop me. "Tell me where she is."

"I've been serving Master for years," Price sneers. "Master promised to turn me, but then he chose her! Now she'll never leave his side. She can't. She doesn't want to. Why would she?"

"What?" I demand, my mind racing. I'm sure that I would have felt it if DeLeone had murdered Aya, and I'm absolutely positive that I would know if he turned her.

But then again, I've never had a relationship like I have with Aya. I've never let anyone drink from me and I've never experienced this kind of connection. Is it possible that our bond wasn't as strong as I thought?

"I tried to touch her once," Price continues. "Before I lost everything. And look how Master punished me!"

"You lost your license to practice law over five years ago," Jayden interjects.

"That's right. After he turned her. I hated her for it. It should have been me. I tried to make Master see that she was not his loyal servant and he took away everything I had."

"I don't think this guy is all there," Adrienne looks skeptical.

"Wait," Aravella stares Price down. "Master promised to turn you, but then he turned the girl five years ago?"

"More than five years. But Master says that if I repent he'll still give me his gift."

"What's the girl's name?" Aravella continues and I'm not sure where she's headed with this line of inquiry.

"Nala," Price spits out. "Princess Nala, can't do anything wrong."

Nala! She's alive? I wonder if Aya knows yet. And I wonder what condition Nala is in.

"We're looking for Aya," Jayden replies before thinking.

"Aya?" Price sneers. "Aya was worthless. She had nothing, she wasn't even pretty. Master cast her out."

"Well he changed his mind," Adrienne taunts Price. "Now he has Aya too. He's going to change her. We're trying to stop him."

"What?" Price hisses. "No. That's a lie. That can't be true. Master is going to change me!"

"It's true," Aravella continues. "He took Aya and now he's going to turn her."

Price screeches like an animal and I know that Adrienne's gamble has paid off. Price is going to betray his Master.

"Virginia," Price is weeping openly now. "That's where he takes them. He likes to throw parties there. Special parties with little girls and boys. Usually just human but he always brings Nala. That's where I tried to touch her and he destroyed my human life. He turned me in to the police and I had to plea down and lose everything to keep my freedom. But I hadn't done anything that they weren't all doing there."

"So we're going back to D.C.," I glance back at my sisters. "What are we going to do with this guy? Do we take him with?"

"Yes," Price interjects like we're talking to him instead of about him. "I can work for you. I can do whatever you need; conduct your business, dispose of your bodies, find you children. I can join you. Make me your little brother."

"Look what I found?" Adrienne waves a small pistol in the air. "It was sitting right out on the coffee table. You think it works?"

She points the gun at Todd Price and shoots him, dropping him on the spot.

"Sorry," Adrienne puts the gun down. "I couldn't listen to any more of that. So. Back to D.C.?"

CHAPTER TEN

AYA LACHAT

I don't think he's coming back.

I've been lying perfectly still for what seems like an eternity. Blood and spit has dried onto my face and I haven't even been able to wipe it off. It's flaking off now and I hate to admit it, but Olsen was right. My injury is feeling considerably better. My fever has abated and my hand is no longer throbbing.

I'm going to have to make my move at some point. I've been paralyzed with fear, afraid that as soon as I try to free myself he'll open that door and take the key, my only chance at freedom. I can't stay here forever though. I don't think Olsen is going to let me live for much longer and I don't see my situation improving any time soon.

I take a deep breath and try to steel my nerves before working the key in my sweating right hand into the cuff on my left. It works, it pops right open and I can finally get a look at my hand.

It's covered in dried blood but the effects that Olsen's blood have had on me are remarkable. The wound is already healing over.

My feet touch the ground and I stand up, then immediately need to sit back down because my head is spinning. I swing my feet back and forth on the edge of the bed for a minute to get my circulation going and I take another stab at getting up.

This time it works and I'm on my feet. My torn clothes litter the floor and I'm still naked; I have nothing to wear. I can't worry about that now though. I need to get out of this room.

I tip toe to the door and I try it.

This time it's locked.

I'm not surprised. I think that Olsen is beginning to question the control he has over Nala. I can see that the stronger she is, the less influence he has over her. I only wish that there was some way for me to get through to her.

As it stands, I'm going to have to wait until he unlocks the door again and then make my move. But what could that move possibly be? I don't have any weapons or even any clothing. I don't think I'm fast enough to outrun him even when I'm fit and I'm far from fit.

There's nothing for me to do but wait. Wait and think.

I'm awoken by the sound of the door quietly opening and shutting. I open my eyes and scramble on the bed. I fell asleep and I've forgotten to pretend that I'm still handcuffed.

"Aya," my sister whispers to me. "Father says that you're going to die."

"What?" I sit up and ask.

"You're dying. I don't want you to die."

"Nala, you have to help me. I'm not strong enough to escape. I can't fight him. But you can. Please, don't let him kill me."

"What?" Nala is incredulous. "I don't understand what you want me to do. Aya I can't help you."

"You can," I insist. "But you need to drink. If you drink, you'll know what to do."

"I'm not allowed," Nala replies wistfully. I can tell by her tone that she's interested.

"Look, Nala, you're very sick too. You're starving. It's made you so weak. Just try. A little bit. Do you remember earlier when you fed? You felt better, right?"

Nala considers what I'm saying for a moment. I'm finally getting through to her but I'm well aware of the risk I'm taking. She's unstable and I'm not entirely certain that feeding will make her more sympathetic to me. I don't have another choice though. If Olsen plans to end this I have to take extreme measures.

"Look," I hold up my hand. "There's still some blood. Just try a little bit. He won't know."

Nala looks at the dried blood on my hand and I can see her eyes glow. I bring my palm to her lips and she tastes the flakes on my wrist. Then she licks them more vigorously, then my plan works.

She pulls the dried, clotted blood from the wound where my finger used to be with her front teeth, letting the fresh blood flow again.

It doesn't hurt at all.

I don't get the same euphoric bliss that I get when I share my body with Elodie, but I do get a feeling of warm contentment as she feeds. My sister lies down next to me and drinks from my wound, slowly at first and then more vigorously.

We're lying on our sides facing one another and I can see the color fill my sister's cheeks. Her eyes are bright and alert and her skin glows. My own body doesn't ache anymore. I don't feel any pain and I'm no longer afraid.

I'm taken back to the Before time, before Olsen destroyed everything I loved, even before Nala was on her way to becoming a child prodigy. We're just little girls again, sharing one single bed at night because one of us had a bad dream.

"Nala!" I can hear Olsen shriek, cracking into my reverie, but I can't see him. My eyelids are so heavy.

"How dare you?"

My wound stings for a moment as my sister is ripped from my arms. The warm, drowsy, pleasant feeling I'd been experiencing is gone in an instant. I want to get up, to launch myself at Olsen, but my limbs aren't obeying my commands. They're so, so heavy. I'm struggling to even open my eyes.

Olsen has grabbed my sister and is thrashing her. Nala, for her part, seems to be accepting the beating. I want to tell her to stop, to fight back, but my mouth just won't form the words.

"Give my your wrist," Olsen demands. He's got his little blade out. He is going to drain her again so she's weak.

"No," Nala whimpers.

My ears prick. She's never refused him before.

"Nala! What has gotten into you? Did you let this little slag fool you? Just hours ago she threw herself at me. She wants to take your place. Should I give it to her?"

I hear my sister roar and then there's a brutal fight. Nala has thrown herself at Olsen and she seems to have gotten his knife from him. Blood is spraying all over the room and Olsen is trying to overpower her.

She's too much for him! In the small space of the room she's able to leap around and avoid his lunges until she gets a good opportunity on the back of his neck.

I'm just barely awake when I watch my sister tear her captor's throat out with the teeth she has left. She's like a wild animal and I'm not sure that she knows what she's doing. Olsen is choking on the blood that's filling his partially intact esophagus and he's not even fighting anymore.

His body goes limp and my sister roars into the air, her face covered with blood. She picks me up and I'm like a rag doll in her arms as she carries me out of the room and slams the door behind her, locking it.

I can hear the sound of breaking glass and I'm assuming that it's finally over for the two of us. I'm not surprised that Olsen has more security stationed outside of his home. Nala hisses and runs toward a large window in the conservatory when four figures in black surround the room and shoot her with some kind of taser so I fly out of her arms and she drops and rolls unconscious on the floor.

"Is she alive?" I hear a voice that sounds vaguely familiar to me.

"Barely," another woman answers. "Looks like somebody drained her. It must have been fairly recent; I can smell it."

"Aya? Aya?"

My eyes open, barely. It's Elodie.

"Are you really here?" I ask her. I'm not sure whether I'm dead or alive.

"I'm here, Aya, but you're not going to make it. You've lost too much blood. Do you want me to let you go or will you stay with me?"

I know what she's asking and I don't have to think twice about it.

"Please," I beg her. "Don't let me die like this."

She rips a gash into her own wrist with her teeth and she lets me drink. I can hear some commotion surrounding us in the room but it's like I'm listening from under water. My thirst is never ending and Elodie's thick blood just keeps flowing into my throat.

She's bringing me back to life.

My senses come back to me but I still feel drunk. Someone has draped a blanket over me and I can see Jayden and Aravella standing over my sister, who seems to be restrained with some kind of metal rope.

"Stop," I call out to them when I'm so sated that I can't drink another drop. "Let her go. She saved me."

"Sweetheart she's completely out of her mind," Elodie says gently.

I look over and Nala is thrashing and making animal noises.

"Don't hurt her," I insist. "She's just needs time."

"He's still alive," Adrienne interrupts, returning from the room where we left Olsen. "Barely, but someone needs to finish this job. I have him bound. You remember the deal?" she asks me.

"Oh I remember," I start to get up but my legs are still shaky and I'm wearing nothing but a blanket.

"Stop," Elodie holds my wrist. "You don't have to do this. Not now."

"I want to," I answer back.

"Do you want me to come with you?"

"No, I want to do this alone." I walk back toward the room but I stop in front of the door and think twice. "Nala?" I ask gently. "Do you want to do this with me?"

Nala looks up at me but she doesn't answer. She has tears in her eyes and I can't tell if what I'm saying even makes sense to her so I proceed alone.

He's there, still alive, barely. He's slumped over on the floor, restrained with the same metal cables that hold Nala. His shirt is ripped open and I can see that he's wearing a gold locket around his torn neck.

Olsen has the audacity to laugh when he sees me.

"Looks like your girlfriend came for you after all," he grins.

He's still missing a large part of his throat. It's not healing up like injuries to the immortal usually do. I think that if I were to leave him, Nala's bites would eventually end his life.

But I want to do this myself.

"You wouldn't dare," Olsen says, reading my mind again. "You haven't got the nerve."

I have the nerve, and I have much more. I finish the job, tearing out the other half of Olsen's throat with my new baby fangs. It's so easy; I tear through him like butter. I don't drink though. I just spit. His blood is sour and acidic, nothing like Elodie's. By the time I'm done, Olsen's head is severed completely from his body and he's gone.

He looks so small and weak now, it's almost hard for me to believe that I spent so many years living in fear of him. I reach down and rip the locket from his neck, then pop it open to see what was so important to him.

It contains four small canine teeth and I have a feeling that I know who they belong to.

I return to the conservatory and Nala wails when she sees me.

"What have you done?" she's crying and thrashing again. She's completely out of control and I'm afraid that I'll never get her back.

"Young lady," Adrienne barks. "Nala. Is that your name? Nala, stop that this instant."

To my surprise and relief, Nala obeys her immediately. She seems to react well to her stern presence. Adrienne softens and pulls Nala into her arms to carry her out to the car and she doesn't resist her.

"Let's take another car," Elodie says what I'm thinking out loud as we watch Adrienne carry my still-bound sister away.

I'm perfectly capable of walking now but I still let her carry me.

CHAPTER ELEVEN

ELODIE GLASS

I'll never let her go again.

I'm carrying her in my arms to one of the late Olsen Leonard's cars even though I'm exhausted from turning her. I haven't been this physically depleted since I was human. I knew that turning someone came at a high cost, but I hadn't prepared myself for this.

I won't let Aya see me weak though. Not right now, at least.

She's been through too much already, and I blame myself. I should have listened to her when she argued that she knew what was best for her. If I had turned her when she asked, all of this could have been avoided.

Thank God that her poor insane sister somehow found the strength to destroy that sick fuck who had enslaved her. I glance over to Adrienne, who's carrying her to her own Navigator. Adri still has her tied up in metal cables and now she's resumed sobbing uncontrollably. I can tell that this girl

— Nala is her name — hasn't been feeding properly, probably for several years.

I feel bad for her but something about her is bothering me. Her current condition hints at what actually happened back there before we arrived. Nala is rail thin and covered in scars. Her face is disfigured and she only has a single eye. Her skin is pink though. She must have fed recently.

My sisters assumed that it was DeLeone who ended Aya's life but I suspect that it was her sister. I've already decided that I'm not going to say anything about it just now. We have the rest of eternity to discuss what happened tonight. There's no need to confront Aya with this trauma right now.

For now I'm just happy to have my Aya in my arms, not just for the moment but until the end of time. Aya will never age now. She'll never get sick and she'll never get seriously injured. I'm going to make sure that she never hurts again. She'll be frozen in time, my perfect dark angel, forever.

"You know, we could all technically just drift now," Jayden suggests when we get outside of the house. "Since they're both turned. We don't have to sit in the cars."

"You can't be serious," Adrienne groans. "They don't know how yet. Someone needs to teach them, in a safe place. Plus if this one dissolves God only knows where she'll end up. I think it's safe to assume that it won't be back at our place. Not to mention we have to return this rental or we'll get fined."

"I wasn't serious," Jayden quips back. "I was just saying. These girls aren't human anymore. I guess they're our new sisters now. Are they going to work with us? They're moving in I guess."

Adrienne grimaces back. She clearly isn't sharing Jayden's optimism about our new living arrangements. "We can discuss that later."

"It was just the two of you, right?" Jayden addresses this question to Aya.

"Hmm," she gives it some thought. "Actually I have no idea. That's a good question."

"We better check it out before we leave," Aravella turns around. "It's possible that this guy had a whole house full of women locked up somewhere. The inside was drenched with blood, human and otherwise."

"Right. We'll wait here for you. Text if you're going to need a lot of time and we'll take these girls home."

Aravella and Jayden run back in to give the place a once-over and make sure that there aren't any more prisoners. Aya, Adrienne, Nala, and I are left out in the cool night air. Aya is taking deep breaths of the fresh air and Nala is wailing in Adrienne's arms.

"We didn't find anything," Jayden explains when they return. "But we did bring you these." They hand over a pair of dresses, the style of which I haven't seen around in at least fifty years. "So you don't have to wear just a blanket."

Aya slips into her dress, a floral number which is so large that it hangs on her small frame, just behind the car. I can hear Adrienne struggling to try to get Nala into her dress. She doesn't want to take off the one that's soaked in blood. After several long minutes and a string of vulgarities from Adrienne, I hand over the blanket that I had used to wrap Aya and she just wraps Nala in that.

We get into Leonard's black Expedition and Aravella takes the driver's seat.

"Is she going to be like this forever?" Aya asks as soon as all the doors are shut.

"I hope not," I answer honestly.

"I just don't get it," Aya shakes her head. "Why doesn't she fucking hate him like I do?"

"Well she did kill him," I counter. "You finished him off, but if we had just left him like that, he wouldn't have made it. Maybe just another few hours. You just sped up the process. He was too far gone to recover after what she did. I don't even know how she managed without her fangs."

"Oh!" Aya perks up. "That reminds me. Look what I found."

She opens the palm of her hand and my gut twists. It's four little canines.

"Where were they?" I ask out of morbid curiosity.

"He was wearing them in a locket around his neck," she wrinkles up her nose in disgust.

"Well at least now she'll be able to feed herself I guess. That's good."

"You think they can be fixed?" Aya is incredulous.

"Oh sure. Your fangs won't grow back if they're lost but if you find them you can put them back in. It just hurts a little bit. She'll be good as new though."

"What about her eye?"

"I think she lost that before she died, which means that it's lost forever. Sorry."

"That's too bad. God. How could she be so fucking torn up over the guy who did this to her?"

"Sometimes," Aravella answers from the front seat, "captives fall in love with their captors. Victims become obsessed with their abusers. For the prey, the predator can become their whole world. Your sister's entire existence was this monster for so long, fearing him, trying to please him, suffering under his hand… she probably feels adrift now. How does her life continue without him?"

I can hear the bitterness in Aravella's voice and I know that she knows what she's talking about from firsthand experience.

"Joyfully?" Aya spits back. "Free from torture?"

"Isn't that a bit hypocritical, coming from you?" Aravella taunts Aya.

"That's enough," I stop this conversation before it turns ugly. I'm going to have to keep an eye on these two. Something about Aya is triggering the worst in Aravella and I don't want the two of them at each others' throats. "Nala has been through a lot," I soothe Aya. "It's not like there's a manual for how to properly survive the ordeal she's undergone. It's not really a surprise that she's processing her grief and trauma in unpredictable ways."

"Yeah, that's true," Aya settles down. "Do you think that she'll ever be able to be happy again? Sometimes I feel like I get a glimpse of the Nala that I know and then at other times it seems like she's completely lost any sense of self that she ever had."

"Well," I consider the question, "I don't know. She's definitely going to need a lot of support if she is going to have any kind of recovery. And I wouldn't expect it to happen overnight. We're going to have to have some patience, give her some time."

"I guess time is one thing that we have plenty of now," Aya settles in close to me as Aravella speeds through the night, back to our townhouse.

"Every moment I have from now on is yours," I promise as I squeeze her close to me. She gives me a wan, sleepy smile before her eyelids droop and close and she falls into her first dreamless slumber before the sun even begins to rise.

CHAPTER TWELVE

AYA LACHAT

My eyes open. There's no light at all, but I can faintly make out the corners of an empty room. My body is pressed up against Elodie's and we're in some kind of soft bed that has sides, kind of like a toddler bed.

I sit up and I don't recognize the space we're in. There are no windows and all I can see is a single stone staircase that leads up.

"Did you sleep well, my love?" Elodie asks, sitting up next to me. She's wearing only her briefs, she's topless and her feet are bare.

I'm looking around the room trying to figure out where the hell we are.

"In our crypt," Elodie sees my confusion. "Well we call it that but it's a basement with no light leak. We have to slumber during the day now and we're in my coffin. I didn't shut the lid because I was afraid you'd wake up first and freak out. Usually I shut it though."

"Oh," I look around and realize that the soft sides are velvet padding. "It's, like, an actual coffin."

"You can have your own or we can get a bigger one built for two people, whatever you prefer," Elodie explains.

"Okay. I guess I'll think about it. So I have to sleep every day in a coffin now?"

"You don't have to, most of us just prefer it. It's comfortable and if someone somehow finds us during the day they won't disturb us. Most humans know instinctively not to touch a body in a coffin."

"Has that ever happened to you?"

"Not that I know of. But I like the added security. We're vulnerable when we slumber."

"Okay. I guess I have a lot to learn."

"It's true but don't worry, I'm going to show you everything. You can shapeshift now! And fly!"

"I can turn into a bat?"

"No, sorry. You can turn into smoke though."

"For real?"

"For real."

I'm thrilled. I wanted to turn because I wanted the power and invulnerability that came with being immortal, but now that I'm hearing about all the other little perks and details I'm very excited to try out my new skillset.

"I wonder why Nala never just shifted into smoke and left Olsen."

"She might have not known how. Sonny had to explain it to me. Or she might have known that Olsen would find her if she tried to leave and she was more afraid of what he'd do when he retrieved her."

"Maybe," I nod. "This dress is gross. Can I still take baths?"

"Why would you not be able to take a bath? You're a vampire, not the Wicked Witch of the East. Water won't hurt you."

"Smart ass," I grin and slug Elodie playfully in the shoulder. "Would you mind running me one then? This dress smells nasty."

Since the moment I woke up I've been painfully aware of my new senses. I can smell things much more powerfully than I could before when I was a woman, especially this revolting old dress. I can smell the sweat of the women who wore it before me and I can smell blood. The only things that don't smell at all are Elodie and I.

Elodie steps out of the coffin and picks me up again, carrying me up the stone stairway into the kitchen pantry, where the door is hidden and where Yeti is waiting for his breakfast.

"Well hello," I greet him as he rubs himself all over Elodie's legs. "Did you miss me?"

"He missed his tuna," Elodie jokes. "But he's going to have to wait another minute. I've already been given a job."

She carries me upstairs into the big bathroom in my old room and sets me on the side of the tub as she runs the water. I strip out of the granny dress and suggest that we burn it, to which she immediately agrees. I pour some bath oil in and slip in, rubbing the oil into my skin to get rid of the scent of blood and decay.

"Hey," I stop Elodie as she's stepping out the door, "where do you think you're going? Come on. Get undressed and get in here with me."

"Okay," Elodie smiles. She slips out of her clothes and steps into the hot, vanilla scented water with me.

I reach over to her and rub the oily water into her skin. She leans back and lets me and I let a devilish grin creep across my face.

I want to try out my new body.

I keep rubbing her all over and she remains still, letting me tease her. My hands slide up and down her slippery breasts and abs, getting closer and closer to her pussy until I reach the curls of it. Then I slip one finger in gently.

The tub is big enough for me to straddle her. I climb on top of her and lower myself gently on to her lap. I know that I'm technically dead now but I feel more alive than I ever have. I begin to slowly rock myself back and forth on Elodie, working her with one hand while I use the other on myself. The water is splashing out of the tub and I don't care. She feels amazing underneath of me.

Elodie has her head leaned back over the edge of the tub and she's biting her lip and grasping the rim of the bath, holding on like she's barely able to restrain herself from grabbing me and forcing her own fingers into me.

It's what I want too, but first I want to draw things out a little bit. To torture us both. It doesn't take long before I can't resist her though. I stroke and rub us both harder and faster until I come, and when she hears me call her name she finally grabs my wrist with one hand and thrusts the fingers of her other deep inside of me. My body clenches and trembles around her and it's several moments before I return to my senses.

Once we're both spent, the water is still hot and I stay in her lap, holding her and stroking the tip of her breast absent-mindedly.

"Elodie," I say softly, my cheek resting against her shoulder. "I want to do what you do."

Her body stiffens and she doesn't reply immediately.

"I want to cleanse the world. I think that's my calling. Olsen wasn't enough. I need to remove everyone like him."

She takes a deep breath before she responds.

"You might not find it so easy when it isn't personal," she says. "Even with my background, sold as a thrall and then raised as an assassin, I struggled with the first few. Only knowing that they were one hundred percent guilty and unpunished gave me the fortitude to go through with it."

"I can do it," I insist. "I get a dark rush from the thought of making these people pay. There are too many of them and not enough people fighting them. I'm sure that this is what I want to do and I'm also sure that I won't have a problem doing it."

"Okay," Elodie concedes. "We can talk about it."

I trace my finger over her chest as my mind drifts.

"You think Nala will ever recover?"

"Oh, love, I don't know. I wish that I did but I really can't tell."

"What about that woman? Beryl? The one who took the girl we found? Maybe she can do something."

"Maybe. I can ask Aravella. Nala seems to have attached herself to Adrienne for the time being."

"I don't think Adrienne likes the extra responsibility."

"Oh," Elodie laughs, "I don't know about that. Sometimes she likes to act like a hardass even though she's really enjoying something. I think she's got some kind of complex that makes her feel like she's not allowed to indulge in any kind of pleasure. You know, military gal. Everything is a job or a responsibility or whatever."

"Well it seems to work for Nala. She's so different from when she was a girl. Olsen really fucked her up. I'm furious about what he did to her. What he took from her."

"You're right," Elodie agrees. "She'll probably never be the girl that you once knew again. But then again, you're not the same person either. You've changed a lot, even just over the past year."

"That's true," I concede. "The old Aya never in a million years could have imagined a life like this. I couldn't even protect myself. Protecting and avenging other people certainly wasn't on my radar. I guess that my death brought me the freedom to live the life I want to live."

Elodie wraps her arms around me and pulls me in close.

"I love you forever, Aya."

"I love you forever too."

CHAPTER THIRTEEN

AYA LACHAT

SIX MONTHS LATER

"Shall we convene to the living room? I've got wine."

I'm having fun playing hostess. Everyone takes a seat around my living room, either in a chair or on the sofa, and I bring everyone a glass of red. My sisters like to make fun of my wife's new living situation, which they claim is girlish and frivolous, but I can tell that at least Jayden and Aravella appreciate my housekeeping and other creature comforts.

It's our turn to host our monthly meeting, which lately has turned into a weekly meeting, and Jayden is projecting a presentation that they've prepared on their phone onto the wall. I don't know how they do it. They died before I was born but they somehow understand technology that I never even know existed.

I'm included in every meeting now. I have jobs. Not, like, I accompany Elodie on her jobs. I have my own jobs! I get assignments every week. I do research and I follow suspects. I assassinate rapists and murderers. I've never felt so alive.

I was born to do this. I died to do this. And I don't think it's just because of what happened to me. I truly believe that I've finally found my calling. I've never felt so fulfilled, with either my personal life or my professional life.

Nala is included in this meeting too, but only because she latched on to Adrienne the moment that she entered the house. At the moment she's sitting on the floor at her feet, which Adri is acting like is a totally normal thing to do. Adrienne is stroking Nala's hair and speaking softly to her. Adri's body language is stiff and awkward. I don't think she's very accustomed to receiving any kind of attention from women. Sometimes I have trouble deciding which one of them is weirder.

Things have not been easy with Nala. She was originally staying at the big house with my sisters but she's such an agent of chaos now that we had to take her. She can't ever, ever be alone. She disappears, she accidentally starts fires, she'll start screaming at nothing at completely random times... she certainly does not give one single shit about targets or assignments.

The meeting begins with Aravella describing a target that she neutralized in the past week. It was a plastic surgeon who was drugging women at fancy bars. He'd take them home and then video himself raping them. That wasn't the end of it though; he's proceed to blackmail them with the videos. He'd already been investigated by the police multiple times, but they kept claiming that there was no evidence that the sex wasn't consensual.

As if a videotape of an unconscious woman wasn't evidence.

Let alone dozens of tapes.

"He tried to buy me off," Aravella is laughing. "Like his money could fix everything. I'm assuming that he was offering me the money that he'd extorted from his victims. He died begging."

"Where did you dump him?" Adrienne asks, stroking Nala's hair absentmindedly.

"In the lake. He's fish food now. It's got to be better for them than all that pollution anyway."

"Did you destroy the tapes?" Jayden asks.

"Tapes, phone, hard drive. All of it, just like you told me. No one else will ever view that material. I also checked his cloud accounts and deleted those before I left. Thank you for explaining that, I didn't even know that was a thing."

"Maybe we'll get you participating in the twenty first century yet," Jayden jokes. "But now, Elodie. How are things going with your target?"

"It's a go. This guy came onto my radar when I was reviewing anonymous reports to CPS. Multiple sources kept claiming that he was taking in foster kids, then they would get skinnier and skinnier and dirtier and dirtier, then they would disappear from school. Social workers kept *investigating* with phone calls, then marking the reports as unfounded. I went to check out his address and it's sending up red flags. He supposedly currently has eight foster kids but none of them are ever visible outside or even in the windows. I'm not sure what he's doing with them yet, but I'm sure it's not good."

"When are you going to make your move?"

"I need some help to get into the house. If those kids are still alive, there are at least nine people living in that house. I need a reason to get the kids out to kill him, it's not a big space."

"Hmm," Jayden considers the problem. "That's tricky. You haven't seen any evidence that the kids are still there?"

"No but it smells like there are a lot of people living there. I just can't tell where he's keeping them."

"You have to go in late, like 3 or 4AM," I suggest. "When everyone is almost certainly asleep. Then you can see if they're all just in regular bedrooms or locked in the basement or God knows what. Then you can figure out how to get the kids out for the a night so you can do whatever needs to be done."

"You're right," Elodie agrees with me and I bask in the validation.

I was initially worried that I wouldn't be allowed to work, that I wouldn't receive any assignments or my ideas wouldn't be taken seriously. That's far from what's happened though. I know that I'm a valued member of the team.

By the time we're done, Elodie is planning a break and enter, Adrienne is investigating a serial rapist on the local army base, and I'm going to learn how to create fake identification documents. It was a productive meeting and I'm feeling good.

"You know, that's the calmest I've seen her since the night of the rescue," I comment to Adrienne, who is still petting my sister. "I think it might do her good to spend a little time with you."

My suggestion lands like a lead balloon. Adrienne dismisses the idea immediately, then leaves the meeting early before I can even offer everyone a refill on her drink. Nala is visibly distressed and retreats to her room, which was my room before I moved in with Elodie.

Later that night I go to her room to check on her and to lock her in for the day. As usual, I find her sleeping on the floor of the closet. I bring her a pillow and cover her with the blanket, wishing that I could do more for her.

"I just wish that I knew what to do to help her," I lament to Elodie later when we're in our room. The night is still young and we have some time alone together.

"We'll figure something out," she offers. "I just wish that Adrienne wasn't so stubborn. I think she's more afraid of losing control over herself than she is of whatever Nala might do."

"Is losing control over yourself so bad," I smile and begin to unbutton Elodie's shirt.

"Oh, I don't know. I used to go to great lengths to control myself around you."

"But not anymore," I tease. "You still drink from me but you don't want to bloodlet anymore."

"There's no reason," Elodie explains. "There is no my blood and your blood anymore. Only our blood. It's the same blood that we share."

"Just the two of us," I purr.

"No," Elodie shakes her head. "I know about Nala. I know what she did, Aya."

"She had to," I look up at Elodie, surprised by her admission. I had thought that was Nala's and my little secret, the only one I kept from Elodie because I was afraid of what she would do to Nala. "I asked her to do it. It was the only way for us to destroy him."

"I guessed," Elodie pulls me close and kisses me.

"You're not angry at her?"

"What happened wasn't her fault. Not any more than it was really yours or mine. We all did what we had to do, and look where we are now."

"Right where I want to be," I answer, leading her underground.

"Right where we belong."

ABOUT THE AUTHOR

Rojana lives in the beautiful high desert of northern New Mexico. When she's not busy reading or storytelling, she enjoys practicing archery and trail riding.

More on www.rojanakrait.com

facebook.com/rojanakrait

instagram.com/rojanakrait

tiktok.com/@rojana.krait